PRAISE FOR TH̲
OF ALLISTER, ALABAMA

"Prepare for the read of your life!"
—Perpetual Motion Machine Publishing

"Part mystery, part ghost story, this humorous whodunnit will have you humming Elvis tunes and watching for the King himself to come gyrating through your door."
— Jason Jack Miller, award-winning author of *Hellbender* and *The Devil and Preston Black*

"A fast-paced, fun, and compulsively readable romp. The Burg gave us Stephanie Plum, Las Vegas gave us Lucky O'Toole, and now, Allister, Alabama, presents us with Cleo Tidwell."
— Lane Robins, critically acclaimed author of *Maledicte, Kings and Assassins*, and the Shadows Inquiries series (as Lyn Benedict)

"Mystery, murder, mayhem, and … Elvis? Cozy in for a laugh-filled evening as Susan Abel Sullivan spins a ghost tale with Southern attitude and good style that you won't be able to put down."
— Heidi Ruby Miller, author of *Greenshift* and *Ambasadora*

"Cleo Tidwell is a Southern belle with spunk. You'll love this heroine and her quirky family and be clamoring for more!"
— Rebecca Roland, author of *Shards of History*

"A unique, must-have addition to your to-be-read stack!"
— Kelly L. Stone, author of *Grave Secret* and *Time to Write: No Excuses, No Distractions, No More Blank Pages*

"Susan Abel Sullivan could very well be the Janet Evanovich of the paranormal mystery genre."
—Sherry Peters, author of *Silencing Your Inner Saboteur*

The Haunted Housewives of Allister, Alabama

A Cleo Tidwell Paranormal Mystery

SUSAN ABEL SULLIVAN

World Weaver Press

Published by World Weaver Press
Kalamazoo, Michigan
www.WorldWeaverPress.com

Cover design by Eileen Wiedbrauk

"Getting the Curse" copyright © 2007 Susan Abel Sullivan.

First Edition: October 2012

ISBN: 0615700896
ISBN-13: 978-0615700892

To a spooky little girl like
Roberta ...
Boo !

Susan Abel Sullivan

THE HAUNTED HOUSEWIVES
OF ALLISTER, ALABAMA

To my sister, Laura Abel Kennedy,
who told me to write what I know.

ACKNOWLEDGMENTS

Sergeant Matthew L. Evans with the Largo Police Department in Florida for answering my many questions about small town police work. Any errors are solely mine. My publishers, Eileen Wiedbrauk and Elizabeth Wagner at World Weaver Press, for taking a chance on me and Cleo. Jeanne Cavelos, Director of Odyssey Writing Workshops, for feedback, coaching, and support. Maggie Della Rocca, my Odyssey roomie, for introducing me to Janet Evanovich novels and cheering me on every step of the way. My mom, Jean Abel, who took me to Graceland. The Novelist Group at TNEO 2009 for critiques, especially Abby Goldsmith, Rebecca Roland, and Rita Oakes. My Beta Readers, Shannon Wilder, Rebecca Franklin, Rhonda Martin Berry, Maggie Della Rocca, and Laura Kennedy, for their invaluable feedback. And my husband, Andy Sullivan, for supporting my passion for fiction writing.

PRELUDE:

WELCOME TO MY WORLD

CHAPTER ONE

Late September

1

My name is Cleopatra Kilgore Tidwell. As a middle class Southern gal born and raised in small town Alabama, I was brought up with certain social rules. You don't wear white after Labor Day, you don't decorate your lawn with pink flamingos, and you most certainly don't hang black velvet paintings in your home.

So when my husband Bertram and I were recruited to help his mother pare down her Elvis collection and pack up the rest of her stuff for her upcoming move to a senior's condo, I was a bit judgmental about all the tacky Elvis doo-dads.

Okay, I was a good bit judgmental. Don't get me wrong. Out of the three mothers-in-law I've had, Georgia is hands down my favorite. But really? A black velvet painting of Elvis Presley? That was supposedly haunted. She might as well have hung a dogs-playing-poker print smack dab in the middle of her living room. It was just not done in Allister unless you were a redneck or trailer trash.

And Georgia was neither, bless her heart.

My mother, Martha Jane, always says, "Hindsight is wiser." I didn't know at the time that the "haunted" Velvet Elvis would lead to murder, mayhem and a media circus. Or that my whole worldview on the subject of psychics, angels, the occult, and disembodied spirits would be turned on its head. Yep, I was in for a rude awakening. Uh huh.

2

My gorgeous mother-in-law, who at sixty-two could still turn younger men's heads, plucked a framed 8x10 photograph from the end table beside her couch. Her spacious ranch home was in complete disarray from the three of us sorting through a lifetime of belongings for her upcoming move to a smaller abode. But Georgia herself was the epitome of neatness, her blonde hair done up in a 60s flip, her navy slacks neatly pressed, and not a smudge of dirt or dust on her hot pink knit top.

"Oh, Bertram, I absolutely must take this photo to the condo with me."

"Now, Mama, you know you can't take everything with you."

Bertram stroked his beard, a clear sign he was thinking up some alternative for his mother. He'd opted against his usual suburban uniform of khakis and polo shirt and was wearing jeans and a Jimmy Buffet t-shirt touting the song, "It's Five O'Clock Somewhere."

"How about you trade something in your gonna-keep pile with that photograph?" He rose to his full six foot four height, his knees cracking with the effort. He pointed to the spot on the golden shag carpet where we'd gathered a growing pile of Elvis memorabilia. "Like this Velvet Elvis?"

He hoisted up a two by three foot acrylic painting of Elvis preserved for all posterity on black velvet and bordered with a gold frame that would have been right at home in a Liberace museum. This was the often parodied Elvis: white rhinestone-spangled jumpsuit, chiffon scarf, dark, longish hair in the early seventies style, thick mutton-chop sideburns, and a hint of a jowl. For an odd moment, I thought I heard Elvis saying, "Priscilla," in my head. And then it was gone.

"But that's the painting I bought last month when I went to Graceland," Georgia said. "A little fella was sellin' 'em by the roadside. Said it was haunted. I paid a thousand dollars for it."

Oh, Lordy, Martha Jane would be fit to be tied if she heard this. A thousand dollars for something only a bonafide Elvis fanatic would want and hideously tacky, to boot.

Bertram frowned. "A thousand dollars, Mama?" He was still holding the painting, staring at Elvis's one eye as if he could silently discern its dubious secrets. I was just relieved the trashy thing didn't belong to us.

"Well, yes, hon. If this was the real deal, I wanted to be the next person to witness it. I wasn't about to let another Elvis collector get their hands on it." She nodded at me as if I were a kindred spirit.

"How is it haunted?" I said. I'm tellin' ya, some people will believe anything.

"Well, the little fella said it sang 'Heartbreak Hotel' at night after he and his family had all gone to sleep. A pitiful soul. He reminded me of those men you see by the interstate holding up the will-work-for-food signs."

Bertram set the painting down on the thick carpet again, propping it against the wall, but one hand lingered along the upper edge of the gilt frame. "If they were all asleep, how'd they know it sang anything?"

"Because he videotaped it. And he also told me it showed Elvis leavin' the painting."

I didn't doubt for one moment that this was all a gimmick to dupe the gullible, but it could be entertaining to see someone's amateur efforts at pulling a con. "Did he give you the tape?"

"No, darlin'," Georgia shook her head sadly. "Said it burned up in a trailer fire."

It was on the tip of my tongue to say, "Yep, sure it did." But I kept my mouth closed. Martha Jane used to say, "If you can't say something nice, don't say anything at all." Not that that ever stopped her.

Bertram couldn't seem to keep his hands off the painting's gold frame. "Which one is more important to you, Mama? The signed photograph or the haunted painting?"

Georgia sighed. "I guess I'll keep the photograph. I'd truly hoped I'd get to commune with Elvis's dearly departed spirit, but nothing's happened so far. Maybe someone else'll have better luck with it."

Bertram hefted the thing, his biceps bulging. "Then I'll just set it over here in the gotta-go pile."

For a medium-sized painting, it seemed to weigh a lot.

Georgia hugged the photograph to her bosom. "Cleo, honey. Set down what you're doin' and come take a look at this."

I was happy to oblige. We'd been at it for awhile and I was ready for a break. I had no idea one person could accumulate so much stuff, most of it Elvis related.

She passed me the old black and white photograph. It was from the early sixties. Georgia, Elvis Presley, and a lanky, blond mystery man posed together in front of a swimming pool surrounded by lush, tropical plants. Georgia was in the middle, the guys on either side of her, their arms draped across one another. The three of them looked pretty chummy together. Georgia reminded me of Connie Stevens and Sandra Dee with a little Doris Day thrown in, the all-American girl. Elvis was young and still beautiful.

The King's scrawl jittered across the bottom half of the photograph.

Georgia.
We certainly had fun in Acapulco.
Yours, Elvis.

16

I pointed to the mystery man. "Who's this?"

"Oh, that's Lee Munford. He was part of Elvis's Hollywood entourage. He and Elvis would stay up late talking about the occult and life after death."

Good to know. Like that bit of trivia would ever come in handy. Uh huh.

Georgia was not to be deterred from trying to take it all with her.

"Bertram, hon, it's so hard to choose which things to keep and which to let go. Are you sure you two can't store some of these in that roomy Victorian Cleo just inherited?" She gestured grandly like Vanna White on *Wheel of Fortune*, indicating enough Elvis memorabilia to stock a Graceland gift shop.

Say no, say no, say no, I thought, mentally crossing my fingers. My great-aunt Trudy, who left us her house a few months ago when she died at the ripe old age of ninety-nine, would roll over in her grave if she knew we might use it to store Elvis crap. Elvis had been a vulgar upstart in her way of thinking.

"Mama, we've been over that. Cleo and I have nothing against the King, but we're just not into him like you are."

Whew! Actually, we weren't into him at all. I could rattle off a laundry list of Elvis aversions that Bertram had from growing up with an Elvis nut for a mother. Trust me, it was enough to put anyone off Elvis for life.

Georgia lovingly wrapped the picture in white paper. "Cleo, did I ever tell you that Elvis dyed his hair? He was actually a natural blond. Or that his middle name was Aaron?"

"Why yes, Georgia," I said as sweetly as I could, "I believe you did." *Several times.*

For a moment she had a startled expression. I'd probably derailed her entire thought process. But she recovered quickly and said, "So how are you two love birds celebrating your third anniversary?"

Bertram and I exchanged knowing glances, favoring each other with a little smile. I shrugged and said, "We're spending a quiet evening home alone. Nothing fancy."

Nothing fancy! We were only going to celebrate the Super Bowl of Romance in our new home. Married three years and we still had the heat of newlyweds.

"Well, that's sweet, hon. I wish you both a lifetime of happiness."

3

Champagne buzzed through me like the soft whirr of cicadas on a hot summer's night. Our third wedding anniversary had been absolutely exquisite up to this point. A candlelight dinner for two in the formal dining room of our new Victorian home. Kansas City steaks, grilled to perfection. Cherries Jubilee and not a single scorch mark on the antique lace tablecloth. Bertram looking absolutely yummy in a charcoal gray suit. And me all gussied up in a slinky red dress, my blonde hair curled and pinned up off my neck. We'd broken out the good china, silver, and crystal for the occasion.

Bertram had burned a CD of romantic songs. As he cleared the dessert dishes from the table, "The Way You Look Tonight" segued to Elvis Presley's version of "Can't Help Falling in Love." He must have gotten that one from Georgia, since we didn't own any Elvis music. But it was a romantic song. What sort of gift would Bertram give me this year? He'd presented me with a box of Godiva chocolates and the entire set of Maude Adams mysteries on our first anniversary. And tickets to see Jimmy Buffet at the Fox in Atlanta last year. I was aquiver with anticipation.

And then he toted out the Velvet Elvis.

"Happy Anniversary, Cleo."

A laugh bubbled out of me. Oh, what a good one. We'd remember this anniversary for years to come.

"No, really, Cleo," Bertram said, his brown eyes troubled. "Happy Anniversary."

And then it hit me. This *was* my anniversary gift. I stared at 70s

Elvis in his white jumpsuit and mutton-chop sideburns, painted so, um … artistically … on black velvet, trying to think of something—anything—to say. The only words I could come up with were: *Oh my God.* If I had to make a list of gifts I'd least like to receive, a velvet painting of any kind would be at the top, right above tickets to Muppets on Ice or maybe a ceramic gnome for the front yard. It wasn't so much the hideousness of it as the shock of the unexpected. It was if I'd been expecting to go to dinner at a five-star restaurant only to be taken to McDonald's for a Happy Meal. And if it had been a gag gift, I could have played along, but this was our wedding anniversary.

The silence was stretching out to an uncomfortable span, accentuated by the ticking of the grandfather clock in the adjacent parlor. I had to say something, and I had to say it now. But I didn't want to hurt Bertram's feelings, not on our special night.

"It's, uh … Bertram, I don't know what to say."

Bertram propped it against the back of one of the gold upholstered dining room chairs, and we admired the thing together. How cozy.

"After we helped Mama move," he said, his arm draped around my shoulder, "I just knew I had to get it. It had *you* written all over it."

"It did?" I was trying so hard to be careful with what I said.

"Yeah. Like neon lights. And you can tell all your friends about it being haunted."

"I can?" I didn't want to tell my friends about it at all. I didn't want to tell *anyone* about it. I think I'd die from embarrassment.

"Sure. You'll be the talk of the town. Who else can say they own a genuine, haunted painting of the King?"

"No one?"

"No one, but you." Bertram gave me a squeeze. Even with high heels on, the top of my head barely reached his chin.

I could hear it now. I'd be the joke around town. *Oh, that Cleo*

Tidwell, married three times. Her husband gave her a Velvet Elvis on their anniversary. Isn't that the tackiest thing you ever heard? And then they'd chortle like a pack of hyenas.

But I looked up into my husband's handsome face at that moment, and my bafflement and concern got shoved to the back burner. His brown eyes were so full of love.

So I said, "Thank you, Bertram," standing on tiptoe and throwing my arms around his neck. And even then, he had to lean down to kiss me, his beard tickling my lips. But it was a five-alarm kiss that made my toes—and other parts—tingle. Bertram scooped me up Rhett Butler-style and carried me up the grand staircase to our boudoir, where we scattered a couple of cats off the bed.

The Velvet Elvis couldn't have been farther from my mind.

4

When I came downstairs for breakfast the next morning, all seemed right with the world. I had on my favorite L.L. Bean navy walking shorts, a white scooped-neck knit top, and a pair of navy Keds. My unruly hair was pulled back into a ponytail with a gross grain hairband. My make-up was Cover Girl perfect. And Bertram and I had had a spectacular night in the bedroom.

But what should I find in the formal dining room but my husband of three years balancing on one of Great-aunt Trudy's antique chairs before the fireplace, a hammer cocked in one hand and a nail poised against the cabbage rose wallpaper? And right before he was supposed to head out to work.

Oh, I could just kill him! Those delicate chairs weren't made for a six foot four, two hundred and twenty pound man to stand on them.

"What are you doing?" I said, each word in staccato.

He jerked around to look at me, and I heard a distinctive crack from the chair.

"I know the *perfect* place to hang your painting," he said. "It came to me this morning in the shower."

"In the dining room? Of a Victorian house? Wouldn't it be better in ... that back room upstairs?"

"No," Bertram sang out all cheery, "you'll want this prominently displayed so you can show it off."

And then he pounded the nail home.

Oh. Oh. Oh. I couldn't bear to watch. This *so* went against the social rules I was raised with.

Bertram set the hammer on the mantle and actually scampered across the gleaming hard wood floor to where we'd left the Velvet Elvis the night before. Then he practically traipsed back to the scene of the crime with it. I winced as he stepped upon the antique chair again.

"Bertram, couldn't you have used a step ladder? That chair can't hold your weight. It's fifty years old, for crying out loud."

"No time," he sang out, totally unfazed. He hung the painting, leveled it, and then stepped down to admire his handiwork. "Perfect."

"Uh, Bertram?"

"I also got a great idea for a new half-time show this morning. I don't know why I never thought of it before." Bertram was the Director of Bands for Allister State University and he was much more proficient with a musical instrument than he was with handyman tools.

He left the chair and hammer where they were and disappeared in the direction of the butler's pantry. "We'll do a tribute to Elvis. The alumni will love it."

The things that make you go: *hmm*. If it hadn't been for the Velvet Elvis, I wouldn't have thought twice about a show dedicated to Elvis.

Bertram breezed out of the pantry into the big open foyer, a Dr. Pepper in one hand and a granola bar in the other. He broke stride only long enough to kiss me on the forehead. "That was some night last night, Cleo. See you at lunch."

As soon as his convertible backed out of the drive, I whisked the step ladder out of the laundry room and climbed up in front of the velvet-offense-against-good-taste. The King still sang silently in profile, rhinestones glittering, microphone held high. I listened, hands poised on either side of the gold frame. Nothing. Nothing but house noises, like the hum of the fridge in the kitchen, and the ticking of the grandfather clock, and a board creaking upstairs from our fat cat Cosmo.

"Darlin', you're comin' down," I told the painting.

It didn't answer. Good thing, too, or I probably would have fallen off the step ladder and sprained something.

I grasped the frame to lift it off the wall, but couldn't get it to budge. Geez, maybe I should have eaten my Wheaties. I tried again. Ergh, the thing was too heavy to move. What was it made out of? Gilded lead?

Maybe I could use my powers of persuasion to convince Bertram to relocate it tonight. In the meantime, I could live with it on the wall. It wasn't like anyone was coming over today, at least not for a social call.

I had just snapped the step ladder closed when the doorbell did its dull ding. Goodness, who could it be so early in the morning?

The who was Marty Millbrook, my second ex-husband. His color scheme would have made the sisters of Phi Mu squeal with joy. Green polo shirt, pink and green plaid shorts, navy belt, and pink slip-on tennis shoes. How many times had I told him that redheads shouldn't wear pink?

"Well, hey, Cleo. I'm glad I caught you at home."

I pulled him inside and gave him a big hug. It's no secret that I still adore Marty. But he's like a second sister … or a gay brother … or hell, I don't know. What I do know is we survived our divorce to become great friends.

"You're up and at 'em early this morning."

"Just trying to catch that ole worm." His face lit up with a boyish grin.

Our house is a combination of Victorian and Craftsman design. At one time, the big open arch between the larger parlor and the dining room probably sported a thick velvet drape hung on a rod. The drape could be tied off for roominess or left closed for privacy. But the drape was long gone, and anyone standing at my front door had a clear view of a large portion of the dining room.

Marty now leaned way out to his left, his expression incredulous. "Cleo, that Velvet Elvis in your dining room has got to go. I thought you had better taste than that."

"I do." I gave him the scoop.

"Straight men." He shook his head in sympathy. "But you are a lucky girl in all other ways. That Bertram is quite a catch."

"Yes, isn't he?" I almost purred thinking about all those ways.

"All right, sweetie," Marty said, pulling a folded up piece of paper from his shorts pocket. "I'll get to the point. The historical society is having a historic home tour to raise money to buy and restore the old Parnell place on Main Street. We're calling it a Haunted History of Allister. Of course, none of the homes are haunted, but we're modeling it after the one in New Orleans. Naturally, I thought of you and this house."

"Naturally. So, when is it? On Halloween?"

"Nope. Tuesday, the twenty-first. From five to nine p.m. So, what do you say, Cleo? Can I count on you and Bertram?"

"Somebody else dropped out, didn't they?"

"You got me, Cleo. But your house is great. Come on, do it for the historical society. Pretty please?"

Oh, no. Not the begging. Not the puppy-dog eyes. Marty knew how to penetrate my defenses. It was the only thing of mine he could penetrate, bless his gay little heart.

"All right. We'll do it."

"Great! I knew I could count on you, Cleo." He unfolded the

paper in his hand and passed it to me. "Fill out this bio and fax it to me by tomorrow. I need to upload it onto our website ASAP."

I sneaked a peek at the questionnaire.

Year built?

Who originally owned your home?

Are there any ghost stories associated with your house? Any special possessions significant to the house?

Marty was saying, "You can decorate for Halloween or not. Whatever you're comfortable doing. But, sugar, I recommend you ditch the Velvet Elvis. That's what I call truly scary."

5

And speaking of scary, my sister, Molly, popped over from next door where she runs a Bed and Breakfast out of her historic home. No make-up unless you count the mascara smudged under her eyes. No jewelry. Bed hair. Her shapeless *Large Expressions* blouse wrinkled and smudged with chocolate.

"God, it sucks to be me," she said, tugging on the spiky ends of her short, blonde hair.

"Richard the Bastard?" It hurt my heart to see my former cheerleader, popular-girl sister look so bedraggled all the time. But with four girls to take care of as a single parent and the former love of her life shacked up with a twenty-two-year-old stripper named Candy, I could hardly blame her.

"Yeah, Richard. And Mr. Vassals. I mean, Aaron." She paused, sniffing the air like a hound on a scent. "Where are your Krispy Kremes? And don't hold out on me, Cleo. I am not a woman to be fiddled with."

"We're all out."

Molly shot me a look that said I was on dangerous ground as she blazed her way into my kitchen.

"Seriously," I said. "We're all out."

"I know how you keep junk food stashed." She snatched open, and then slammed, each cabinet door in her hunt. "Where's your stash? Where is it?"

"If I tell you, will you calm down and tell me what's going on?"

"Absolutely."

"Okay, go in the parlor; I'll bring you your fix. But I want you to know, it's against my better judgment."

"Yeah, yeah, yeah, just bring me the goodies."

I grabbed a couple of king-sized Snicker bars from my kitty-cat cookie jar and was opening the fridge when I heard, "Oh my God! What is a Velvet Elvis doing in your dining room?"

"Oh, that." I added a couple of Cokes to our mid-morning snack and headed toward the parlor. "It's just a little thing Bertram gave me." I deliberately mumbled what I said next.

"What? I didn't understand you."

I plopped down on the couch adjacent to the leather loveseat where Molly sat, but not before moving aside a dozen little jingly cat toys. The upholstery sported a lovely coating of orange cat hair, but I thought it went well with the hunter green walls and the gold drapes dressing the picture window.

"That's because I didn't want you to."

Molly tore off the wrapper of her Snickers. "And why's that?"

"Because it's mortifying."

My sister pierced me with a look. "Spill it, Cleo."

"Oh, all right. It's my anniversary present."

"No!"

"Yes. And he hung it up there himself this morning. I tried to take it down, but it weighs a ton. I'm surprised the nail is still holding it."

"That is so unlike Bertram." Molly used her candy bar like a pointer. "So, what are you going to do?"

I shrugged. "Dunno. Something. I just know I don't want news of it spread around town. I have to think of a way to get rid of it without hurting Bertram's feelings. Especially since Marty wants our house on the historic home tour now."

Molly face lit up. "Oh, I'm so glad you're doing it. Now both our houses will be on the tour. Are you sure Bertram wasn't giving you a gag gift?"

"Pretty sure," I said in sing-song snark. "I don't think he would have hung it on the wall if it were a joke."

"Good point."

"So what's going on with Richard and Aaron?"

Molly smoothed out her empty candy wrapper. "Richard's been hitting me up for money ever since we received our inheritance. The S.O.B. is supposed to be paying me child support, but he wants *me* to sell the lake house and give him half. But I inherited that after our divorce, so it's not an asset he gets to split. What I really want to know is, what's that stripper wife of his doing? Sitting on her ass and watching *Jerry Springer* all day?"

Yikes. Richard really was a bastard—a bastard having a chronic mid-life crisis.

"And Aaron? Did you take my advice and go talk to him after the P.T.A. meeting?"

"Yeah, but I've lost my mojo. I could see it in his eyes. I'm just a student's mother, not someone he'd actually want to date."

"Well, don't give up. I mean, look at me. I think this third time is the charm."

Elvis Presley singing "I Can't Stop Loving You" popped into my mind. Weird. I didn't even know I knew that song. Must have heard it at Georgia's. I glanced at the Velvet Elvis. And did a double take. I could have sworn his profile now faced the opposite direction.

Molly was about to speak, but I interrupted her. "Um, does the Velvet Elvis look different to you?"

"In what way?"

Boy, I felt like a dodo now. Molly obviously didn't see any difference. "Um, I don't know. It just seems different."

"Different from what?"

"Different from a moment ago."

"What's going on, Cleo?"

"Well, this is totally stupid, but the painting's supposed to be haunted."

"Are you serious?"

"Oh, yeah. Georgia bought it from some roadside vendor on a trip to Graceland, and the guy told her it was haunted. And she fell for it."

Molly crossed her arms. "That is a bunch of hooey, Cleo. Ghosts only exist in stories. And even if there were such things, why the hell would they want to haunt a tacky painting when they could inhabit some fabulous antebellum mansion or a county courthouse?"

"Good point."

"I think your imagination's working overtime. That thing's no more haunted than this Snickers wrapper is."

"You're probably right."

"Of course, I'm right. What's it supposed to do, anyway?"

"Sing 'Heartbreak Hotel' in the dead of night."

"Well, there you go. I guess some people will believe anything."

"Yep."

"But Cleo, if it does ever sing for real, call *The Oprah Winfrey Show.* You'll be famous."

Right. I'd rather be caught dead than admit to anything like that. I was already having to do damage control from all my marriages. I sure as hell didn't need to tarnish my reputation further. Which was why I needed to figure a way to get that thing off the wall and stashed out of sight before anyone else saw it.

6

But I didn't figure a way. The thing was just too damned heavy to get it off the wall without hurting myself or damaging the house, should it slip out of my hands. And Bertram was still too googly-eyed about the painting for me to ask him to move it yet. I really was in quite the pickle. Hide the eyesore and hurt my husband's feelings, or leave it be and risk social humiliation? Boy, what a quandary.

The other thing I didn't do was fill out the historic home tour bio for Marty. In truth, I actually forgot about it. Between tackling glamorous chores like scrubbing the toilet, coaching the ASU majorettes, and teaching private twirling lessons, it slipped my mind.

And when I finally did remember it the next morning, I couldn't find it to save my life. It wasn't on the little table by the front door where I'd left it. I didn't remember moving it. Surely Bertram hadn't filled it out.

Oh crap! I'd forgotten to even tell him about it.

So I figured that would be a good way to start the day. Fill Bertram in on the historical society fundraiser and see if he knew where the bio might be. But on my way to the kitchen, I detoured through the parlors and dining room, opening the drapes to let the morning sun in. And no matter where I stood in those front downstairs rooms, it seemed as if the Velvet Elvis's one-eyed gaze followed me.

Creepy.

But not necessarily a sign of a haunting. Just an optical illusion. But it didn't stop me from wanting to throw a sheet over it. In fact, that sounded like something I could do after breakfast. I had a Laura Ashley five-hundred-count, Egyptian cotton sheet that would look lovely thrown up on the wall. Didn't everyone decorate that way?

When I entered the kitchen, Bertram was merrily making breakfast at the gas range. My first thought was that he was making pancakes.

Bertram threw me a good-natured glance and a smile. "You know what I have a hankering for this morning?"

I peered at the griddle. Not pancakes. "Grilled cheese sandwiches?"

"Nope. A fried peanut butter and banana sandwich." He levered the spatula underneath one and expertly flipped it to brown in bubbling butter.

"Didn't Elvis eat those?"

"I don't know. Maybe."

"I thought you didn't like banana sandwiches of any kind because your mother made you eat them with mayonnaise when you were a kid."

Bertram tamped the golden-brown bread with the spatula. "Well, that's true. But I woke up wanting one just the same. And I'm making you one, too."

"Well aren't you just the sweetest thing?"

Before this morning, a fried pb&b sandwich would have held zero appeal to me, but they actually smelled good. Of course, Southerners tend to fry everything. I've rarely had anything fried that wasn't good. Besides, if I didn't like it, I'd never have to eat it again.

"Say, I misplaced an important paper, and I was wondering if you've seen it?"

Bertram turned off the burner, flopped a golden sandwich on a plate, and passed it to me. "Was it the Haunted History of Allister form? Cool idea. I think it'll be fun." He slipped the remaining butter-soaked sandwich into a Ziploc baggie.

"Yeah. I thought I'd lost it. Marty would have a cow."

Bertram kissed my forehead. This was his signature, running-out-the-door move. "Marty would have a zebra ... with pink stripes."

I grinned. "Yep, that, too."

Bertram grabbed some napkins, then snagged a Dr. Pepper from the fridge, and headed for the door. "Gotta run, sweetheart. See you at lunch."

"What'd you do with the form?" I didn't want to spend the rest of the morning turning the house upside down looking for it.

He called out from the foyer. "I went ahead and filled it out while you were at the Y last night, then faxed it to Marty."

Sweet. One less thing to do.

7

The phone rang a couple of hours later. I figured it was Molly calling to kvetch about her love woes. Or maybe Martha Jane asking me to take in another stray cat.

It was neither.

"Mrs. Cleo Tidwell?" a woman said.

"Yes?" I said cautiously.

"My name is Faye Eldritch. You don't know me, but I saw the highlight about your house on the Allister Historical Society website this morning ..."

"Uh huh." I wished she'd get to the point. I really needed to run to Piggly Wiggly before heading out to ASU.

"And my spirit guides told me to contact you immediately ..."

Spirit guides?

"You and your husband are in grave danger—"

Danger? "Is this a prank? Did Bertram put you up to this?"

"I assure you, Mrs. Tidwell, this is no prank. But the good news is that for only $39.95, I can cleanse the evil from your house."

The evil from my house? "What are you talking about?"

"The painting of Elvis. It's evil. You must—"

I hung up.

And dashed upstairs to my office, a corner room in front with quaint, hinged windows, a coal-burning fireplace, and blue walls. I Googled the historical society's website, then clicked on their tenth annual historic home tour. Our house was the first one.

Cleo and Bertram Tidwell, owners of the McKay-James house at 618 Founder's Row, might not have any ghosts residing in their hundred-year-old Victorian, but they do possess a haunted painting of Elvis Presley done on black velvet. Bertram Tidwell relays this story: "As soon as I saw the painting, I knew it would be the perfect gift to give my wife on our third wedding anniversary."

As to whether or not the painting is really haunted, Bertram had this to say: "Absolutely. When it's dead quiet, if you stand close to it and hold your breath, you can hear the King."

Which begs the question, "And what does the King say?" To which Bertram replied, "I'm so lonesome, I could cry ..."

I wanted to bang my head on the desk. We were going to be the joke of the tour, not to mention the talk of the town. Marty must have laughed his ass off as he uploaded our info onto the website. I was going to call him right this moment and tell him to take out that crapola about the Velvet Elvis.

But he called me first.

"Hey, Cleo! I had my doubts when I got Bertram's fax last night. But I gotta tell ya, we've already been getting a very favorable response to the tour. Very favorable. It's downright genius. People are even asking if the painting will talk when they view it, so you and Bertram might want to come up with a way to rig it so that it does. I think this'll be the most successful tour yet."

Oh, great. Talk about a hard place and a rock. Gee, which should I choose? Swallowing my pride and raising money for charity? Or pull the plug on the whole thing and go douse the painting with lighter fluid and toss a match at it? Hmm ... tick tock, tick tock ...

Yeesh, I couldn't pull the rug out from under the tour if the Velvet Elvis was generating so much positive response. I wasn't *that* self involved.

"I was just looking at the website," I said. "You did a great job. I'm looking forward to the tour." Yeah, liar, liar, pants on fire. "Hope y'all raise a lot of money."

"Me, too. See you soon, luv."

Guess I was going to have to bite the bullet and live with the painting for a few more weeks. Martha Jane always says that nothing worthwhile is easy. This whole Velvet Elvis thing was going to put that to the test. After all, it was just a piece of artwork, however undignified and lacking in taste it might be. Besides, it was just a small town historical tour, it wasn't like the whole world was gonna know.

Yeah, right.

PART I:
ALL SHOOK UP

CHAPTER TWO

Three Weeks Later
Friday, October 17

1

Little Jamie Sue Deaton, one of my home-schooled students, tossed her silver baton into the air, spun around three times, and then caught it flawlessly. I applauded from my coach's chair on the driveway. The morning held a nip I knew would burn off by ten o'clock. I was quite comfy in gray coach's pants and an ASU sweatshirt with a white polo shirt underneath.

October in Alabama is a mix of summer and autumn—sweltering heat and humidity some days, clear blue skies with cool, crisp air on others. Leaves don't tend to change color till November, if at all. The gingko tree in the front yard was still a month away from bursting into glorious, golden color. While the azaleas, the camellia, and the boxwoods that made up the hedges on either side of our property stayed green year round.

"Very good, Jamie Sue. I can tell you've been practicing."

The little girl beamed from the praise. "Yes, ma'am. Mama said I'd get a Coke and a candy bar if I practice an hour every day."

"Well, it's paying off. I want you to work on your fishtails between now and next week."

A rusted-out station wagon turned onto Founder's Row and trundled along the street. The engine back-fired and a plume of black smoke jettisoned from the tailpipe. The car was definitely at odds with the stately Victorian homes in my neighborhood. As it passed the vacant Queen Anne for sale next door, the front passenger window rolled down with the jerkiness of a hand crank.

Oh, great. Yet another redneck drive-by. All in a day of fun at the increasingly popular Tidwell house.

The station wagon lurched to a halt, effectively blocking the driveway. A puffy-faced woman, her head taken over by sponge rollers, leaned out the window and shouted, "Can we see your Velvet Elvis?"

"Sorry," I hollered back. "No early birds."

The woman frowned, reminding me of a bull dog's face. "But we drove all the way from Mississippi."

"I'm sorry. We're not a museum. The historic home tour is next Tuesday. There's a Motel 6 down by the interstate." I assumed that's where they'd want to stay.

The station wagon shuddered into motion, vomiting smoke from its tailpipe again. As it rolled past the boundary line between my house and Molly's, puffy woman shot me the bird. Fortunately, Jamie Sue was packing up her batons and didn't see it.

Mrs. Deaton's SUV pulled up at the curb, and Jamie Sue bounced over and got in.

I waved good-bye. "See you next week."

As I gathered my folding chair, batons, and stopwatch, a couple more cars trundled down the street, slowing when they got to my house. But no one stopped or shouted anything from the window—always a big plus when you've become a minor celebrity over something as tacky as a haunted Velvet Elvis. But the infamy, no matter how distasteful, was for charity. Something I had to remind myself of constantly.

2

The sheet had fallen off the Velvet Elvis again and lay puddled on the blue-tiled hearth in the formal dining room. Now that he was uncovered, Mr. One Eye seemed to follow my every move. No matter where I stood, he seemed to be watching me. What was that song of paranoia from the 80s? "I Always Feel Like Somebody's Watching Me"?

Uh huh.

I fetched the step ladder yet again, along with some push pins, and tacked a navy blue sheet to the picture frame. I even used a hammer to secure the thumb tacks. The King could stay covered until the Open House. Just because the historical society was selling a lot of tickets because of the painting's notoriety didn't mean I had to look at it from now until then.

Once that task was done, I checked the answering machine in the kitchen. We'd been getting so many calls, I'd taken to turning the ringer off and screening all incoming messages. The red light blinked like a neon sign in Vegas.

I hit play.

The machine said, "You have thirty-seven messages." And that was just in the past hour.

Beep.

"Is Elvis the only dude y'all talk to, or have you heard from Jimmy Hoffa, too?"

Beep.

"Cleo, this is Shelly Clark. Did you know you and Bertram are on YouTube? It's from when y'all were on Bippy. Call me."

Beep.

"Uh … yeah. I hope I have the right number. I'm in Panama City, and I swear I just saw the King playing Goofy Golf."

Beep.

"This is Bob and Susie Patterson in Oakland, California. We'd like to buy your house, but only if the Velvet Elvis remains."

Beep.

"My name is Joe Rossi, and I'm a professional artist. For the bargain price of only three hundred dollars, I'll paint a velvet Priscilla for you so Elvis won't be so lonesome."

Beep.

"This is Faye Eldritch again. Please call me back, Mrs. Tidwell. Your house needs cleansing. That painting is evil."

Beep.

"Miss Cleo Tidwell," a friendly Southern woman said, "the Fabulous Fried Okra Queens of Allister would love to have you as a member of our way-fun little group. Give me a call, and let's talk about you meetin' the other girls. Oh, this is Queen Bee Purdee Delicious, otherwise known as Julia McKee. Call me. You'll love us!"

Beep.

Oh the irony. When I was younger, I couldn't get the time of day from the Junior League, but now that I was almost thirty-nine, the Fried Okra Queens were practically begging me to join. I'd seen them in local parades wearing their pink wigs, sparkly crowns, bodacious evening dresses, and pink high-top tennis shoes. Unless it was Halloween, a costume party, or a show, I did not want to be seen in public in that kind of get-up. It was too undignified. I can remember so many times as a child when I'd be ready to head out the door to school and Martha Jane would go, "You're not wearing that out in public. Cleo, how many times have I told you? You don't wear flowerdy underwear with white pants." Or "Those feathers on your top make you look like a hooker. Take it off and put something else on." Martha Jane, ya gotta love her.

The rest of the messages were more of the same. The final communiqué, however, was in a class of its own.

"That painting doesn't rightfully belong to you," said a woman with a serious Southern accent. Her voice was so devoid of warmth, I thought the machine was going to ice over. "We've been searching for it a long time, and just because you found it, doesn't mean it's yours. Hand it over or we'll put a hurtin' on you."

And that was it. No name. No way to identify who she was. I certainly didn't recognize the voice. Even though I knew deep down it was just some kook yanking my chain, my stomach clenched and my hands went clammy. Other than the puffy-faced woman shooting me the bird, this was the first threatening overture, and it spooked me that it could kidnap my emotions so effectively.

I leaned back against the breakfast bar. It amazed me that something so banal as a Velvet Elvis could inspire so many crazy people. Or maybe I'd never really known crazy and was meeting up with the real deal for the first time.

I hesitated deleting that last message, then thought, *Why give more power to a kook?* So, I got rid of it.

The back door opened and Molly whisked in, a magazine rolled up in one hand. I glanced over at her, then had to look again. Low-rise jeans hugged curvaceous hips, and a snug top displayed a fair amount of cleavage. Artfully applied make-up accentuated her blue eyes and peaches-and-cream complexion. And her blonde hair had bounce.

"Who are you and what have you done with my sister?" I grinned. Molly might still be a plus-size, but now she had Va Va Voom, a lá the pre-divorce era.

"He asked me out!" She smiled like the cat who ate the canary.

"Who?"

"Aaron Vassals."

"Details, woman."

"Our first date is tomorrow night—"

Disappointment and happiness warred in my heart. A date meant Molly wouldn't be coming to my family dinner party tomorrow night, but I was psyched that the guy she was sweet on had finally noticed her.

"—and I'm bringing him here. He's an Elvis fan and wants to see your famous painting. I hope that's okay."

Yeesh. It wasn't like the cat wasn't already out of the bag. "Yeah, okay, the more the merrier," I said with heavy sarcasm. "I'm just surprised he's into Elvis."

"Yeah, me, too. But I don't care. He asked me out!" And she whirled around my kitchen like a ballerina.

"So, whatcha got in your hand there?"

"Oh my God! You and Bertram are in *Snazzy Magazine*." She thumbed through the tabloid to a dog-eared page. "Look. It's from the *Bippy Barndale Show*."

"*Snazzy*? Let me see that." Oh, dear Lord, I was going to need to break open the Pinot Noir and it wasn't even lunchtime yet. I'd mightily resisted doing a stint with Bertram on the public access show known around town as the Bippy Barndale Busybody Hour but Marty had talked me into it. In for a penny, in for a pound and all that happy crappy.

Bippy, heiress to the Olson Manufacturing fortune and a local celebrity with her own cable talk show, courtesy of her daddy's millions, had sat catty-corner from us on her TV set in a cushy wingback chair upholstered in a velvety, avocado green, a throwback to the Dick Cavett and Merv Griffin days. She'd worn an honest to God turban and a shiny, gold pantsuit that had nearly blinded me in the bright studio lights. And for all her money, no one had ever told her that tweezing her brows bald, and then drawing them back on with a make-up pencil was a big beauty no-no.

Bertram had sat next to me, holding the bottom edge of the Velvet Elvis on his thighs so that the painting completely hid him from view. For a moment, it had seemed as if Bertram had disappeared from the hips up, and Elvis had taken his place.

Apparently, someone in the studio audience had snapped a picture of that brief instant with their cell phone and then sent it to *Snazzy* ... as well as uploaded a video to YouTube. Gee, would the fun never end? Only a few more days till Mr. One Eye could go bye-

bye. Until then, I'd just grin and bear it. After all, the historical society was going to make a lot of money from this fundraiser. *Uh huh, keep telling yourself that.*

"Well, I don't want to keep you," Molly said, handing me the magazine. "I know you've gotta head to work soon. I just wanted to drop this by."

I thanked her and said I was looking forward to meeting Aaron. Then I puttered around the kitchen a bit before tackling domestic tasks like scooping cat poop from the litter boxes in the laundry room and gathering clean clothes from the dryer to take upstairs. But first, I stopped by the dining room.

The five-hundred count, Egyptian-cotton sheet lay puddled on the floor again, and the Velvet Elvis watched me from on high.

3

I backed out of the drive and headed off to Allister State University in my cute little PT Cruiser. I think I hit every red light along the way. Each time I waited in traffic, I thought about how I'd first met Bertram in marching band when we'd been undergrads at ASU. I'd been a majorette, and he'd been the handsome drum major. Even though we were both from Allister, our paths had never crossed. He'd gone to private school while I'd attended Allister High. We'd dated off and on in college for two years until I'd met Stuart Benedict at a fraternity party. I wound up marrying Stuart, only to divorce him a year later when the drug addiction he'd been hiding became evident. But by that time, Bertram was out in Texas, working on his Ph.D. in music.

At the sixth red light, I glanced in the rearview mirror while I waited for green. A black Ford pickup idled behind me. Couldn't really tell if the driver was a man or a woman. I decided to go with man 'cause of the broad shoulders. He wore a ball cap tugged low on his brow and a pair of reflective sunglasses. The driver must have met my gaze in the mirror because he revved his truck a couple of times like he was raring to go. I quickly looked away. I hate passive-aggressive jackasses.

The light finally changed, and I zoomed forward.

But when I made a couple of turns off Main Street, the truck stuck to my rear like a turd on a fat cat's ass.

Now, I was getting a little freaked.

So, I took a roundabout route, one where I backtracked a few times and meandered as if I were out for a Sunday drive, even though it was Friday midday. No matter what I did, I couldn't lose the black pickup. The asshole on my tail was going to make me late for work, and that pissed me off.

So, I decided to head on over to the university. It was broad daylight, after all.

I pulled into my parking space and turned off the engine. The truck sidled up behind my car, effectively blocking me in.

Oh, no. This couldn't be good.

I grabbed my cell phone and flipped it open, ready to dial 911.

The guy in the truck just sat there. Oh, he was glaring at me through those sunglasses because I could see him looking at me in the mirror. My watch said 1:05 p.m. I should have been in the band hall fifteen minutes ago.

Okay, this was creepy, but I needed to get on in to Goodlett Hall.

So, I stepped out of the car.

The driver's door on the pickup opened. And a woman slid out. I say woman because she had a big bosom, but in all other respects she looked like an overweight man, even down to the nearly shaved head which explained why the ball cap rode so low.

"You Cleo Tidwell?" she said with some serious attitude. At least it wasn't the same creepy voice on the answering machine.

"Maybe. Who's askin'?" Oh, I was so brave. Uh huh. My voice had a little tremble in it.

"You the one that's got that Velvet Elvis, the one that's

haunted?" She took a step towards me, reminding me of a prison matron.

I took a step back. "Why do you want to know?"

"'Cause Spike and me—Spike's my honey—we have Elvis's love child through alien inception … you know, like on The X-Files? And when we saw you on TV, tellin' how Elvis talks to you through a painting, well, we just knew we had to contact you. 'Cause we're like…," she let it dangle as if searching for the right word, "cosmic twins."

I was thinking more like kooks, but who was I to argue with a woman twice my size?

"That's nice. I'm happy for you—"

"Darlene."

"Huh?" I took another step back.

"Darlene. My name's Darlene."

"Right. Well, Darlene, I'm late for work, so if you don't mind—"

"You don't believe me." She crossed her arms under her humongous boobs.

"Oh, don't be so sure." I took two more steps back. "Say, why don't you email me all about it? What do you say?" A few more steps and I was nearly to the bumper of the white SUV parked in front of me.

"I don't have your email address."

"Ask the aliens!" And I sprinted across the asphalt to the music department.

4

Bertram was hunched over his desk, scribbling furiously on a yellow legal pad, when I entered his office. Disheveled heaps of sheet music and marching-band diagrams cluttered his workspace. A portable CD player squatted atop a stack of papers, acting like a paperweight, and an alto sax lay atop another. His laptop balanced in the middle of it all.

I stood in the doorway of his office for a moment, remembering our college days when all the girls in band had referred to Bertram as "the Greek god." And he was still a good looking devil. His olive complexion allowed him to tan easily, and his chestnut-brown hair tended to lighten to a reddish-blonde in the summer. His deep brown eyes could melt me with a single look.

"Hey, handsome," I said, all prepared to launch into my harrowing escape from Darlene and the creepy phone message from the Ice Queen.

Bertram's face lit up. "Let's go to Graceland!"

I grabbed a chair and pulled it around the desk so I could sit next to my hubby. "You're awfully chipper. Are you on something?"

"Just high on life, baby." And he yanked me to him and stole a kiss. Even though we were at work, he still managed to get my engines thrumming.

"So, what brought this on?" I said.

"Graceland or the high on life?"

"Let's start with Graceland."

"I was thinking today how it's been a long time since I've seen it."

"Really? You told me it would take a team of wild broncos to make you set foot in Graceland ... ever."

"Did I?" He looked genuinely surprised.

"Um, yeah."

"Hmm. That's weird. I have the oddest feeling that I've been there before ... like when you're dreaming but you're not yourself." He shook his head as if the clear the cobwebs from his brain. "Maybe I'm working too hard on the Elvis Extravaganza."

"That's probably it. I'm sure the older alumni are going to enjoy it."

"Speaking of which." Bertram refreshed his laptop and pulled up email, clicking on the most recent one. "The seamstress finished the drum major's jumpsuit. Doesn't it look authentic?"

Not only authentic, but identical to the one in the Velvet Elvis—white, rhinestone-spangled, bell-bottomed, and topped off with a cape. Made me wonder if Elvis had been a caped crusader on the side.

Bertram tapped the legal pad with a pen. "Came up with a few embellishments for the show this morning."

"Embellishments?" Hmm. We already had the majorettes in poodle skirts twirling hula-hoop batons to "Jailhouse Rock." For "Burning Love," they were gonna whip off their skirts to twirl fire-batons in their orange-and-white-sequined costumes. We'd added capes to the marching-band uniforms, courtesy of the Alumni Band Club, and our drum major, Dwight Holcombe, would be wearing the white jumpsuit, as well as an Elvis wig. I wasn't sure how we could embellish it any further without going all Super Bowl Half-Time Show with it. And we had neither the time nor resources for something like that. Nor the need.

"Yeah. I want the band to march into the stadium carrying your Velvet Elvis."

"What?"

"We'll prop it up in the stands like it's watching the game. Like a good luck charm. Or a mascot."

"Huh? We've already got a mascot."

"You can never have too many mascots. It's an Alabama tradition. Auburn Tigers and War Eagle. Crimson Tide and 'Bama Elephants. The ASU Fighting Ferrets and—"

"Velvet Elvii? That's not a mascot. Bertram, you're not making any sense—"

"We'll get the dance team to dress up as basset hounds and prance around on the field to 'Hound Dog.' And for the finale, I'll come out with a microphone in rolled up blue jeans and a leather jacket, and sing 'Blue Suede Shoes' while the *Flying Elvii* parachute into the stadium like *Honeymoon in Vegas*. Damn, but I've always wanted to meet those guys."

Really? This was news to me. "Bertram, are you okay? Did you whack your head on a tuba?"

Bertram looked at me like I was the nutty one. "I'm fine, Cleo. Really."

"If you say so."

Could you catch Elvis Mania? And if so, was there a cure?

5

The afternoon was close to being over as I headed back to the parking lot after marching band practice. I had a lot of errands to run to get ready for tomorrow night's dinner party. But when I reached the PT Cruiser, I thought I was going to have a hissy fit right then and there. Someone had soaped the C-word on my windows.

Well, son of a biscuit!

It must have been Darlene. I guess I should have been thankful for small favors. She could have sliced my tires or put sugar in the gas tank. Yeesh! And I'd never gotten a chance to tell Bertram about her or the Ice Queen's phone message. Maybe she and Darlene were in cahoots. Right. And maybe I was being paranoid.

Of course, it's not paranoia if someone's really out to get you.

6

A detour to the car wash did the trick. Rivulets of water dripped from the Cruiser as I shot into a parking spot at the Piggly Wiggly. I really wanted to whiz in, get my shopping done, and get out again without having to shoot the poop with anyone I knew. With all the hoopla over the Velvet Elvis and the historic home tour, going out in public could balloon into a serious time bandit nowadays. Everyone and their brother wanted to know all about the painting, and if I thought it was really haunted, and where they could buy tickets for the tour. I just wasn't in the mood for all that today, especially after

Darlene's little shenanigan.

Snagging a cart, I wheeled into produce, ready to play Speed Shop. I zoomed around the store, almost running over a woman with a walker when I swung around the end of the bread aisle too fast. With only frozen foods left to go, I was almost done.

As I stood beside a freezer debating the merits of Ben & Jerry's versus a lemon meringue pie, I heard a familiar voice say my name on the other side of the aisle, followed by, "Married three times before her second high school reunion. Can you believe her husband gave her that horrid Velvet Elvis for their wedding anniversary? And they're featuring it in a historic home tour? What'll they do to top that next year? Showcase a trailer park?"

I knew that voice anywhere. Cathy Wilson Godwin. Who'd married a local plastic surgeon and had the hooters to show for it. Geez, we were twenty years out of high school, and she was still a snooty bitch. The last time I'd seen her I'd been buying thong panties at Eberhart's and had been forced to leave them in the gourmet food aisle because, Lord knows, I did not want Cathy Godwin to know what kind of underwear I wore. It would wind up being everyone's business.

I really didn't want to run into her now, or pretty much ever.

The woman she was talking to said, "Well, bless her heart." And then they both laughed, an ugly mocking sound.

I hunkered down over my cart and zoomed toward the checkout. My dessert selection could wait. On second thought, maybe I'd just leave the cart and come back tomorrow. Yeah, that was the ticket.

I was just about home free when Cathy said my maiden name as if she hadn't seen me since high school. "Cleo? Cleo Kilgore?"

Oh, great. My day just got better. *Riiiight.*

I halted in my tracks and slowly turned to face her.

Cathy's tennis outfit was too clean and white for her to have actually played tennis in it, and her make-up was Merle Norman perfect. Don't even get me started on her hair, and nails, and all the jewelry she was wearing. I mean, who gets dolled up like that just to buy groceries? Cathy Godwin, that's who.

"Why Cleo, I *thought* that was you. How's your husband these days? What's his name? Barney? Bernard? Byron?—"

"Bertram. He's just fine," I said through gritted teeth while forcing a smile.

"Oh, that's right. Bertram." She laughed as if she'd just made a joke. "It is hard to keep them all straight since you've had so many."

I had to hand it to the woman. She had some cajones.

"Say, I was just heading up front to get a Coke. Would you like one?"

She seemed taken aback at that. As if I'd forgotten how she'd kept me out of Keyettes in high school.

"Uh, sure. Diet would be nice."

I trotted over to the Coke machine. Even though Cathy irritated the stink out of me, it wasn't proper for me to get into a cat fight with her in public. I could hear Daddy telling me, "Never let on that you don't like someone in public." It was taking all of my moral fortitude to restrain myself, though. Cathy making fun of Bertram was like waving a red flag at a bull. I was about ready to gore her.

And with that in mind, a moral dilemma presented itself as the second twelve-ounce can came barreling out of the machine.

To shake or not to shake?

That was the question.

I heard arguments from opposing counsel.

Crazy Cleo: *Shake it. Shake it good!*

Rational Cleo: *But you'll stain that white dress.*

Crazy Cleo: *Remember how she had you black-balled from the cheerleading squad?*

Rational Cleo: *Let bygones be bygones.*

I said, "Who are you kidding?" and some people walking into the store looked at me like I was nuts.

So I shook up the drink despite my daddy's words of wisdom.

The afternoon was looking up.

7

It was dark when I got home with the groceries. Not a single house light was on inside or out. Molly's house was dark to the left. The vacant house was dark to the right. And the street light didn't quite pierce the gloom of our wrap-around porch.

Where was Bertram? He was usually home by this time. But his convertible wasn't in the driveway.

I got out of the car, my batons in one hand, my keys in the other, and my purse on my shoulder. The gingko tree beside the drive rustled in the breezy night, casting dappled shadows on the PT Cruiser. I wanted to get the front door unlocked and some lights on before I started bringing in the Piggly Wiggly bags.

No sooner had I stepped up onto the porch when a soft, Southern male voice said, "Miz Tidwell?" and a man-sized shadow disengaged itself from the wicker love seat.

I shrieked, jumping about two feet into the air, batons flailing. I think my stomach did a free-fall down to my toes. The batons hit pay dirt, thudding against something fleshy. The reverberation traveled up my arm.

"Whoa there, little lady," the man said. "I didn't mean to scare you. I just wanted to talk to you about your Velvet Elvis."

"Stay where you are! Don't come any closer!" I stood poised like Uma Thurman in *Kill Bill*, batons held high, ready to strike. Yeah, like I was so threatening.

"I don't mean you any harm."

"Good! Then don't move while I unlock the door, or I'll whack you again."

I rammed the house key into the dead bolt, shoved open the door, zoomed inside, and switched on the porch and parlor lights while slamming the door shut and locking it. "The police are coming!" I peeked through a clear panel in the stained glass.

"Look," the man said, stepping into view. "I don't want any trouble."

He was a big man and had one of those physiques where his belly made him look eight months pregnant while the rest of him was slim. His thick, coal-black hair was slicked back into a pompadour and mutton-chop sideburns jutted down his cheeks and jaw. A nylon baseball jacket covered a t-shirt sporting an *I'm with Elvis* iron-on. His jeans were buckled low on his hips to accommodate his done-lop.

Oh, brother. Another Elvis kook. I guess it wasn't enough for them to leave phone messages or soap dirty words on my car anymore.

"The historic home tour is next Tuesday night," I shouted through the door. "The Velvet Elvis will be on view then and not a minute before. Now, I suggest you skedaddle unless you want to answer uncomfortable questions from the police about why you were lurking on my front porch in the dark when no one was home."

"Yes, ma'am," he said, sounding contrite. "Sorry to have scared the bejeezus out of you. I'll be in touch." And he turned on his boot heel and disappeared into the night.

I leaned against the door, my heart still off at the Indy 500. Where was my husband? I called his cell phone but no answer. I really didn't want to go out and get the groceries by myself. So I called D.K. Greenwood, my old high school chum with the Allister P.D., and asked him if he could send a car to drive by and check out the neighborhood.

While I waited, I played back all the new messages on the answering machine.

There were eight stories from strangers saying they'd seen the King having a Frosty at Wendy's or waiting for a Greyhound at the bus station. Five requests to see the painting before the tour, including one from a Dupree Hardcastle with The Church of the Blue Suede Shoes. Call it a hunch, but I had a feeling I'd just met ole

Dupree.

Sean Johnson, an executive producer with the Sci-Fi Channel's *The Dead Speak*, had left a message reconfirming the filming of their show at our house on the night of the 25th. It wasn't a show I normally watched, but I was aware of it. They employed a psychic who sniffed out ghosts in people's houses and belongings. I thought it was all a bunch of hooey, myself. Initially I'd balked at their first overture. No way were we going to be on a national TV show because of a velvet painting. But they'd thrown money at the problem, and well, as Bertram put it, I could be unhappy in Allister about our fifteen minutes of fame or I could be unhappy in the Bahamas on a second honeymoon with money to spare. When he put it that way …

The last message was Bertram saying he was going to be home a little later than usual tonight.

The doorbell rang, signaling that the police had arrived. They searched the yard while I got all the groceries out of the car. It was nice knowing my tax dollars were going to good use.

"All clear, ma'am," said the nice patrolman. "Give us a call if he shows up again."

"Thank you, officer."

I figured it was Miller Time after the scare I'd had, so I grabbed a beer from the fridge, then trotted into the living room to become one with some leftover pizza and the TV remote.

The one beer became three, and by that time, I had channel surfing down to an art form. I happened across an old Elvis Presley movie. Those nifty little buttons on the remote let me access some informational doo-hickey that comes with having cable, and I found out—Presto!—that I was watching *Fun in Acapulco*. I kept my eyes peeled for Bertram's mother, which wasn't easy, considering I wanted to curl up on the couch and go to sleep.

The next thing I knew, someone was shaking me, saying, "Wake up, darlin'. You fell asleep on the couch."

I opened my eyes to behold the King himself in my living room. No pompadour for this Elvis, he had that full, seventies-style hair with the tell-tale sideburns, the white rhinestone-studded jumpsuit and matching cape, the gold scarves around his neck, and the wide belt that looked like it belonged on a prize fighter, instead of a pop singer.

I reached out with awe and said, "Elvis?"

And Bertram said, "What do you think? Looks like the real deal, doesn't it?"

"Oh my God! Bertram! What did you do to your hair? And what happened to your beard and moustache?" I tried to sit up, but the room spun, so I stayed put.

Bertram grinned. "Dyed it and shaved it. The sideburns glue on. And don't you just love the jumpsuit? It's the one I had made for Dwight to wear for half-time." He sidled closer, leaned down near my face and said, "Thought I'd bring it home for a little test drive first, if you know what I mean, baby."

Oh, brother. An amorous Elvis. All I needed at the moment.

"Um, Bertram, I'm three sheets to the wind. I'm gonna need help getting upstairs."

What I'd meant to convey was that I was drunker than a skunk and just wanted to sleep in our bed, but what Bertram heard was: *Yeah, baby. Let's get it on. Just help me up those bad-ass stairs first.*

So when we finally made it to the bedroom, Bertram put the moves on me, all the while singing, "Love Me Tender."

But I one-upped him. I passed out again.

I don't think he even knew the difference.

CHAPTER THREE

The Next Day
Saturday, October 18

1

Bertram lathered up his face for a shave at the white ceramic pedestal sink while I perched on the closed toilet seat next to the antique claw-foot tub. He had nothing on but his skivvies, and the view was magnificent.

"Are you going to grow your beard and moustache back?"

"Eventually."

I like a man with a moustache, but I liked the man behind it more. "And what about your hair? Are you going to keep dying it black?"

"Maybe."

That was a cryptic answer. "But you don't look like you."

"Really? I do to me." He ran the razor across his jaw.

"Who do you see in the mirror?" I held my breath, afraid to hear the answer.

"Elvis."

I gasped. I couldn't help it.

Bertram whirled to face me, pointing the razor. "Gotcha!" He laughed. And then I laughed. "Had ya goin' there, didn't I?"

"Yeah, you did."

And for the rest of the morning Bertram seemed like his old self. He didn't sing Elvis songs, didn't glue those silly sideburns on his face, didn't try on the Elvis jumpsuit one last time, didn't eat a triple-bypass-inducing breakfast, didn't tell me he wanted to visit Graceland, didn't babble on about the Flying Elvii, and didn't give the painting a second glance. After lunch he took off in his convertible, saying he had some errands to run, but that he'd be back in plenty of time for the dinner party.

2

With Bertram out of the house, it was time to face the Velvet Elvis again. I gazed up at it, wondering if I should just plaster a Hannah Montana poster over it.

"I can't get you off the wall," I said out loud to nobody. "And I can't seem to keep a sheet thrown over you. Hmm. How can I camouflage you?"

Elvis hadn't "moved" again, but the one eye did seem to be looking down at me even though his face was tilted toward the upraised microphone. And was the corner of his mouth tilted south just the tiniest bit?

Nah. I was being silly. The damn thing was *not* haunted. Georgia had just been suckered.

I had it! I could prop a mirror up on the mantle. It wouldn't completely hide the painting, but it would at least look more period proper than a Velvet Elvis. I toted the mirror down from the attic. The gilt frame, not unlike the painting's frame, was heavy, but not as heavy as Elvis. I hoisted it up onto the mantle from the step ladder, propping it to lean back against the velvet painting.

And voila! All I could see of Mr. One Eye was the top of his head, some black velvet, and the top of the frame. Sure, it looked a little awkward as far as decorating goes, but it beat the alternative.

That taken care of, I hummed old Three Dog Night and CCR

tunes, a bounce in my step as I vacuumed up tumbleweeds of cat hair, gathered up scads of little jingly cat toys from downstairs, lint rolled the upholstery, and ran a dust cloth over the furniture and kitchen counters.

The security chime on the back door cheeped, followed by my sister saying, "Hey, it's me. How 'bout a Coke break on your front porch?"

3

Molly sipped a Diet Coke on the very wicker love seat that Dupree Hardcastle had parked his butt on the night before. I was amazed at the change in my sister. Two weeks ago she would have been drinking regular Coke while snarfing down Krispy Kremes. And she would have been wearing super large, shapeless clothing, not the stylish, form-fitting dress that hugged her ample curves. But the biggest change of all was in her attitude. Whiny, depressed Molly was out and sassy, fun Molly was in.

"Tonight's the night," Molly said. "Hot damn, tonight's the night!"

"The kids?"

"Are at Richard and Candy's this weekend. And even though I need the money, I don't have any guests checking in till tomorrow afternoon. So we'll have the entire house to ourselves once your dinner party is over." She smiled slyly. "I hope you won't think it rude if we eat and run tonight."

"Absolutely not. A girl's gotta do what a girl's gotta do. You just have to promise to give me the details."

"Full disclosure." She laughed like a teenaged girl again, her eyes sparkling. "Cross my heart."

I spotted a white hearse creeping up the street our way. You don't see many white hearses. It crossed the imaginary center line and pulled up in front of our house so that the driver's side was to us.

The window rolled down, and whoever was behind the wheel held an electric megaphone in front of their face.

An old man's pinched voice blasted across the yard. "Repent of your sins now, sayeth the Lord your God. The Devil has come to your house."

Oh, for the love of all that was holy.

The magnet sign on the side of the hearse read:

Burn in Hell Adventist Zion Church
Reverend P.K. Hambright, Minister
Services daily
"Ye must wash in the blood of the lamb."

Great. Just what we needed. Holy Rollers.

The preacher's voice boomed again. "Ye must cast the sickness out so that thy sight may be holy. The beast whose number is six-six-six dwelleth in your heart's desire."

It was bad enough to have this guy roll up at my curb and preach to me via megaphone. But to top it off, he didn't make a lick of sense.

Molly gawked in amazement.

"Welcome to my world," I told her. To Mr. Holy Roller, I shouted, "Okay. Thank you. Have a nice day."

"Repent now before it's too late or ye'll be sorry when you suffer the fiery tortures of hell for all eternity. Burning and screaming in torment forever and ever and ever—"

"Please move along, sir, before I call the police."

"—and ever and ever—"

I motioned for Molly to come inside with me. "I'm calling the police," I hollered. "Now."

We went in and the white hearse moved on. Boy, if the historical society wasn't raising a lot of much-needed funds, I would have pulled out of the tour days ago. But I love old buildings and wanted to help them if I could, even if it meant putting up with some annoying inconveniences for a short time.

"Uh, Cleo. Why is there broken glass all over your dining room?"

"What?"

The mirror I'd put on the mantle lay in a zillion pieces. A few large pieces of glass had gouged my beautiful hard wood floors. With the way things were going, I did *not* need seven years of bad luck tacked onto my life. I had plenty as it was.

As we swept up the mess, I told Molly about my plan to camouflage the Velvet Elvis, at least until the open house.

"Do you think one of your cats might have knocked it off?" she said, carefully picking up jagged chunks of mirror and dropping them in the trash can.

"It's possible," I said slowly. "But improbable. The mantle is too high for them to jump directly onto it. I suppose they could have leapt from the table. But I don't know why they'd want to get up there in the first place. It's weird. That mirror was leaning back, not forward. And it's fairly heavy. I know because I had to lug it down from the attic."

"Well, I'm sorry your mirror is shattered, but Aaron did want to see the Velvet Elvis."

"Oh, and he'll get to." I dumped a dustpan full of glass into the trash. "Boy, how does a piece of glass break into so many tiny pieces?"

"It's like spilled milk. There's always seems to be more than there should be." She carefully pulled a slab of glass out from under one of the iron radiators all the way clear across the room. "Aaron wanted me to ask you something before dinner tonight."

"Yeah?"

"He wants to know if you'd be interested in selling the painting."

"Maybe, but not until after the open house and *The Dead Speak.* You wouldn't believe some of the phone calls we've been getting. One couple offered to buy the house as long as the Velvet Elvis came with it."

"Well, if they're anything like that Holy Roller, I probably would believe it."

"Oh, I haven't told you about what happened yesterday." I filled Molly in on Dupree scaring the bejeezus out of me and Darlene being scary.

Molly shook her head. "Some people just don't understand the concept of boundaries. So, are you excited about being on a national TV show?"

"I would be if it weren't for the velvet atrocity over there. Do you think we could qualify for federal witness protection for harboring such a velvet-offense-against-good-taste? We'd be right up there with people who keep their Christmas lights up year round and yards with ceramic gnome gardens out front.

Molly snorted a laugh.

"So, you seem to have gotten your groove back," I said, happy to change the subject.

"Just call me Stella." My sister grinned, posing like a 1950s pin-up girl. "It's Aaron. I feel like a new woman. And we haven't even gone all the way yet."

"Well, he's sexy as hell. And damn, but the man's got a fine ass."

"I'll tell him you said so." Molly waggled her eyebrows.

"Don't you dare," I said in mock indignation.

"During dinner." She laughed. "Oh, wouldn't Bertram find *that* amusing?"

"Just remember, paybacks are hell."

"Oh, I remember. I think I still owe you for tattling on me about skinny dipping with Wayne Johnson that time his parents were out of town."

Ah, the good ole days. "Yes, well I'm sure there are a few other things I could tell Daddy and Martha Jane that would make their ears burn. Or Aaron's."

We grinned at each other with affection. What's sibling rivalry without one-upping each other?

4

I glanced at the clock for the gazillionth time in the past fifteen minutes. The table was set, the beer was cold, the fried chicken was hot, the biscuits were warm, and the potato logs were greasy. Everyone was due to arrive any moment now, and Bertram still wasn't home. I dialed his cell, but just like last night, all I got was his voicemail. Where was he? What was keeping him? I was getting exasperated. Bertram was usually so considerate. This wasn't like him at all.

Multiple car doors slammed out front. I ducked into the little half-bath under the stairs and touched up my lipstick. My hair had just the right amount of wave, my make-up wasn't shiny yet, and my pink button-down and navy chinos were still pressed and unwrinkled. The clasp on my pearls had migrated south, so I tugged it to the back of my neck. Perfect. I forced a smile in the mirror. Except my smile didn't meet my eyes.

Well, too bad. It was show time, and I was up for the part of the consummate hostess.

Usually the doorbell would have rung by now, so I opened the door to see what was keeping everybody.

A 1955 pink Cadillac with a white roof, white interior, and white-walled tires commandeered our driveway. Georgia, Molly, Aaron, Daddy, and Martha Jane, who insisted that we use her given name because, in her words, she was "too young" to have children our age (even though she wasn't), all stood before the Caddy while Bertram caressed the hood. I stepped out on the porch. Bertram's convertible was nowhere in sight.

"Isn't it a beauty?" Bertram said as I approached with the sort of caution reserved for wives who think their husbands are cooking up some sort of half-baked scheme.

"Let me guess," I said, trying not to trip over the big crack in the walkway since I couldn't seem to take my eyes off the antique car in the drive. "You're going to use this in the show?"

Bertram snapped his fingers and pointed at me, a big grin on his face. "Hey, that's not a bad idea. We could drive the Homecoming Queen around the field in it."

"Well, if you didn't get it for the show, what did you get it for?"

"Why, darlin', the King had a Caddy just like this."

Before I could say, "So?" Georgia piped in with, "Elvis bought a pink Caddy for his beloved mama, Gladys. It was originally blue, but he had it painted pink just for her. And can you believe she never drove it?"

Georgia was dressed in a sleeveless knit top and a darling pair of black pedal pushers. Her cute little purse, most likely a Graceland Gift Shop purchase, sported the face of a young Elvis.

Now it was Aaron's turn to stroke the car. I'd only seen him from afar when Molly dragged me to a P.T.A meeting to scope him out. He looked just the way I remembered him, dark-skinned as if he were of Italian or Middle Eastern descent, his build slim, yet muscular, and his black hair thick and wavy. And when it all came together he somehow managed to make a polo shirt look more GQ than preppy.

He let out an appreciative whistle. "Must have set you back a few sheckles."

A few? Bertram and I hadn't even discussed this. Not even a little bit. This was a total surprise on my end.

Daddy ran a hand across the pristine white roof. Like the Caddy, Dad's got a full head of white hair. And he turns pink when he gets out in the sun. "Gonna have to build yourself a garage now, Bertram. Can't have a baby like this sitting out in the elements."

Molly leaned in for a closer view. "I've never seen a pink car before. It's kinda cute."

Molly's Va-Va-Voom quotient was soaring off the charts, from the high heels she wore and the cleavage-enhancing dress that molded to her curves in all the right ways. It practically had *I love sex* written all over it. There was no way Aaron was going to be able to resist her. Frankly, I was surprised he hadn't wanted to skip the dinner party entirely after seeing her in that dress.

Martha Jane opened her mouth, then shut it. I think she was too stunned to say anything. Which is saying a lot for Martha Jane, whose tongue can be sharper than a Ginsu knife. She was also probably reeling from fashion sensory overload what with Molly putting it all out there, so to speak, and Georgia's gaudy quotient tipping the scales at "Go Home and Change." Understatement was Martha Jane's mantra when it came to attire.

And that's when it hit me. Bertram's car was *gone*. As in: bye-bye. As in: see ya later, alligator.

"Did you trade in the Sebring?"

"Yep," Bertram said, as if any dunce would know this. "Helped knock down the price a bit."

I could feel the steam building in my skull. If I didn't get away from the Caddy soon, I was going to blow up.

"Chicken's gettin' cold," I said through gritted teeth. "Let's all go in and eat."

5

Aaron gestured at the Velvet Elvis with his spork. "Do you really think it's haunted by the King?"

I'd seated Aaron, Molly, and Georgia opposite the painting. Daddy and Martha Jane had their backs to it. Bertram and I sat at either end of our long dining room table that was also another Great-aunt Trudy item. We were all eating, drinking, and being merry. Well, everyone, except me. I was fuming at Bertram for trading in his car without at least discussing it with me first, and I was furious that he'd brought it home when we had company so that we couldn't talk about it until everyone had left.

I said, "No, that's a bunch of hooey," at the same time Bertram said, "Yep," and Georgia said, "I thought so when I bought it."

"Why is that, Mrs. Tidwell?" Aaron said, meaning my mother-in-law.

"You can call me Georgia, honey." Bertram's mother batted her eyelashes and flashed a winsome smile. I could tell Aaron's charms were working on her, too. "The little fella sellin' it by the roadside seemed so sincere." She sighed. "But nothin' ever happened. I never heard any music. Never saw the King leave the painting. Not sure what I would have done if he had. Maybe died of euphoria."

"Bertram, what makes you think it's haunted?" Aaron heaped another helping of coleslaw on his plate. Boy, the man sure could eat. And not a bit of fat on him that I could see.

Bertram glared down the table at me. I guess he was mad at me for being mad at him. "I'm taking the fifth on that one."

"Elvis was into the occult, you know," Georgia said. "When we filmed *Fun in Acapulco*, he was always keeping company with yogis and reading books about numerology and life after death. He was determined to live forever."

"Georgia and Elvis did a movie together," Molly said for Aaron's benefit. Boy, was she ever sending out hot-girl vibes. The air around her almost crackled with energy. And she had her chair so close to Aaron's I don't think you could have slid a pipe cleaner between them.

"That's not all we did together, honey," Georgia said. "Elvis and I went out a few times. He was actually rather shy in person."

Daddy jumped in. "Some people say Elvis faked his death and still lives. There's a whole website devoted to it. Lives is an anagram of Elvis."

"How could the man *not* be dead?" Martha Jane said with disdain. "All those pills, all that gluttony. He was a walking time bomb."

"How 'bout you, Cleo? Why do you think it's hooey?" Aaron's

questions made me feel like we were all being interviewed by Bippy Barndale again.

The Miller Lite I was drinking packed a punch. "Oh, puh-lease. Why would Elvis, or anyone for that matter, be haunting a god-awful acrylic painting on black velvet? Wouldn't the man be haunting the toilet at Graceland, instead?"

Molly kicked me under the table. At least, I think it was Molly. I'm sure she didn't want me to ruin her chances of hot monkey sex with Aaron later on. Who was I to rain on her parade? I could be having hot sex with my Elvis-impersonator husband later on. Yep. And if I were really lucky he'd wear the jumpsuit. *Riiiight.*

An awkward silence settled over the table. I'd just insulted Aaron, Georgia, and Bertram in one fell swoop. Me and my big mouth. So I stuffed it full of fried chicken to keep it occupied.

"It's a beautiful portrait of Elvis," Georgia said to break up the dead air. "I like the way the artist painted him in profile, microphone in hand, as if you're watching him in concert. You can almost see the sweat glistening on his face."

"Thank you, Mama," Bertram said, a brouhaha brewing in his normally gentle brown eyes. "I'm glad someone appreciates it."

"Well, frankly, Bertram," Martha Jane said, waggling a drumstick at my husband, "a Victorian dining room is not the place to hang a velvet painting of any kind. It's uncouth."

You tell 'em, Martha Jane!

All heads swiveled my way. Had I said that out loud? I wanted to sink into the floor and disappear. Loose lips sink ships ... and marriages.

"So," Aaron said casually, "what do you think you'll do with the painting after the historic home tour?"

Bertram answered before I could say anything as if we were in a race to see who could speak first. "You know, I've been thinking of moving it up to the bedroom. There's this bare spot on the wall across from our bed."

"Oh, no. That thing is not going to violate the sanctity of our bedroom."

Yikes! This was quickly becoming Showdown at the Tidwell Corral. Aaron probably thought he'd come to dinner at the nut house.

Molly chimed out, "Who wants pie in the parlor?" before Bertram and I could launch into a full-blown fight.

6

I counted to fifty in the kitchen, while Molly settled everyone in the parlor with a helping of apple cobbler. Bertram had charged upstairs. I hoped he wasn't going to be rude and sulk while we had guests. I needed to pull it together myself and get back in the game. A good hostess did not fight with her spouse or insult her guests. And I'd done both. Martha Jane was probably ready to disown me, thinking she'd raised me better than to act like this. Lordy, but I was sure to get the sharp side of her tongue later.

I took a deep breath, preparing to make my entrance, when Bertram's voice boomed through the house, singing the opening lines of "Blue Suede Shoes" as though it were karaoke night at the roller rink.

I rushed into the parlor.

My husband cavorted before our family, wearing the rhinestone-splattered jumpsuit complete with white scarf and cape. Microphone in hand, he swiveled his hips like nobody's business while a portable karaoke machine supplied the music. I didn't even know Bertram could move like that. I stared, transfixed. He'd glued the mutton-chop sideburns to his face again and even had Elvis's lip curl down.

Had he lost his mind?

Georgia looked like she had died and gone to Heaven. And why not? Her only-begotten son was emulating the King of Rock and Roll. Judging from Daddy and Martha Jane's expressions, Bertram's antics only confirmed that he'd flipped his lid. Third time the charm, indeed. God only knows what Aaron thought of us. That we were a certifiable bunch, most likely.

Fortunately, "Blue Suede Shoes" is a short song. As soon as it was over, I said as neutrally as possible, "Bertram, what are you doing?"

Bertram gave me an "Aw, shucks" grin as if we hadn't just been glaring at each other during dinner. "Have a seat, darlin', and enjoy the show." And then he launched into an energetic "Viva Las Vegas."

Molly and I exchanged looks. Hers said I'd married a cuckoo, and mine said I knew it. I curled up in the white wingback chair, and Molly hunkered down beside Aaron on the leather love seat. Martha Jane tapped her foot, although I knew it was with impatience and not keeping time to the music.

After the third song, Martha Jane popped up off the couch and said, "Thanks for dinner, Cleo. Your father and I hate to run off in the middle of Bertram's … concert, but we're not getting any younger and turn into pumpkins by nine."

This was an out and out lie. Martha Jane is over sixty and has more energy than anyone I know.

Daddy jumped up, too. "Yeah, thanks, you two." He didn't look Bertram in the eye. He was either embarrassed for me or was trying not to laugh or both. "We should do this more often."

Martha Jane shot him a look that said, "Don't encourage the clown." God, what a track record I had: the addict, the gay guy, and the kook. If I kept this up, I was going to run out of challenging types to marry.

Bertram clicked off the karaoke machine for a moment and said in a perfect imitation, "Thank you. Thankyouverymuch."

"We can show ourselves out," Martha Jane said.

After they left, Bertram continued his Elvis revue with "Suspicious Minds." I figured Aaron would politely excuse himself and Molly, but ten songs later, they were still there, Molly sending me distress signals. This was supposed to be her and Aaron's special night, but here he was, engrossed in my husband's Elvis mania. Frankly, it was pretty freakin' weird. What straight man in his right mind passes up first time sex to hear someone's brother-in-law put on an impromptu Vegas floor show? Aaron might be hot as hell, but his weird-o-meter rating had just soared into the red zone.

After a few more horrendously long songs, Aaron finally said, "I'm going to have to call it a night. I've got church tomorrow." He gave Molly a chaste little kiss and told her, "I'll call you tomorrow afternoon." To Bertram he said, "Thanks for the show, man. I mean it. You're one talented dude." And then he left.

I thought Molly was going to cry. She'd gotten all gussied up, her kids were with her ex for the weekend, and she'd had what had seemed like a sizzling date with sex a sure thing. But apparently not. I also didn't know any normal straight men who'd pass up sex just because they had to get up early the next morning for church. There was definitely some trouble brewing in Aaron-land.

Bertram said, "And now for my finale—"

I had to cut him off. It was down to me, my sister, and my mother-in-law, the latter who could have listened to her son's shindig all night. "Hey, Bertram, why don't we call it a night? It's getting late."

He smiled at me in an incredibly beautiful way and said, "No sweat, little darlin'. Elvis has left the building."

I saw Molly out.

"Why did he leave?" Molly wailed quietly once we were on the back deck. "Tonight was supposed to be the night."

"He's obviously not in his right mind. Or maybe he has an erectile dysfunction problem. You just never know."

"Yeah, you're probably right. Maybe he had some embarrassing problem and didn't want to say so."

"Absolutely. Give him another chance. And if he messes up a second opportunity, dump him."

"That's good advice." But her face was sorrowful.

"Look, if it's meant to be, it'll happen."

"You're right, you're right," she said.

"Of course, I am. It's an older sister thing."

We hugged, and Molly slipped off her heels and went home through my backyard to the adjoining gate between our properties.

The downstairs was utterly quiet. I guess my mother-in-law had gone home and Bertram had packed it in. I tidied up and locked the doors, turned off the lights, went upstairs, and fell into bed beside my snoring husband and our two cats. I lay awake for awhile, watching Bertram sleep once my eyes adjusted to the dark.

Who was this man lying beside me? And what had possessed him to buy a pink Caddy and serenade everyone tonight? Was he having a mid-life crisis? He was the right age for it. And why had he given me that god-awful painting to begin with? That seemed to be the start of it all. Was the painting haunted, but in a way we hadn't expected? Geez, Louise! What was I doing blaming Bertram's behavior on a velvet painting? I was grasping at straws. Maybe it was time to seek couples counseling.

7

I snapped awake in the dark, my heart in my throat. The bedside clocked blinked 2:43 a.m. Something wasn't right, but I'd just come out of a deep sleep and didn't know which way was up.

"Bertram?" I whispered, patting his side of the bed.

Empty.

And then I heard it, drifting faintly up the stairs. The opening lines to "Heartbreak Hotel."

Every hair on my body, and I mean every hair, stood at attention. My breath hitched in my chest while the drum of my heart threatened to drown out all sounds. I lay paralyzed as if stuck to the sheets. And meanwhile, the song wafted lazily through the night.

What the hell was going on downstairs? And where was Bertram?

A sixteen pound cat bounced onto my stomach like a furry bowling ball with legs. I sprang out of bed, then made like a slinky and slunk down the staircase, my heart a yammering, my hands as cold and clammy as luncheon meat.

A single lamp in the parlor illuminated Bertram sitting crossed-legged on the dining room table, a video camera set up on a tripod beside him and aimed at the Velvet Elvis on the wall above the fireplace.

My first thought: *What the hell is Bertram doing on the table?*

My second thought: *Holy shit! The Velvet Elvis really is singing in the dead of night.* But I leaned around the corner to look in the parlor and noticed the red light on the stereo that indicated a CD was playing. What was Bertram up to?

Softly, hesitantly, I said, "Bertram?"

Nothing. He didn't twitch. He didn't blink. Just stared at the painting as if he were watching Monday Night Football.

So I said his name again, but a little louder.

No reaction.

The song ended, then started over. He must have had the CD player programmed to repeat.

"Bertram!" I flipped on the dining room chandelier and light blazed forth.

My husband shuddered, but didn't look at me. I trotted over to the CD player and ejected the music.

"Bertram!!"

He shook his head like someone waking up from a dream. "What am I doing on the table?"

"That's the question I was going to ask you." The house had cooled off during the night, and I shivered in my thin t-shirt and skimpy panties.

Bertram slid off the table and turned off the video camera. "I woke up and couldn't go back to sleep. So I thought I'd fiddle around with some special effects for the tour. I must have dozed off."

"You were sitting on the *dining room table* staring at that painting." I pointed at the guilty party hanging over the fireplace. "You weren't even blinking."

"What can I say, Cleo? I must have been sleep sitting."

"Uh huh."

We were going to have to have a serious talk. But not now. It was almost three o'clock in the morning, and I was too damn tired to get into it with my husband.

But tomorrow. Tomorrow we'd have words.

CHAPTER FOUR

The Day After
Sunday, October 19

1

Bertram slapped my rump with a resounding smack. "Rise and shine, beautiful. What do you say we go to church this morning?"

I peeked at the clock with one eye. Eight o'clock. Bright sunlight slanted in through the blinds. Ergh, after the middle-of-the-night weirdness, it was too early to even be thinking about getting up, let alone going to church. And why did Bertram suddenly want to go? We hadn't been since Easter.

I remembered my resolve to have words with him this morning. But the only word I was able to manage at the moment was, "Erph," and that was sleep-talk for: *Leave me alone, I need to snooze some more.* I rolled over, snugging the covers up to my chin.

Bertram nuzzled my neck. "I know what'll wake you up. How 'bout a little tumble?"

My eyes might be closed, but my nose was working just fine. And what I smelled was Bertram's musky man-scent. If he were any other guy, he'd just stink, but I found his natural odor intoxicating. According to Oprah, it meant we had great chemistry. As if I needed her tell me *that.*

My husband spooned me under the covers, kissing my shoulder while cupping a breast. His Mr. Happy pressed quite merrily against my backside. I think I whimpered.

So much for having words. Although I do believe I cried, "Hallelujah!" a few times. And if I'm not mistaken, that is definitely a word.

2

The antique Caddy dominated our driveway like a long, pink boat that had run aground. I slid onto the white leather seat in my Sunday best, feeling as though I should be wearing gloves and a little pill box hat with netting from the 1950s. Of course, that sort of thing wouldn't go with the black linen sheath dress appliquéd with sunflowers and matching jacket I had on for church, although the black pumps might have fit right in with that era. Some things never go out of style. A pair of fuzzy dice dangled from the rear-view mirror. I gave them a swipe and set them to swinging.

I had a nice view of our house as I waited for Bertram. *Our house.* Not that long ago, it had been Great-aunt Trudy's house. How I'd loved visiting her as a child. The gray house with the purple trim and fish scale shingling on the gables had seemed charming and mysterious. And Trudy had always referred to the front porch as her outdoor room. She'd perch on the slatted porch swing while the four younger Kilgores—me, Molly, Martha Jane, and Daddy—lounged on the wicker chairs and loveseat, sipping sweet tea or Coca-Cola from glasses so cold they practically rained condensation. How I'd longed for a house of my own like hers one day. I'd been so envious when Richard and Molly had bought the bed and breakfast next door to Great-aunt Trudy. But Trudy had somehow known what was in my heart, for she'd left her house to me and had given Molly the cabin on Lake Martin.

Bertram slipped behind the wheel, ending my reminiscing, so

handsome in his charcoal-gray suit. He hadn't been able to get the fake sideburns off even though he said he'd applied plenty of facial glue remover. We were going to be quite a pair pulling up to the Methodist church this morning in a pink Caddy. I was still curious as to what he'd shelled out for the car and why he'd traded his Sebring for it, but was afraid it might start World War III. I really didn't want to get into it with him in the car because it was like getting trapped on a submarine. We could always fight after church.

We drove down Buchanan Street through historic downtown Allister. The city had torn up the old concrete sidewalks and cobbled new ones with ancient bricks from a defunct elementary school. Old fashioned lampposts occupied every street corner, and traffic lights hung from steel poles jutting out over the intersection, eliminating the need for power lines.

Various shops had taken up residence downtown, catering to tourists, locals, and college students. There were antique dealers, a bookstore, a couple of gift shops, realtors, a small art gallery, a toy store, a bar called The Night Spot, and A Touch of Class Beauty Shop. We passed The Imperial—a restored movie theatre, the Bama Burger Shack where they serve the best burgers, fries, and milkshakes in Alabama, and Bellagio, an eclectic and utterly charming Italian restaurant. The Allister YMCA was located along half a block of Buchanan Street. I taught a baton-twirling class there two nights a week.

But the pièce de résistance was the gargantuan First Methodist Church that stood four stories high and spanned an entire city block, reminding me of a European castle. All it needed was a moat and drawbridge to complete the fairy-tale picture.

When we drove right by it without turning into the parking lot, I said, "Hey, you passed the church. Where are we going?"

"Aaron invited us to attend his church."

"Aaron?"

Lapsed Methodists, Bertram and I were doing good just showing up for Easter and Christmas Eve services at our own church, let alone visiting someone else's.

"Yeah, last night. I think you were in the kitchen."

"Uh huh. And what possessed you to say yes? Didn't you tell him we already have a church-home?"

"I figured it wouldn't hurt to give it a try. We might even like it." He glanced my way as if to gauge my reaction.

I didn't quite know what to say. This was so unlike Bertram. But Bertram hadn't exactly been himself recently, either. The restaurants, businesses, and government buildings of Buchanan Street rolled by the Caddy's window in a fluid stream of brick, concrete, and glass. I clutched my purse a little tighter, trying to understand what the heck was going on with my husband.

"So which church *are* we going to?" Allister only had about thirty churches. Baptist, Lutheran, Presbyterian, Church of Christ—

"Church of the Blue Suede Shoes."

"Oh, for Pete's sake, Bertram. That's not a real church. Aaron must have been pulling your leg."

"Then why did he give me this?" Keeping one hand on the wheel, he reached into his suit coat with the other, withdrew a business card, and handed it to me.

If you love all things Elvis
Then we'd LOVE
To have you join us
at
The Church of the Blue Suede Shoes
Allister Chapter
1115 Ellwood Heights
Bring this card and a guest for an introductory visit

"Because he's playing a joke on you." Molly had said he was into Elvis, but come on, this was a bit ridiculous.

"But what if he's not?" Bertram glanced my way, his expression serious.

"Bertram, we're not even Elvis fans."

His face clouded over. "Look, will you do this for me? You don't have to go back again if you don't like it."

God, if I didn't go, I'd come off as the bitch of the year. "All right. You win. But I'm not singing any Elvis songs."

3

We drove up the mountain, the Caddy straining from the steep incline. Allister is located in the foothills of the Appalachians. The town is long and narrow like a bloated snake. Allister's downtown and historic neighborhoods are situated in a bowl-shaped valley ringed by mountains. There's Blue Mountain to the north where the Kmart is located. But the mountain to the east is just called "the mountain" and that's where we were at the moment.

Finding the right house wasn't hard. Cars lined both sides of the street about mid-way down the block. We added the pink Caddy to the mix. If I hadn't known an Elvis cult met in this neighborhood, I never would have surmised it from the home's outward appearance—gray vinyl siding and red brick, with white trim and a dark gray roof. Tiny front porch. Split level, the ground floor most likely a finished basement with living quarters on the second floor. Nothing stood out that said: *Elvis fanatics meet here.*

Bertram escorted me up the brick steps to the front door. We rang the bell. I wondered what exactly we were going to say when someone answered it. *Hello, one of your members gave us this card ...* or ... *You don't know us, but we're here to get kooky with ya.*

A petite woman with a warm smile opened the door. "Well, hello there," she said.

Bertram showed her the card. She nodded as though she'd been expecting us. "Welcome to the Church of the Blue Suede Shoes. My name is Mavis Matthews. Won't you come on in?"

Once inside the teeny split-level foyer, the gentle murmur of a small crowd of people talking amongst themselves wafted up from the lower level as did the delicious chocolate-aroma of coffee. Too bad I didn't drink the stuff.

Mavis closed the door. "And who might y'all be?" she said in a perfect hostess tone, cocking her head slightly. I pegged her to be in her early forties. She reminded me of a little bird with her bright eyes, clipped way of moving, and the tuft of hair that wouldn't lay down on the top of her head.

"I'm Dr. Bertram Tidwell. And this is my lovely wife, Cleo."

"It's a pleasure to meet you both." She gestured to the lower staircase. "The service will begin shortly in the room downstairs, where you'll also find the restroom and the coffee maker. Please make yourself at home and remember that we do not allow photography of any kind. Thank you."

Politely dismissed, we headed downstairs.

What would have been a family room in most houses had been converted into a shrine to the King. Bertram's mother had nothing on these people. Framed photographs, paintings of Elvis—some even on velvet—and movie posters peppered the walls. The room was set up like a store-front church. Folding chairs in orderly rows faced an elevation carpeted in red shag where a keyboard, a pull-down movie screen, and a portable lectern had been set up. Twinkly Christmas lights and soft lamps illuminated the space. About twenty men and women stood around talking to each other, dressed as if they'd stepped out of either the fifties or an Elvis impersonator convention. One fellow was even African-American, a rarity among Elvis fans. Most of the women had on contemporary clothes, but one gal was wearing a rhinestone-speckled jumpsuit. It took me a moment to realize she *was* a gal.

A tall fellow in a gold lamé tux pushed toward us. I recognized the big belly and the pompadour. This was the guy who'd scared the bejeezus out of me the other night.

"Doctor and Mrs. Tidwell," he said, extending his hand. "Dupree Hardcastle, chairman of this here little group. Please accept my apologies about unintentionally startling you the other night, little lady."

Bertram gave me a quizzical look, and I realized I hadn't told him about what had happened.

"Yes, well, I'm not used to coming home after dark to find a strange man lurking on my porch."

Dupree flashed a wry grin. "Nor am I in the habit of lurking on people's porches. I'd love to chat longer, but the service is about to begin."

He beelined to the dais as the others began taking seats as if on silent cue. I noticed Aaron on the front row sitting next to the female Elvis. He glanced back at us and waved. She followed his gaze, a sour look on her face. I'd be sour, too, if I had to wear that get-up.

Dupree gripped the lectern with both hands. "Welcome to the Church of the Blue Suede Shoes, where we give glory to the King and his sainted mother, Gladys.

"We have a couple of guests with us this morning. Dr. Bertram Tidwell and his wife, Cleo. Make sure to give them a friendly hello after the service. And Gladys-Gal Mavis Mathews has reminded me to inform y'all that there's still room in her minivan for anyone who wants to make the annual sojourn to Graceland in December.

"I'd like to start this morning's dedication with a reading from the Book of Parker. Colonel Parker, that is."

He shuffled some papers and cleared his throat. "Yes. Here we are.

"And Colonel Tom Parker, the King's manager, did say later in the week after Elvis had left this mortal coil, 'Elvis didn't die. The body did. We're keeping up good spirits. We're keeping Elvis alive. I talked to him this morning and he told me to carry on.'"

Dupree paused, surveying the small crowd with a practiced eye. I wondered if he'd been a preacher in a previous life.

"Please stand and let's all sing 'What Now My Love.'"

Mavis Mathews seemingly materialized at the keyboard as everyone floated up from their seats. I felt pretty silly, but stood, too. Someone thrust a sheaf of papers into my hand. Sheet music. Like that was going to entice me to open my mouth.

The song began slowly with a stately beat. Everyone seemed to know the words by heart, including Bertram! I stared at him gape-mouthed. The lyrics fit right in with the Colonel Parker reading.

The song built to a majestic crescendo. I had to admit the group had some accomplished tenors. Bertram hit the deep bass note at the end as if he'd practiced with these people. And for all I knew, he might have. I wouldn't put it past him, what with him trading in his convertible for a pink Caddy and putting on a karaoke show for our dinner guests last night. Did I even know my husband any more? Had he been taken over by some pod people?

As soon as the music ended, everyone sank into their seats. Dupree sprang to the lectern. "Thank you, Miss Mavis, for that lovely accompaniment." He studied his notes for a moment.

"And Elvis so loved the world that he consumed it, cheeseburger by cheeseburger, until he died upon the john, having given his soul to his fans. Three days later, he did not rise from the dead, but as you heard the Colonel's own words, he did not die, either."

Dupree scanned his congregation. "What are we to make of this? What, I ask you? Well, I'll tell you. The Colonel himself said it: 'We're keeping Elvis alive.'

"Alive. And it is our mission, nay—our duty—to find the King and resurrect him to his former glory. Can you say, 'Viva Las Vegas,' good brothers and Gladys Gals?

"And now, Brother Jeb, if you'll dim the lights, we'll take in a clip from *A Star is Born*. Yes, I know it's not an Elvis movie. But Elvis was offered the lead and turned it down at Colonel Parker's urging. Let us now watch a role that should have been the King's."

Oh, my God. These people were seriously cuckoo! From reading their business card, I'd thought they were just a social club for folks who loved Elvis, but they were so much more than that, and none of it was good. I glanced at Bertram. He was entranced. Or enthralled. Or both. Argh! What was it going to take to get him out of here? A fried peanut butter and banana sandwich?

The lights winked out, and the bathtub scene in *A Star is Born* bloomed on the movie screen up front. I leaned over to Bertram and whispered, "Can we go now?"

He went, "Huh?" Several people shushed us.

"Can we go now?"

"Aw, Cleo, it's just starting to get good."

I rolled my eyes, not that anyone could see it in the dark. "Can I have the car keys?"

"Why?"

"Because I'm going home."

"Just a minute."

Bertram never once looked my way during this whispered exchange. The minute turned into three, into five, and finally, fed up, I slipped out and left. I honestly don't think Bertram even knew I was gone. I opened my purse to use my cell phone to call Molly to see if she could come pick me up, but then remembered I'd left my phone at home to recharge the battery. Oh, well. I was going to have to walk home, and down from the mountain at that, but I guesstimated that it would only take me half an hour.

Yeah, wrongo bongo.

However, thoughts about the length of the walk evaporated when I glanced at the pink Caddy on my way past it down the sidewalk. Even though the temperature was a pleasant eighty degrees or so, I shivered from a sudden chill as if I'd been doused with ice water.

Someone had soaped the windows. *He belongs to us, bitch.*

4

Here are some important life lessons: Don't walk home in heels. Don't head off in a huff without a house key if you haven't got a spare hidden somewhere. And don't leave an antique car where some loony can soap the windows.

I had blisters on blisters when I limped up Molly's front walk. Her wicker porch swing had never looked more inviting. I kicked off my shoes, rang the bell, and collapsed on that swing in an unladylike heap. My pantyhose had worn away on both heels about twenty blocks ago. My feet throbbed, and even the wind stung my toes where the blisters had popped. I needed a tube of first aid cream and an entire box of band-aids. And some chocolate. Maybe an entire box of chocolate.

I hadn't been sitting more than a couple of minutes, but it seemed like twenty. I probably needed to ring the doorbell again, but it might as well have been a hundred yards away. I reached out as if stretching would make it happen. Uh huh. Mind over matter. Ring that bell.

Nope. Wasn't going to happen. I was going to have to get off my butt. A wave of frustration washed over me, and I popped up and shucked off that pantyhose in a frenzy outside in front of God and everyone. Not that anyone was out at the moment. But they could have been. And in my fit of agitation, I zipped over and pressed the bell again, the concrete cool under my feet.

"What are *you* staring at?" I asked the jack-o-lantern in the window.

Molly answered the door. "Good Lord, Cleo. What are you doing out here barefoot and in your Sunday clothes? And what's that in your hand? Pantyhose?"

I breezed past her. "Got any chocolate?"

5

A bag of Halloween candy and a pack of band-aids later, I sprawled across Molly's antique couch in her front parlor with a tall glass of sweet tea. A coal-burning fireplace with an ornately carved wood mantel competed with three bay windows and a pair of French doors as the focal point of the room. The delicate little table beside the couch sported a lace doily and an assortment of ceramic figurines as well as a rose-colored glass lamp. A beat-up, one-eyed, mohair teddy bear from the 1920s shared the French Provincial couch with me. The room seemed too fancy to eat in, but we were grown-ups, after all.

Molly had given her girls strict orders not to disturb us unless her B&B guest arrived. She'd sealed off the room by sliding both sets of pocket doors closed. I marveled at Victorian ingenuity.

"So you saw Aaron at that Church of the Blue Suede Shoes, huh?" Molly nibbled on a piece of Melba Toast. "I should have known it was too good to be true. A guy that good looking and never married? Bound to be something wrong with him."

"I don't know if being a major Elvis fan is a minus, but I do know those folks are a few slices short of a loaf. And speaking of that, who's following me around and soaping car windows? I thought that crazy Darlene woman was the culprit, but now I'm wondering. And what does 'he belongs to us' mean? Who is it referring to?"

"Crazy people have their reasons, but they don't always make sense to us. And you're attracting Elvis kooks right and left."

"God, I will be so glad when the home tour is over and things can return to normal."

"Only a couple more days, Cleo. I'm hoping to drum up some B&B business from it. In fact, the guest checking in today said he was coming here for the tour."

"Yep, you profiting from my mortification makes it better." Yes, it was snarky, but Molly knew it was just me grousing and didn't take it personally.

"He's arriving two days early. Either he's a dedicated Elvis kook or a serious historic home buff. Or maybe both."

I tried to imagine the type of person who'd be into those two interests. And drew a blank. "So what are you going to do about Aaron?"

"What can I do?" Molly reached toward the bag of candy on the mahogany coffee table, then snatched her hand back. "He either wants to see me or he doesn't. It might be the twenty-first century, but men still like to do the pursuing. As soon as a woman gets assertive in the romance arena, the man thinks he's being chased. It's unfair, but true."

"Wow. This is a far cry from how you were last night."

"I've had a chance to think about it. It's not like Aaron's the only fish in the sea."

"You go, girl. That's the attitude." I checked my watch. An hour had flown by. "Well, I better run on home. Thanks for the tea and emergency chocolate."

I was all ready to rise from the couch and found I'd become one with it. Oh, it was too comfortable to leave. I didn't want to have to go and face the music at home. But I made myself get up. And realized there was no way I was wedging my poor feet into those pumps again. "Can I borrow some flip flops? And my spare key?"

"Sure, Cleo. And keep the candy. Now that it's been opened, it'll just be a temptation to me."

I hobbled out to the entrance hall, while Molly dashed upstairs to get some shoes. The doorbell rang, so I went ahead and answered it since my sister was occupied.

A short man clearly of Irish descent waited on the front porch. He had a slim build, green eyes, a profusion of red hair, and pale skin with serious freckles. I bet he stood no more than five foot six without the Western boots. His good-ole-boy attire, right down to the camouflage hunting cap, didn't seem to jive with the kind of guests who patronize a B&B. I pegged him to be around forty-five, give or take a year. He smiled and his teeth were pearly-white perfect.

"Am I at the right place? The Founder's Row Bed and Breakfast?" His accent was about as Southern redneck as you can get.

"You sure are." I opened the door wider and gestured for him to enter. "Come on in."

He let out an appreciative whistle as he stepped inside. "Mighty fine place you got here, Ms. Saenger."

"Oh, I'm Ms. Saenger's sister, Cleo."

"I'm proud to meet you, Cleo." He held out his hand. "Elmer Inglebright."

I clasped his hand, and damn if I didn't feel good. Julie Andrews-the-hills-are-alive-with-music sort of good, or a pack-of-puppies good, or finding-an-unbroken-sand-dollar-at-the-beach good. I just felt … good. And happy. Not-a-care-in-the-world happy.

"It's a real pleasure to meet you, Elmer." And I meant it.

"The pleasure's all mine." He released my hand, and my everyday worries came tumbling back like quarters out of a slot machine. "My sister will be with you in a moment."

"I'm in no rush." He ran a hand over the carved-oak balustrade of the staircase. "They just don't build houses like this anymore."

"They sure don't."

"Nowadays, they're just slapped together. No artistry. No craftsmanship. No *soul*."

"You're right about that. But you really think a house has a soul?" What an intriguing idea.

"Absolutely. And not just houses. Anything hand-crafted has a soul. The artist imparts some of their energy into the creation. That's why mass produced stuff feels hollow in comparison. No soul."

Did that mean the Velvet Elvis had a soul? I shuddered to think about it.

He peered at me closely. "Say, ain't you the gal with the haunted

Velvet Elvis?"

Speak of the devil. "Yep, that's me."

"Well, I was wonderin' if I could ask you a favor?"

"A favor?" Yeesh. I'd just met the guy and he was already askin' for favors?

"Yes, ma'am." He flashed his pearly whites again. "You see, I'm a bone-a-fide collector of the rare and unusual. Here's my card."

He fished a business card from his Western plaid breast pocket and handed it over.

Elmer Inglebright

Collector Extraordinaire

Sarasota, Florida

888-COL-LECT

"Oddities are my specialty"

"Hmm. A collector." *Of oddities.*

I'd say he was a bit of an oddity himself.

"Yes, ma'am. You have to admit a haunted Velvet Elvis is pretty odd."

"Uh huh."

"I was hopin' you might see fit to give me an early audience."

"An early audience?" Oh, boy. Another Elvis kook. Guess I'd answered my earlier question.

"Yes, ma'am. I'm interested in buying your painting. Top dollar. But I'd like to get a look at it before the tour on Tuesday."

My first instinct was to say no flat out, top dollar or not, but then I remembered how good I felt shaking his hand and decided there wasn't any harm in letting one person see it ahead of time. And he seemed like a nice fellow.

"Okay." I put his card into my purse. "But let me get back to you on the when."

"Thank you. I appreciate it."

Molly came tromping downstairs. "Sorry it took me so long, Cleo. They were in the back of my closet." She saw Elmer just then and added, "Oh, you must be Mr. Inglebright. I'm Molly Saenger. Welcome to my inn. I hope your stay here is a pleasant one."

She held out her hand and Elmer gently clasped it. My sister's eyes widened and her expression turned rapturous. She let out a little moan, then regained her composure, fanning her face vigorously with the flip flops as a deep blush blossomed all the way from her cheeks down to her bosom.

Elmer released her hand. "Mighty pleased to meet you, Miss Molly."

Now it was my turn to stare. Elmer was gazing at Molly with a similarly rapturous expression. Was my sister releasing pheromones into the air? Molly patted her chest. "Oh. Oh, my. *Oh ... my.*"

Without breaking his gaze, Elmer said, "Well, I'll just go get my things from the car."

"Okay," Molly said a bit breathlessly. "And here's your key. You're in the Camellia Room, second floor. You can park around back."

Elmer took the key and headed out the front door.

As soon as his car started, Molly clutched my arm. "Oh my God. I just had an orgasm."

6

Bertram was flopped on the pea-green couch in jeans and a t-shirt, watching football with a beer in his hand, when I hobbled in. I'd left my shoes on Molly's porch. Frankly, I never wanted to see or wear them again.

"Cleo, where have you been?" He jumped up, his voice full of concern.

I should have counted to ten before speaking, but I was full of piss and vinegar. "Where do you think? Over at Molly's. She's got a spare key."

He noticed my torn up feet. "Oh, Cleo, honey. What have you done? I didn't know you were going to walk home. I thought you'd just gone to the bathroom."

"For an hour?" Okay, so it was more like a fifty-five minute walk home, but I was rounding up.

He took a step toward me, and I held up my hand like a policeman. "Stop right there. I don't want to see you, talk to you, or hear you. Right now I'm mad enough to spit nails. The Elvis mania, the pink Caddy, and now this Church of the Blue Suede Shoes. It's the straw that broke the camel's back. I'm going upstairs to lie down. I'd advise you to keep your distance. But later, we're going to have to have a serious talk, Bertram."

From the look on his face you'd have thought this was news to him. Which only made me madder. I was like a riled up hornet.

I limped to the staircase and gripped the banister.

"Want me to help you upstairs, honey?"

"No!"

"Okay," he said in a hurt, little boy voice. Oh, for crying out loud. I was at the end of my patience. I headed up the stairs, wincing with each step, the flip flops smacking against the bottoms of my feet. When I reached our room, I closed the door, dumped the bag of candy on the dresser, and pulled off my jacket and dress, leaving them wadded up in a pile of black linen and sunflower appliqué on the floor. Then I climbed into bed and promptly fell asleep.

I woke up an hour later from all that sweet tea I'd consumed. Afternoon sun streamed through the windows. Geez, but the house was quiet. No cats crying, no football on TV, no Elvis tunes. I sucked in a deep breath, let it out. Okay, my bladder was telling me to hurry it up already. I rolled out of bed and minced across the floor, pausing only long enough to slip on some sweats and a t-shirt.

As soon as I opened the door, two orange fur balls streaked past me to jump on the bed. I made my way into the master bathroom across the hall and took care of business. Then I swallowed a couple of Advil and squeezed half a tube of first aid cream on my blisters. It was time to have that little chat with Bertram, the one I knew we needed to have but had been putting off. But when I rounded the corner to the stairs, a computer-printed note was taped to the newel post. *I'm sorry*, a frownie face below it. I found another note at the mid-way point on the little antique table before the bay window where the stairs make a hair-pin turn. A cascade of rose petals spilled down the rest of the steps.

"Bertram?"

No answer.

I followed the rose petals to the ground floor and through the French doors into the dining room where two dozen red roses and a gold box of Godiva chocolates awaited me on the dining room table. An envelope was propped up against the flower vase.

Cleo.

I tore it open. The card within sported two bulldogs snuggled cheek to cheek. On the blank space inside, Bertram had written:

Cleo, please forgive me. I've been a complete horse's ass. I went out for a drive, but when I get back we'll sit down and talk. I don't want to lose you. In the meantime, kick back and enjoy the flowers and candy.
Love,
Bertram

Awww. How sweet. Maybe there was hope for us after all. The only thing marring this touching sentiment was that it was displayed before the Velvet Elvis, as though Bertram's apology were an offering to the god of rock and roll. I couldn't help but sneer. Everything had been great until that painting had come into our life. I'd thought about selling it on eBay after the tour. The media circus surrounding it had generated quite an interest. But maybe I'd sell it to Elmer Inglebright. He seemed like a nice guy. Certainly polite. And he didn't scare the bejeezus out of me or leave wacky messages on my answering machine or soap my windows.

Yeah, I might just do that.

So I took Bertram's advice and kicked back in the recliner, my bare feet on a gold throw pillow, the box of Godiva in my lap, the roses and a cup of hot cocoa on the end table beside me, and a Marge Hanover mystery in my hand. It didn't get much better than this.

7

Bertram walked in a half hour later with a six pack. He offered a tentative smile. "Oh good, I see you've been enjoying the Godiva."

Boy, had I ever. "Uh huh. Thanks. You didn't have to go to all that trouble."

But we both knew he did. I still couldn't quite get over Bertram's clean-shaven look nor the mutton-chop sideburns. I'd known him with a beard and moustache for so long that he looked like a different person to me now. And I suppose, in light of all that had happened recently, he *was* a different person in many ways.

He knelt beside the recliner, cracking open a beer and offering it to me. I waved it away.

"Look, Cleo. I'm sorry. About everything. I'm sorry I bought the Caddy without telling you. I'm sorry I took you to the Church of the Blue Suede Shoes without any forewarning. I'm sorry you had to walk all the way home today. And I'm sorry if I haven't seemed like myself lately. When a man hits forty, he takes stock of his life, and sometimes he finds it lacking."

Lacking? What more did Bertram want? He was in good health, had a good job, a beautiful home, and up until our anniversary, a good marriage. So, maybe his hair was a bit sparse on top. There were worse things.

Bertram laced his fingers with mine, took a sip of liquid courage.

"I've been in love with you ever since we dated in college. I lost you back then to Stuart, then later to Marty. I don't want to lose you again."

Golly, he was gazing up at me with those big, brown, puppy-dog eyes of his. It's hard to resist an apologetic man on bended knee, no matter how mad I might be at him. I could feel my anger ebbing like the tide rolling out to sea. Forty years from now, we'd look back at this moment and laugh our asses off, thinking what knuckleheads we were.

I kissed Bertram's hand. "You're not going to lose me. In fact, I was thinking that after the tour and the TV show, I'd sell the painting to the highest bidder, and we'd take the money and—"

"I promised the painting to the church," Bertram blurted out.

"What?" I snatched my hand from his.

"I promised—"

"I heard you." Oh, boy, was I ever feeling riled up again. "I'm assuming you mean the church we attended today?"

"Yeah." Bertram knocked back the rest of his beer.

"Bertram?" And I put every bit of incredulity into my voice that I could muster. Generations of Kilgore women have mastered this ability to a tee. "How could you? That painting was a gift from you to me."

"Yeah, but I know you don't like it." He gestured toward the dining room where it hung over the fireplace in all its hideous glory. "Aaron and Dupree asked me after the service today—"

"Asked you what?" I really was fit to be tied. I might not like the painting, but it was still mine to do with as I wished. Or, at least, I thought it was.

Now Bertram sounded a bit miffed. "Do you mind not interrupting me while I'm speaking?" He let out a huff. "They asked if they could have it for their church. And since I knew you hated it,

I thought I was doing you a service, helping you save face, so you didn't have to admit how much you detested a gift I'd given you." This last bit was so frosty it was a wonder I didn't have icicles on my face. In contrast to Bertram's frigid indignation, my temper was rising. I figured I had about ten seconds before I read my husband the riot act.

Nope. More like two seconds.

"You're right, Bertram. I hate that painting. There! I said it. Finally. I hate it. Hate it, hate it, hate it. It's the most hideous, god-awful thing I've ever been given."

I was on a roll now and wholly helpless to stop. That's the bad thing about losing your temper. You often say and do things in the heat of the moment that you later regret. But for now, it felt good to get all this off my chest.

"But it's my painting," I continued. "Not yours to give to someone else, no matter how much I might not like it. Not to mention, we promised the historical society that it would be displayed during the tour since they've had such a positive response to it." I finished this last bit with my own self-righteous huff. Yes, I utterly detested the Velvet Elvis, but a promise is a promise, no matter how uncomfortable it made me.

Bertram scrutinized me, his brown eyes as hard and cool as dog crap on a cold day. I fought the urge to fidget under his intense gaze. It was *my* painting. It was.

He finally said, "Are you through?"

"Yes. Yes, I believe I am." We might as well have drawn a line in the sand.

He stood up, towering over the recliner, and for just the teeniest moment, I was a little scared of him. Anger radiated from him in undulating waves, invisible, but palpable.

"Cleo, you're a piece of work. You know that?"

I had no response to that. I mean, hello? He was the one trying to give away my gift.

"I'm going to Mama's. Don't wait up for me, as I'm not coming home."

He stomped upstairs and packed a bag while I slumped in the recliner, stunned. Bertram and I had never had a fight where he'd been mad enough to spend the night away from me. I wanted to beg him not to go, to stay home. We could patch things up. But I couldn't muster the words. Saying I'm sorry is something I'm lousy at.

He tromped downstairs as loud as a moose, stalked out the front door, revved up the pink Caddy, and burned rubber out of the driveway. I packed my own bag and went next door to Molly's, making sure I toted the rest of the six-pack with me.

I didn't want to be alone with the Velvet Elvis.

CHAPTER FIVE

The Day Before the Historic Home Tour
Monday, October 20

1

I greeted Monday morning bleary-eyed and hung over, still wearing the sweats and t-shirt from the day before, my hair a rat's nest, my throat and tongue parched. Getting toasted the night before and passing out at Molly's had seemed like the way to go at the time, but now I was regretting the dubious wisdom of drowning my sorrows in Miller Lite. Just because my husband had stormed out was no reason to live life like a country song.

When I entered Molly's formal dining room, Elmer was already seated at one of the cozy little tables, dining on a full Southern breakfast. This was not the norm for my sister's B&B guests. She usually set a basket filled with muffins, fruit, jams, and juice outside their bedroom door.

Elmer gazed at Molly as if she were Botticelli's Venus. Molly glanced at him shyly as if she'd just noticed him, and I swear it was like watching two love-struck teenagers.

"Good morning, Elmer." I took a seat at the table adjacent from his.

He didn't seem surprised to see me. "Well, hey, Cleo. How are you this fine morning."

"Oh, I'm peachy. Just peachy." I injected all the irony I could into those five words.

Molly handed me a Diet Coke in a can. Just the way I like it. I absolutely cannot function until I've had my Diet Coke in the morning. "Would you like eggs, bacon and biscuits, Cleo? Or pancakes?

"No. I'll just nurse my drink here."

Molly heaped a few more pancakes on Elmer's plate.

"Why, thank you, Miss Molly." His expression bordered on worshipful.

My sister—a mother of four—blushed. Elmer had quite an effect on her.

I discreetly checked whether he wore a wedding ring. Nope. No finger jewelry at all. Maybe Elmer was the answer to Molly's prayers for a decent man who would love her.

"So, Cleo," Elmer said. "I don't mean to be pushy, but when would be a good time to preview the haunted painting?"

Ergh. Like I didn't have enough on my plate with Bertram taking off and the open house tomorrow night. But I'm a Southern gal, raised to be accommodating, so what came out of my mouth was, "How about this afternoon around three?"

I was planning to take a personal day from work anyway. I really didn't want to face Bertram in front of three hundred band members and have to pretend that everything was hunky-dory.

"I'll be there. And once again, I appreciate it." Elmer lit into his artery-clogging meal with gusto. For a short, wiry guy, he sure could eat.

I finished my drink and headed home. But not before borrowing a Hannah Montana poster from one of the nieces.

2

Once inside my own house, Maury and Cosmo rubbed against my ankles, making happy "prrrt, prrrt" sounds. After feeding them, I dug several push pins out of the junk drawer in the kitchen. Then I marched into the dining room with the poster, unrolling it like a scroll. I was going to have to buy my niece another poster, but it was a small price to pay to hide an eye sore. It seemed like old times as I climbed the step ladder once again.

"You and I are going to have to stop meeting this way," I told the painting.

Mr. One Eye did nothing. Boy, if it really was haunted, it sure didn't do much. Bertram and I were going to have to rig up something to make it sing or talk. That is, if Bertram ever came home. A little sniffle bubbled up, and I wiped a single tear away. Married three years and never a serious fight. Until now.

The poster covered the Velvet Elvis perfectly. I pressed a pin into each corner, then climbed down to admire my handiwork. Hannah Montana beamed across the room at me. It was still tacky, but not as tacky as a velvet painting. And certainly much more pleasing to the eye.

That done, I rescheduled my private-lesson students and then called in sick to work. I told Bertram's assistant, Betty Lou, that I'd picked up a twenty-four hour stomach virus. She made sympathy sounds and then asked if I wanted to be patched through to my husband. I feigned ill and hung up.

3

Ten o'clock came and went, and Bertram didn't call. Then I remembered the ringer on the phone was still off, so I turned it on and re-played the long list of messages on the answering machine, in case he had. There was nothing from him, but the Ice Queen had called again. Oh, joy. Uh huh.

"We want what's ours, shug," she said, her voice cold enough to freeze a shot glass of schnapps. "I suggest you hand it over unless you want things to get ugly."

Oh, for crying out loud. Did this lady not realize that I had no way of knowing who to turn it over to? Not that I would do that. I wasn't about to give the Velvet Elvis to some kook who threatened me with creepy phone messages.

And just who was she? The sound of her voice set my nerves to jangling.

God, she could be anybody. The French-fry girl at McDonalds. The laundress at the dry cleaners. A Wal-Mart cashier. A waitress at Billy Bob's Bodacious Bar-B-Q.

I played on through the rest of the messages. The last one was from Marty.

"Hey Cleo!" he said, all cheery. "Just wanted to let you know we've already sold five hundred tickets for the tour. And largely because of your haunted painting. We've already broken all previous fundraising attempts. Here's a big thank you, luv. See you tomorrow."

Good to know all our travails were at least aiding a worthy cause. Otherwise, the Velvet Elvis would have been history weeks ago.

4

Fake cobwebs stretched across the dining room and faux flames flickered in the chandelier. I plunked three black candles into a candelabrum to go on the stone fireplace mantel in the double parlor. But it was when I was hanging the tiny ornaments on the gnarled Halloween tree that I felt the weepies coming on again. Bertram and I normally put the decorations up together every year.

I dabbed at my eyes with a tissue. Bertram still hadn't called even though the afternoon was halfway over.

On TV, Oprah said, "Our show today is how to tell if your husband's having a mid-life crisis. Stay tuned as Dr. Phil sheds light on this often heart-breaking topic."

I perked up at that. Maybe Bertram was just having a mid-life crisis. Too bad I couldn't sit down and watch it since Elmer was due to arrive any minute. But I could record it. As I set TiVo to capture the show, a *plink plink brrrrrWHAP* emanated from the dining room.

The lower push pins must have popped out, because the Hannah Montana poster had rolled up like a window shade. The Velvet Elvis almost seemed to smirk. Or maybe sneer.

"Hey, One Eye. You just saved me the trouble." God, *I* was going to have a mid-life crisis if I kept talking to a painting. The doorbell did its arthritic ding.

Elmer stood on the welcome mat, just another good ole boy in his Western shirt, jeans, and pointy-toed boots.

I opened the door. "Come on in."

Maury and Cosmo, who usually made themselves scarce when company arrived, appeared as though from nowhere, rubbing up against Elmer's ankles as if he'd doused his jeans with catnip.

"Hello, kitties." He knelt down to cat level, scratching behind their ears. Both fur balls purred so loud, it sounded like someone had put miniature outboard motors inside their bellies. "You're friendly fellows."

Not usually. "You've got a way with cats."

He shrugged. "I just like critters. And they like me." He patted the cats, then rose from the floor. Orange cat hair clung to his jeans.

"Do you want to use a lint roller?"

"Nah. A little cat hair is just decoration." He flashed a charming Irish grin.

"The painting's this way. In the dining room."

Maury and Cosmo followed on Elmer's heel like he was the Pied Piper of Allister. I was a little jealous. The cats didn't follow me around like that.

Elmer pointed to the rolled up poster. "What's that tacked to the top?"

"Oh, just a little something I was trying. It's removable."

"I've been following your story in the press. Your husband ..."

"Bertram."

"Yes, Bertram, said Elvis spoke to him from the painting?"

Argh, I was never going to live this Velvet Elvis thing down. "Well, that's what he said, but I don't think he was serious."

"You're not sure?" Elmer crossed his arms over his chest.

"Look. I know you said you collect oddities. And if you want this thing because it's famous from all the media hype, I can understand that. But if you think it's really haunted, you're gonna be disappointed." I gazed up at the King in his gilt frame against the busy cabbage rose wallpaper.

"You don't believe in ghosts?"

I didn't say anything for a moment. "I think there may be ghosts," I said slowly. "I've never come across one, but that doesn't mean they don't exist." I dared ole One Eye to make a move. "Do they haunt velvet paintings? I don't think so. It's just too ridiculous."

Elmer nodded sagely. "Here's the deal. Whatever anyone offers you, I'll pay you more. I'm booked at your sister's place for a week, so take your time. I know the painting's committed to the historic home tour. But in the meantime, collect offers. Then remember, I'll top the highest bidder. Cash."

Wow, I guess he wanted the Velvet Elvis bad. I was impressed he'd made an honest offer instead of trying to bamboozle my husband into donating it.

"That's quite an offer."

"I play to win."

"Nothing wrong with that."

"So, I have one final question."

"Yeah?"

"Is your sister currently seeing anyone?"

I wasn't expecting that. "Uh, not exactly. Or I should say, not seriously."

Elmer smiled as if I'd just made his day.

5

My cell phone jingled a half hour later. Molly. "Yeah?"

"Can you come right over?"

"Sure," I said, intrigued.

Molly was gently rocking on her wood-slat porch swing, a moony look on her face.

"Elmer asked me out," she said dreamily.

"Did you say yes?"

"Oh, yeah."

"He touched you again, didn't he?"

"Uh huh," she said, her voice languid.

I plunked down on the swing beside my sister. "That is so weird. When I shook hands with him, I felt good, I mean, really good, like going-to-Disney-World good. But you … you have the Big O."

"Yeah, bodes well, doesn't it?"

We both chuckled over that. "So when's the big date?"

"Tonight. Dinner and a movie. He wants to see some Chuck Norris flick, but Cleo, if he holds my hand, I really don't think I'll care *what's* on the screen."

"I don't think you will, either."

My phone jingled again. Maybe Bertram was finally calling.

Nope. Georgia.

I fired out a bunch of questions with machine gun rapidity. "How's Bertram? Is he all right? Did he ask you to call?"

"He's fine, dear. And no, he didn't ask me to call—"

My heart plummeted to my stomach.

"—but there is something I need to tell you. Can you come over to the condo?"

"I'm on my way."

6

"Jailhouse Rock" blasted out into the hall from my mother-in-law's condo. I pounded on the door to be heard.

The music stopped.

"Yoo hoo! Georgia? It's Cleo," I hollered.

Georgia sang out, "Come on in."

My mother-in-law was decked out in jeans and a sleeveless red-checked shirt. She'd teased her hair into a sixties flip. It made me wish sixties fashions would come back in style.

"What a cozy place you've got here, Georgia." Her living room could have doubled as the Graceland Souvenir Shop, only with a couch and couple of chairs thrown in, but hey, if it made her happy.

"Why, thank you, dear. My only regret is that I wish I'd done this sooner. A condo is so much easier to keep up than that big ole house I was rattling around in. And we have a social committee that plans all sorts of fun outings, like going to the movies or the community theater or out to dinner. In fact, I'm leaving tomorrow for a trip to Hollywood. I'm afraid I'm going to have to miss your Historic Home Tour."

I parked my butt on the couch. A fringed Elvis throw covered the entire thing.

"So, a trip to Hollywood, huh?" Oh boy, if there were two things I didn't want to get Georgia yakking on about, they were Elvis and Hollywood. "So, what was it you wanted to tell me?" I said, trying to derail my mother-in-law.

"I'm making myself a Vodka Collins," she said. "Would you like one?"

"A Coke would be great."

Georgia made drinks in her cute little kitchenette. "Bertram has always been musical. Just like his daddy."

"I didn't know Fred was musical." Fred Tidwell, God rest his soul, had not been able to sing on pitch if his life depended on it. And Bertram had never mentioned his father playing any musical instruments. The one thing Fred had really excelled at had been selling insurance. Georgia had been well set with an array of policies when Fred keeled over from a stroke two years ago.

"My dear," Georgia said, handing me an ice-cold tumbler. I noticed she still wore her wedding band. "I'm sure there are all sorts of things you don't know about this family." But she said it very pleasantly. "You and Bertram have only been married a mere three years. That's practically no time at all."

I took a polite sip and sputtered as the drink burned its way down my throat. "Holy smokes, Georgia! There's rum in here."

My mother-in-law knocked back half her Vodka Collins. "You're going to need it, darlin'."

My brows arched. What could Georgia possibly tell me that I'd need liquor to hear?

Georgia perched on the edge of a blue wingback chair. "Remember when I said at dinner the other night that Elvis and I had gone out a few times while we were filming *Fun in Acapulco?*"

"Um hmm." I took another sip. It still burned, but at least warm fuzzies were radiating from my stomach to parts distant. I was going to have to be careful. I hadn't eaten today, and the rum was going to go straight to my head if I wasn't careful.

"There's something I want to show you."

While Georgia retrieved the something from her bedroom, I busied myself by studying the Elvis coasters on the coffee table with *All Shook Up* written across them in red. I had to admit, Elvis had been a good looking fella before the drugs, alcohol, and gluttony had taken their toll.

I swallowed another gulp from the tumbler. Now that I was feeling warm and fuzzy all over, I wondered why Georgia had never pursued a Hollywood career after making the Elvis movie. She'd certainly had the right look for the time.

Georgia returned and handed me a manila envelope. Inside was a baby picture of Bertram and his birth certificate.

"Nice phonograph, I mean, photograph of Bertram. What a cute baby." Oh, dear Lord, my lips had lost their feeling. I patted my mouth. Just how many shots had she put in my drink?

"Look more closely at his birth certificate."

The Elvis cushion at the end of the couch was looking mighty comfy. I could almost hear it telling me to lay my cheek upon it and take a little nappy-poo.

Georgia peered at me closely. "Oh, dear. I might have made your drink too stiff. Stay with me, Cleo."

"Okey dokey, Jo-Ja." I held up the certificate, but the words were kind of blurry. I did make out a *Father Unknown*. "Fred's not his daddy?"

I let out a jaw-cracking yawn. Figured I'd close my eyes for just a few seconds. No big deal. My eyes just wanted to rest a moment from all the Elvis paraphernalia. The hum of Georgia's refrigerator seemed amplified by about a hundred times. Or maybe I was hearing cicadas. But why would I hear cicadas indoors?

Georgia's voice was coming as if from a deep well. "Cleo, honey? Cleo? You mustn't tell Bertram. He doesn't know."

And then I slid right on into dreamland.

… I'm sitting in the old Let's Make a Deal *game show theater, just one of many in an audience where everyone wears a costume. Feathered chicken suits, a man in a nun's habit, a French maid, an Elvira get-up—you name it and someone's wearing it. The atmosphere crackles with energy as folks jump up and down, waving signs, and whooping and hollering for all they're worth.*

Monty Hall, dapper in his 1960s business suit, thrusts a microphone in my face and says, "Nice costume, Toots."

"Huh?" I look down at myself and am completely stunned. I'm wearing a white, rhinestone-studded jumpsuit just like the woman at the Church of Blue Suede Shoes. And my hair. I pat my head. My long blonde hair is gone and in

its place is short man-hair—and fuzzy sideburns. Ugh! I feel about as stupid as I look.

Monty says, *"Are you ready to play* Let's Make a Deal?*"*

My tongue could have been wrapped in an old gym sock, but I manage to spit out, "Sure." My voice is ten degrees below zero and sounds so familiar. But I can't quite place it. All I know is that it's not my voice.

Monty smiles a toothy, game show host's smile and reaches into his suit coat. He whips out a wad of cash and waves it under my nose. "Ah, nothing like the smell of money. Right, Toots?"

"Uh—"

"Now you can have this cash, but I'm not going to tell you how much I'm holding, or you can trade for what's behind door number three."

The audience cheers and confetti drops from the ceiling. A chant sweeps through the crowd. "Door Number Three! Door Number Three!"

Monty says, "Tick, tock, tick, tock. Cat got your tongue?"

"Um—"

"I can see that you drive a hard bargain." He stuffs the money back into his suit coat, then slides his hand into his pants pocket. A few coins jingle, then he withdraws the hand, but it's balled into a fist.

"You're a woman of discriminating taste. You can have what's in my hand or what's behind door number three, and remember, we're only an hour-long show."

The voice that's mine, but not mine says, "What's in your hand?"

"Thought you'd never ask. Peace of mind."

"A piece of my mind?"

The audience laughs, an ugly, roaring sound.

"No, Sweet Cheeks," Monty says. "Peace of mind." He uncurls his fingers, but the palm's empty.

"There's nothing there."

"Well, of course not. Peace of mind is an abstract concept. Really, Toots, you've got to get out more."

Laughing faces loom large all around. Monty leans in, his breath smelling of whiskey, only now he's Dupree Hardcastle, pompadour and all. "That really is a nice costume you're wearin'. Mind if I see what's under it after the show? We could have a really groovy time, you and me."

I squeeze my eyes shut as the lunatics around me chant, "Door Number Three!" But I get the bed spins, so I open them again. Dupree has morphed into Aaron Vassals, Mr. G .Q. himself.

"You're the sister I really wanted, but you had to be hooked up with him." *He nods toward the stage and there's Bertram, prancing about in an Elvis jumpsuit, karaoke microphone in hand.*

In my mind, I hear myself say, "Bertram. I want Bertram back." But what I actually say is, "Door Number Three."

Aaron says, "Carol Merrill—I mean, Dr. Bertram Tidwell—will you please show Miss Sweet Cheeks here what she has won?"

"Happy to, Mr. Hall." Bertram dashes off the stage and up the aisle, the microphone cord impossibly long. When he gets to me, he strikes a pose, his face in profile, the mike held high. "Guess who I am? Your very own Velvet Elvis, in the flesh."

"No! I want Bertram. Where's Bertram? ...

... "Bertram!"

"I'm right here, Cleo," came his rumbling bass.

I opened my eyes and there he was, sitting on Georgia's couch and leaning over me.

"Is it really you?"

"In the flesh."

I wrapped my arms around his neck as if I'd never let go. I even think a few tears slid down my face. We sat like that for a little bit, just holding and rocking each other, while Georgia busied herself elsewhere in the condo.

Bertram disentangled himself from me and said with mock exasperation, "Cleo, what are you doing passing out on Mama's sofa in the afternoon? And Betty Lou said you called in sick."

"I haven't eaten all day on account of how upset I was. And then your mom made me the stiffest drink I've ever had." Which isn't quite true. That distinction is reserved for the five shots of tequila I had one night playing Trivial Pursuit with second husband Marty

Millbrook and his soon-to-be lover, Bob. I'd passed out in mid-sentence, falling right out of my chair to land in an undignified heap on the kitchen floor. Not that Marty or Bob paid any attention. They'd only had eyes for each other.

"You were upset?" Bertram said gently.

"Yeah. Pretty much. Aren't most women when their husbands walk out?"

"I wasn't leaving you. I just needed a little ... distance to cool off."

"And did you? Cool off?"

"Yep."

He tilted my chin and kissed me, a nice, we're-in-this-for-the-long-haul sort of kiss, but it still lit my fire. We *were* going to make it to our fourth anniversary. We were. I was sure of it. Then I remembered where we were, and I broke it off gently.

Bertram gazed down at me, his eyes smoky. I must have lit his fire, too. "Let's get you home. We'll pick up your car later."

7

The jingle of my cell phone jangled me out of a light doze. I was in the passenger seat of the pink Caddy, Bertram behind the wheel. We were headed home. I checked the cell's screen. Molly.

"Cleo, you didn't answer my last call. Where are you?"

"On the way home." I noticed the little symbol that I'd missed a call.

"Well, there's a media circus outside your house. I wanted to give you a heads-up."

"A media circus?"

"Yep, there's a TV-6 News Rover from Birmingham and a local Channel 52 van parked out front. Plus a bunch of sightseers."

Oh, great. "Thanks for the warning."

Bertram glanced over at me. "What's up."

"Bedlam. Freakin' bedlam."

8

Our street reminded me of the mall on Friday night back before the internet. Cars cruised up and down the block, slowing to a crawl in front of our house. Folks hung out the passenger windows and snapped pictures with their Polaroids, and their Canon zoom lenses, and their digital cameras. And the two news vehicles Molly had warned me about were, indeed, docked at the curb in front of house, disrupting the flow of traffic like stones jutting out of a creek.

Bertram maneuvered the Caddy into the driveway. Before we could even get out, several car doors slammed, and reporters hauled ass across our yard. Oh, Lordy. You'd have thought the Velvet Elvis and the historic home tour were the event of the year. Must have been a slow news day.

I slid out of the Caddy and met Bertram on the front walk. A petite blonde in a business suit angled up to us and stuck a microphone in my face.

"Tiffany Madson, TV-6 News. Are you Cleo Tidwell?"

I nodded.

She jerked the mike in Bertram's direction. "And you must be Dr. Bertram Tidwell?"

"Yep—"

She yanked the mike in front of her own face. "Is it true the two of you are getting a divorce over the Velvet Elvis?"

"What?" I said at the same time Bertram said, "No! Absolutely not."

Another reporter, not wanting to get wedged out of the action, practically shoved a mike up my nostrils. "Barbara Wright, Allister Cable. There are rumors that you'll be selling the painting to the highest bidder."

"Where did you hear that?" I said. And meanwhile, sightseers were snapping our picture like we were monkeys at the zoo. Tiffany Madson said, "Is the pink Caddy part of the historic home tour, Dr. Tidwell?" as Barbara Wright said, "Did Elvis tell you to buy it?"

Bertram put his arm around my shoulders and herded me to the front door. "No comment, folks."

We hurried inside as the reporters finished up their sound bites. I hadn't taken three steps into the house when my cell phone jingled. Molly again.

"Oh my God! Aaron called. He wants to help me with the tour and then take me out for a late supper. Can you believe it? Oh my God!"

Geez, it was like listening to someone in high school. "Whoa, slow down there, sister. Now, what happened? Aaron finally called you?"

"Yeah, he called just a moment ago. Said he'd enjoyed our date last Saturday and wanted to go out with me again."

"On a weeknight? Isn't that a strange date night for a teacher?"

"Yeah, maybe. But he's so hot! And we never got to do the deed."

"Okay," I said. "You're thinking with your hoo-ha and not your head. Do you really want to go out with someone who preferred an impromptu Elvis revue over getting you in the sack? I mean, come on, is that normal for a guy?"

Molly sounded a bit put out. "What are you saying, Cleo?"

"Look. Elmer asked you out for tonight. He seems like a good guy. But Aaron ... well, there are a bunch of red flags when it comes to Aaron. You even said so yourself yesterday."

"Yeah, I did," Molly said with what sounded like reluctant resignation. "But there's something irresistible about him. How can I not go out with him?"

Oh boy. Molly really was thinking with her hoo-ha. "Look. I'm just trying to keep you from getting hurt. If you want to go out with Aaron, then go out with Aaron. Heck, play the field. Go out with Elmer *and* Aaron. And don't forget what Elmer's touch does to you."

"Oh, I'm not planning on breaking my date with Elmer. That's definitely on, come hell or high water."

"Okay, that sounds sensible."

We said goodbye.

Bertram had been watching me with a bemused expression. "Five bucks says she gets him in the sack."

"We're talkin' about a guy who gave up sex because he had to get up early for church the next day. But if you want to throw five dollars my way, be my guest."

"Well, we'll just see about that," Bertram said with mock seriousness.

"Uh huh. Sucker." I snickered and darted past him, but he yanked me off my feet in a big bear hug, and we both collapsed on the hard wood floor in a fit of laughter.

We wound up in the sack about five minutes later.

9

A chill October wind sent a shiver up my back as Bertram and I walked hand and hand under a ripe harvest moon, leaves crunching under our feet. The sightseers had returned to their homes and hotels, and the streets were empty at this late hour. The only eyewitnesses were the jack-o-lanterns glowing from neighbors' porches. The air had a crisp freshness that made me think of hay rides, carnivals, and football games. I sucked in a deep breath, thinking hot cocoa time was just around the corner.

Since Bertram seemed like himself again, I filled him in on who Elmer Inglebright was and his offer to top the highest bid for the painting. Bertram squeezed my hand under the lamplight.

"Look, Cleo. You don't have to try to hide your dislike for the painting. It's yours to do with as you wish. If you want to sell, I'm okay with that."

We'd reached our house. I'd left the front porch light off to cut down on gawkers. Bertram leaned back against the trunk of the gingko tree, and I cuddled in his arms, the top of my head not quite reaching his collarbone.

"I'm so glad. I don't want to fight." I reached up and caressed my husband's smooth cheek. I was still getting used to the idea of a clean-shaven Bertram.

An all too familiar Southern drawl just about scared the crap out of me.

"Well, hey there, Tidwells," said Dupree Hardcastle from the dark. "How are y'all this fine October evening?"

A shadowy, pregnant-man figure stepped out from under the crepe myrtle tree between the sidewalk and the street.

"Geez! Don't sneak up on people like that," I said.

"Sorry," he said, not sounding sorry at all. "Didn't mean to startle you. I was just out for a stroll."

Stroll, my ass. This guy had been waiting for us. And this made the second time he'd scared the poop out of me.

"So, Dr. Tidwell, have you given any more thought to joining the Church of the Blue Suede Shoes?"

"I have. While I appreciate the invitation, I'm going to have to decline."

"Well, that's a pity. We were sure you'd make a wonderful addition to our little family. Between you and me ..." He left the sanctuary of the crepe myrtle and approached us. "The membership voted unanimously on your behalf. First time that's happened in a long while. Maybe ever."

"Er, yes, well, that's most flattering. But I still must decline joining your group."

"You know, your Velvet Elvis would make a stunning contribution to our blessed artifacts collection. And if you donated it, you could take a tax deduction."

"The painting is not Bertram's to donate," I said.

"Well then, little miss, my missive should be directed at you."

"The answer's no." I was certainly not giving it away to the Blue Shoe Loonies. "Now, if you'll excuse us, Dupree, we're calling it a night."

"Of course. Think about what I said. Some people would kill to have a Velvet Elvis like that."

Yeah, crazy people.

I shuddered at the thought.

CHAPTER SIX

The Big Day
Tuesday, October 21

1

A car horn tooting the opening notes to "Heartbreak Hotel" plucked me from a deep slumber at eight o'clock in the morning. I stumbled out of bed and shrugged on my robe. Gawd! Didn't these people have lives?

The thick odor of fried bacon assaulted me as soon as I stepped out of the bedroom onto the second floor landing. Oh, boy. Bertram must have had made himself another heart-clogging breakfast. As for me, all I needed was a cold can of Diet Coke to jump-start my way into something resembling joy. Although I'd really be able to cut loose and kick up my heels once *The Dead Speak* commitment was over and done with on Saturday. Five hundred people or so were going to be trooping through my house tonight, so there was always that to look forward to. *Riiiight.*

Once downstairs, I pulled aside the drapes and took a peek outside. Cars lined the curb up and down the street. Some people were actually tailgating, sitting in lawn chairs behind their cars and eating breakfasts from Hardee's and McDonald's, while sipping coffee from a Styrofoam cup or thermos. Others milled along the sidewalk, snapping pictures of the house—*my* house. A woman wearing an "I ♥ Elvis" t-shirt and a much-too-tight pair of spandex pants suddenly pointed at me, and the next thing I knew, a herd of Elvis fanatics was rushing my front door.

Eek!

I fled to the kitchen as my cats fled under the furniture.

2

Four skillets sat upon the stove, one on each burner, bacon grease congealing in every single one of them. Two empty pork packages lay strewn about the counter, along with a partially full carton of eggs, a bunch of broken egg shells, a chunk of cheddar cheese, a jug of milk, a lidless jar of peanut butter, several banana skins, and a liberal sprinkling of bread crumbs. Grease-soaked paper towels lined four plates, each one stacked atop the other in the sink. Splatters of bacon fat dotted everything. And I mean everything. The ivy wallpaper where a splash guard should have been, the stove hood, the microwave, and the window behind the sink. There was even grease on the floor three feet out from the stove. As if Bertram had been going for distance.

I was trying to decide where to start first when the back door banged open and Martha Jane whisked in. She was wearing overalls and toting a cleaning caddy.

"Whew! Someone's been frying bacon," she said.

"Yeah, that would be Bertram."

Martha Jane surveyed the kitchen. "Oh, Lordy. And he made a *big* mess." She plunked the caddy on the breakfast bar, selected a pair of rubber gloves, and snapped them on.

"He's not usually like this," I said.

My mother waved a gloved hand through the air. "Men do not give a thought to the messes they leave for women to clean up. Your dad cannot pick up after himself, not even a teensy bit. I swear to goodness; he can't seem to put a dirty plate in the dishwasher or replace the toilet paper when it's empty or wipe his crumbs off the counter. I just want to snatch him ball-headed some days.

"Okay, Martha Jane." I had finally learned after almost thirty-nine years of life on this planet to just agree with my mother when she went into rant mode. Because she'd argue with you until she got the last word.

"That's some crowd out front. I had to park around the corner from your sister's." Martha Jane whipped out a bottle of 409 from the caddy.

"Yeah, it looks like game day at ASU with all the tailgaters."

"And all for what? To see the gaudiest thing God ever saw fit to put on this green earth."

Didn't I know it!

"Believe me, I would have burned it and then danced on the ashes if it weren't for the historical society."

"Oh, Good Lord, of course not. You're doing the smart thing to raise money for charity. Only a fool would walk away from oodles of money like that."

Martha Jane grabbed a handful of rags from her caddy and sprayed 409 on the grease splatters as if everything were on fire. "Lordy, Lordy, Lordy," she said, referring to Bertram's breakfast handiwork.

"You seem to have this under control so I'm going to go straighten up the front of the house."

"Have at it, Cleo. This'll take me awhile." She flipped on the exhaust fan in the stove hood. "We've got to get the smell of bacon grease out of your house. It's overwhelming."

Yep, it was ... like a greasy diner. I grabbed some Febreze and misted the dining and living room with it. Since the historic home tour was tonight, I figured I should go ahead and remove the Hannah Montana poster from the painting. It was still rolled up like a scroll and tacked above Elvis's head. The rhinestones on his jumpsuit seemed to twinkle in the sunlight streaming through the east bay windows. As I climbed the step ladder once again, I remembered the dream I'd had at Georgia's and shivered.

"Son of a biscuit!" came Martha Jane's voice from the kitchen. "How did grease splatter the cabinet knobs *above* the range hood?"

I'm telling ya, Bertam had been cooking for distance.

The two thumb tacks pulled easily out of the velvet. I started down the ladder with the poster, and wasn't even looking at the painting, when I thought I saw Elvis wink at me from the edge of my peripheral vision.

Whoa! Had I really seen that?

I froze where I was. "Do that again," I said, pitching my voice low so that Martha Jane wouldn't wonder why I was conversing with a gaudy painting.

Nothing.

"Oh, my God," I whispered. "Are you really haunted?"

Nothing.

Like what did I expect? For it to answer me?

"Cleopatra," my mother called out, "you've got ants in your kitchen."

Oh, joy.

I pointed my finger at Elvis. "Listen up. If you pull any shenanigans tonight, I'll exterminate you. I've got a can of gasoline out back with your name on it. And don't think I won't."

The painting did nothing. It was as if Elvis had left the building.

3

I sauntered into Bertram's office at 12:05 with two sack lunches. He was singing along to Elvis's "Suspicious Minds," but clicked off the CD player when he saw me. I noticed with dismay that he was wearing a white scarf around the up-turned collar of his ASU Marching Ferrets polo shirt.

"Well, hey there, little darlin'. Come to see the King?"

Oh no. Not the King again.

"Uh, no. Just my husband." I held up the brown paper bags.

"Oh, great. I'm starved." Now that sounded more like the Bertram I knew and loved.

I pulled a chair around his desk so that I could sit next to him. My, but what a paunch my husband was getting. He was going to have to lay off the bacon and fried sandwiches. And what the hell had he done to his belt? The thing was crusted with rhinestones and gold chains.

"So, is there anything you'd like to tell me?" I said, lighting into my turkey and cheddar on whole wheat. I was thinking of an apology for the mess in the kitchen.

But what I got was, "Did you know I can turn the sprinkler system outside on and off just by thinking it?"

"What?"

"Yep. I've been doing it all morning. Wanna see?"

"Bertram, you don't even have any windows in your office. And besides, that's crazy talk."

"But I can do it."

"Okay, I know what you're doing. You're trying to avoid having to fess up to leaving a god-awful mess in the kitchen this morning when you knew, you *knew*, that we're having a fund-raising tour come through our house tonight." My temper was flaring up like a zit before Prom.

Bertram gawked at me open-mouthed.

I hopped up out of my seat. "And what kind of fashion statement are you trying to make? You look ridiculous, for God's sake. Did you even look in a mirror this morning before you left home? Well, did you?"

"I think we've been away from Graceland too long. What do you say that we go home? This tour's gone on long enough."

"Ugh! I've had it up to here with you, Bertram! I thought we could make this marriage work. But you're just getting nuttier by the minute. I hope to goodness your boss doesn't see you like this or you may not have a job anymore."

Bertram looked up at me with those big puppy-dog eyes of his, then shook his head like a mutt with ear mites. "The Flying Elvii aren't available for the game on Saturday. But the pink Caddy's going to look great on the field."

Now *that* sounded like Bertram. Damn, but it was confusing dealing with someone whose personality fluctuated so wildly from one moment to the next.

He seemed like his old self for the remainder of our lunch hour and on through band practice. But I wondered just who would come home tonight for the tour. Bertram or Elvis?

I think we'd reached a point where it was time to call in some professional help. But I couldn't really do anything about that today. I'd call a therapist tomorrow and see if we could get an appointment for early next week. I really didn't want to go to divorce court— again.

4

Martha Jane peeked through the stained glass window in the front door, one hand gripping the antique door knob.

"Oh, Lordy, look at all of those people. Cleopatra, are you ready? It's five till five."

I pulled back the drapes just a hair and took a look for myself.

The line outside our house started on the front porch and snaked down the front walk to the sidewalk where it continued on down past the vacant house next door. Men, women, and children of all shapes, sizes, and ages murmured outside like bees buzzing. Most of them actually looked normal, but a few had chosen to celebrate Halloween early by wearing fifties attire like blue suede shoes, black leather jackets, rolled up blue jeans, or penny loafers. A few of them had even slicked their hair back in a pompadour. And that went for some of the women, too. Several people sported Elvis t-shirts of various design.

Martha Jane and I had changed out of our cleaning clothes. Daddy had joined us for the tour and the three of us were like a photo out of the L.L. Bean catalog: khaki slacks, button down or polo shirts, and loafers. A stark contrast from most of the people waiting outside.

Marty had suggested that we limit the number of people inside the house at any given moment to sixty. So once the first sixty were in, no one else could cross the threshold until someone left. I just hoped Daddy and Martha Jane could handle crowd control.

Two historical society volunteers stood at the ready on the opposite end of the long double parlor. I'd already forgotten their names, but from their smart outfits, perfect hair, and refined air, my money was on them being from money.

Bertram was supposed to be manning the dining room, but was still upstairs. What was taking him so long? If he came down in the rhinestone-spangled jumpsuit, I was going to kill him. Ditto for singing karaoke.

The grandfather clock in the parlor chimed the hour.

"It's time," I said. "Open the door."

Folks swarmed across the threshold like holiday shoppers at Macy's the day after Thanksgiving, vying for a chance to be among the first to behold the Velvet Elvis of internet and tabloid fame.

Someone shouted, "There it is! In the dining room!" Daddy and Martha Jane got swept away with the crowd as it surged through my house, a river of living flesh in spandex, denim, and polyester.

I pushed against the open door, trying to close it again without hurting anyone. Bertram was suddenly beside me, blocking the flow of lookie loos with his six foot four frame. I could have kissed him. He wasn't in the jumpsuit nor any other crazy outfit. Just navy Chinos and an orange polo shirt. The orange really brought out his tan from being in the sun every day with the marching band.

"Hold it up there, folks," he said in his rumbling, good natured bass. "Everyone will get their turn. We're just going to close the door for a moment. As soon as someone comes out, another can come in."

Marty squeezed to the front of the line despite a few protests. He matched Bertram for preppiness except he had on lime green slacks and a white polo.

"I'm with the historical society, folks." He bussed my cheek and made eyes at Bertram as we let him in and then shut the door against the tide.

Marty took in the midnight-shopping-spree atmosphere with a look of delight. "Hey, isn't this a great turnout? The historical society couldn't be happier. Thanks again for being a good sport and letting us promote the tour with your painting. I know how much you love it." He winked at me on the word love.

"Yeah, yeah, yeah. You owe me, big time."

Bertram headed over to the dining room as my bedraggled parents pressed upstream through the visitors to join me once again.

Marty leaned close. "Talk about yummy. If your man weren't straight, I'd steal him away from you."

"Hey, keep your mitts to yourself," I said, nudging him with good natured enthusiasm.

Marty nudged me back. "I hear ya, sister. Oh, there's Kristie Vanderhorn, Miss Moneybags, herself. She donated several thousand dollars last year. I've got to go say hello." He prissed over to the other end of the room.

A roly-poly woman in a rumpled blouse and denim skirt came up to me and said, "You must be Cleo Tidwell. I saw you on the *Bippy Barndale Show*. You're so lucky to have a husband who would give you such a wonderful gift. I can't tell you how much I envy you!"

I really didn't know how to respond to that. By the time I mumbled, "Gee, thanks," Daddy was letting her out and the next person in.

Now that we'd established a little order, Daddy opened the door and set a card table and two chairs right outside the threshold so that people coming in would have to hand over their tickets and squeeze by the designated gate-keepers to enter. I kept vigil by the stone fireplace at the west end of the double parlor, but had a clear line of sight through the open French doors into the dining room and could see Bertram and the Velvet Elvis clearly. Over the general babble I heard a woman ask my husband, "Dr. Tidwell, does it really sing 'Heartbreak Hotel'?"

"It does, indeed, little lady."

She fanned her face with her bare palm. "Oh, gosh. Do you think it might sing during the tour?"

"It's possible."

Bertram had rigged up an auditory effect for the tour. Don't ask me how. I can barely figure out how to work TiVo. He pressed a remote control in his pants pocket and music seemed to emanate from the painting. I thought it sounded a little tinny, but hey, we *were* a local historic home tour, not a professional haunted house.

As Elvis launched into "Heartbreak Hotel," the crowd in the dining room thickened with exclamations of surprise and enjoyment. Some people smiled wryly, understanding that we were pulling their leg for their entertainment, while others seemed to believe a miracle was happening.

Elmer Inglebright sauntered in, Mr. Urban Cowboy. He'd gone capless, his curly red hair untamed.

"Nice illusion ya got going there."

I smiled. I couldn't help it. For some reason I always felt so happy in his presence, as if I were with the nicest person in the world.

"Thank Bertram. It's his doing."

"I'll be sure to do that."

"So what's it like over at the bed and breakfast right now?"

"Slow. That's why I decided to come on over here. And your

sister has a good-lookin' feller helping her. Figured there was no sense in having two foxes in the henhouse."

How quickly Elmer picked up on things.

"I hope the two of you had a good date last night."

"The best. Ever since my wife died several years ago, bless her soul, I haven't never run across a woman who warms my heart quite like your sister."

Awww. How romantic. And he was a widower. "Well, I hope you'll woo her away from the other fox."

"That's what I hope, too."

Gee, all the world loves a lover.

"Well, if you don't mind," Elmer said, "I'm going to make myself at home on your couch over there for a little while."

"I don't mind a bit. You go on over there and kick your feet up."

"Thank you, Cleo. I'm mighty obliged."

Oh. I hope Molly picked Elmer. He seemed like such a good guy. Aaron was a bit weird. Sexy as hell. But weird.

A woman I didn't know interrupted my train of thought.

"Are you Mrs. Tidwell?" Her voice sounded familiar, and I grappled with placing the combination of throaty and nasal quality it had.

"Yes?" I drew out the yes as if unsure.

The woman hijacked my hand and shook it vigorously. I was pretty sure I'd never seen her before. She was the most monochromatic woman I think I'd ever met: dark blonde hair worn in a straight, shoulder-length bob, cream colored short-sleeved sweater set matched with brown slacks, and brown, low-heeled pumps. No ostentatious jewelry or nails. Nothing that would make her stand out in a crowd. Nothing that signified she had any personality. Just beige, boring and ordinary.

"I'm Faye Eldritch. I spoke to you on the phone almost two weeks ago? I've left several messages for you since then, but you haven't returned any of my calls."

Ah, yes. Now I remembered. She'd offered to spiritually cleanse the Velvet Elvis for the bargain price of $39.95. I'd never have guessed from looking at her.

"So nice of you to make the tour." I tugged my hand from hers.

"Mrs. Tidwell, I wasn't joking when I said you and your husband were in grave danger. I've been sensing a disturbance in the psychic force field around your house—"

Psychic force field?

"—and something bad is going to happen unless you destroy that painting."

Uh huh. Right. "I assure you, Ms. Eldritch, that we have taken every precaution and nothing bad is going to happen."

"But Mrs. Tidwell, that is what I came here to tell you. The bad thing has already happened."

"Could you be a little more specific?"

"Psychic ability doesn't work that way. If we all knew the exact future we'd be millionaires."

That had been my line of thinking. "So if this bad thing has already happened, then what good will warning me do?"

"My goodness, but there are rituals that could be performed, spells enacted, powerful psychic helpers could be called forth."

"I see. And I bet all that comes with a price."

She drew herself up, indignant. "Well, I don't give my services for free. Do you?"

"Say, why don't you go have a seat by that red-haired fellow on the couch while I think about it. Okay?"

"Bless you, Mrs. Tidwell. That's all I want you to do is think about it." And she weaved through the throng toward Elmer. Maybe she'd feel so good sitting next to him she'd forget all about my perceived troubles.

A steady current of people continued to flow through the house. I took the opportunity to zip to the bathroom.

When I came out, a bull of a woman pointed at me and said,

"There she is! That's her, Spike!"

Oh, no. Darlene. And there was no place to hide. If only I'd seen her coming, I could have camped out in the bathroom. But what surprised me was Spike. I'd expected a biker guy with tattoos and pierced eyebrows. Well, I was right about two out of three. Spike was a gal. A beautiful gal, Asian ancestry somewhere in her family tree, with tattoos and body piercings, and long silky hair that cascaded down her back. She was dressed in head to toe black.

Not quite knowing what to say, I fell back on Southern manners. "Er, hi, Darlene. Thanks for dropping by. The Velvet Elvis is in the dining room."

Darlene wasn't one to let things lie. "I'm still waiting for your email address. The aliens never did send it to me."

Oh boy. "Are you sure? Because I told them to give it to you."

Belief and doubt warred on Darlene's face.

Spike finally spoke up. Her accent said Alabama. "So does your painting really sing?"

"You'll have to decide for yourselves. It's right in there," I said, trying to entice them to move along.

"Heartbreak Hotel" started up again. Thank you, Bertram!

Darlene grasped Spike's arm and pulled her through the French doors. "Spike, it's just like *The X-Files*. Come on. We gotta see this."

My sister spoke over my shoulder. "So this is all the fun we're missing."

She and Aaron had let themselves in by the back door.

"You mean you don't have a flock of freaks milling through your house?"

"No, they're all over here. Or checking out some of the other houses on the tour. I'm sure it'll pick up later."

I glanced at Aaron and he dazzled me with a Ralph Lauren poster-boy smile. How did this guy manage to look so sexy all of the time? Guess it was a natural talent.

Molly leaned in close. "Don't look now, but Bippy Barndale just walked in the door. I think that's my cue to leave."

"Traitor." I grinned at her. "Hey, before you slink out, would you go around and turn on all the lamps for me? The light's changing and it's getting dim in here."

"Sure, Cleo. But if I get caught up with having to talk to Bippy…"

"Then go, woman, go. Turn on the lights and slip out."

As usual, Bippy dressed like no real woman I'd ever seen. Her hair was wrapped up in a gold turban and she wore a matching gold lamé jacket and slacks. Her make-up was so thick, I wondered if she applied it with a spatula. And she was jacked up on what had to be four inch heels. How anyone could walk in those was beyond me. I guess having loads of money didn't necessarily give you any fashion sense. And no one with any sense would dare tell the empress that her outfits were gaudy.

I tried to do my own slinky impression into the butler's pantry, checking my watch in the process. Wow! Six-thirty already. It would be dark soon.

"Oh, Cleo. Cleo Tidwell."

Drats! Cornered! I turned slowly and put on a happy face.

"Bippy. Hello."

"What a lovely turnout for the historical tour, wouldn't you say?" She made a sweeping gesture, so melodramatic.

"Yes. Just peachy."

"I really must have you back on the show again. Everyone's been talking about it." She edged closer as though sharing a confidence. "Someone posted a video of it on YouTube."

"Really? We're going to be selling the painting after the tour. As much as I'd like to keep it," I crossed my fingers behind my back, "we've had so much interest in it that it wouldn't be right to deprive the highest bidder of ownership."

Boy, wait till *that* got around. We'd have ourselves a bidding war.

"Oh, what a shame." Bippy frowned and her make-up cracked. Then her eyes lit up and she snapped her fingers. "I've got it. Bippy strikes again! You can auction it on my show and give the proceeds to charity. Wouldn't that be marvelous?"

Well, didn't I now feel like a selfish cad? "That's a fine idea, Bippy, and I'll be sure to think about it."

"Heartbreak Hotel" was playing again. "Oh, you don't want to miss that," I said. "Head on in to the dining room. That's right. Through the French doors." Bippy went forth, the lamplight gleaming off her gold lamé suit as if she were lit from within.

It was now officially night. I pushed upstream against the incoming guests to turn on the porch light amazed at how fast the past hour had flown by. And just as I reached the antique light switch, which was actually a panel of push buttons with faux mother-of-pearl inlays, Dupree Hardcastle and tiny Mavis Mathews walked through the open front door. For such a petite woman, she carried a purse that could almost have been a tote.

Dupree said, "Well, look who it is, Mavis."

There was nothing overtly sinister about his words, but I detected an undercurrent of hostility.

"Dupree. Mavis. Come on in," I said. "The painting's in the dining room. Look as long as you like."

I pushed through the stream of people pressing around us to return to my post by the stone fireplace. To my surprise, Dupree and Mavis followed me. From the dining room, I heard someone ask Bertram if he would mind taking the Velvet Elvis off the wall so as to get a better photograph of it. Bertram said no problem. I was going to intervene and tell my husband to leave it put when Dupree said, "I owe you an apology, Mrs. Tidwell."

He was as tall and broad shouldered as Bertram, and he just happened to stand so that he blocked my view into the dining room.

"Oh, that's not necessary, Dupree." Outside I could have sworn I heard the tinkling music of the ice cream man. Weird. Even though October can be warm in Alabama, the ice cream man pretty much hangs up his hat at the end of August.

Mavis stood beside him, and I wondered if she'd put him up to this. The woman behind the throne, so to speak.

"Yes, ma'am, it is. I've unintentionally scared you twice in my zeal to see your painting, and for that, I am truly contrite." If he'd had a hat, he would have been wringing it between his hands. "It was the wrong thing to do, and I hope you can find it in your heart to forgive me. Please accept this small token of my esteem from The Church of the Blue Suede Shoes."

Mavis opened her tote-sized purse and extracted a commemorative Elvis plate, the figure strikingly like the one in our painting. I was touched by this gesture, yet thought what a great gift it would be for Georgia.

A horrendous crash of crunching metal clanged out in the street. The flow of people coming in the house reversed like the tide, and I was swept out the front door and past Daddy and Martha Jane, the new Elvis plate clutched in one hand, as people encircled the accident scene to gawk under the wash of the street light.

A blue and gold ice cream truck had become one with the back fender of a silver Honda Civic parked along the curb. The truck didn't seem any worse for the wear; if anything, "Camp Town Ladies" jingle-jangled louder than ever. The Honda Civic, however, wasn't going to be driving anywhere without the aid of a tow truck anytime soon. The back end had crumpled up like a beer can on a frat boy's forehead.

"That's my car!" A man cried out. A skinny dude wearing jeans and an Elvis Rocks t-shirt rushed to the Honda Civic and began caressing the hood of his out-of-commission vehicle as if it were a horse that was going to have to be put down.

I hoped no one was hurt. I didn't see any dead or injured bodies anywhere. "Dial 911!" I shouted, although there was really no need because people right and left had whipped out cell phones, presumably to call the police. At least, I hoped they had and weren't calling some loved one to send them snapshots of an accident scene.

The ice cream truck driver opened her door and slid out, and all I could think was *Yowzah!* A hot girl in a white string bikini and high heels stepped onto the strip of grass beside the curb and started hawking ice cream. From the looks of her bikini top, she must have been a little chilly. Pretty much every male in the vicinity over the age of ten felt a sudden need to buy a Drumstick or a Nutty Buddy. They clamored around Miss Hot Girl, waving their money and shouting out what they wanted. It was like the pit on the New York Stock Exchange.

Mr. Honda Civic had apparently been distracted from his grief and had now joined the rest of the mob vying for an ice cream cone, his mutilated car momentarily forgotten. Bertram stepped up beside me on the lawn. "She's quite a treat, huh? You want an ice cream, Cleo?"

I just gave him "the look," the one that said, You're on thin ice, Mister.

Sirens blared, fast approaching. Boy, this had all the makings of the midway at the Alabama State Fair. All we needed were some carnies.

The sirens blipped and a voice over a loudspeaker said, "Folks, clear the road." People were milling in the street as if it were a block party. Bertram and I stepped over to the curb while the police spoke with Mr. Elvis Rocks and wrote up an accident report. Miss Hot Girl seemed to have an effect on them, too, because they both bought ice cream sandwiches and had their picture taken with her. Yeesh!

Now that there was nothing more to see, we headed back to the house. Daddy and Martha Jane were licking ice cream cones on the front porch. Oh, no. I hoped they hadn't let people inside with sticky treats. Molly had come over to see what all the fracas was about. She had an ice cream in her hand, too.

"Aaron had to leave early," she said. "His brother came into town unexpected, and he had to go." She frowned. "I think I'm done with him. He can't ever complete a date with me."

I patted her on the shoulder. "Well, you've still got Elmer. He was around here a little earlier, before the crash."

The tour-goers in the house were all talking about the accident while licking Popsicles and shaved ice. Didn't they know it was rude to bring food into someone's house without asking first? Ergh! I hoped the historical society had raised a lot of money.

Bertram said, "I'm going to go hang the painting again."

He headed off to the dining room. I started for the kitchen to grab a pack of napkins to hand out to everyone, but noticed he seemed to be looking for something, his expression perplexed.

I halted in front of the French doors. "What is it, Bertram?"

"The Velvet Elvis. It's gone."

CHAPTER SEVEN

The Night of the Big Day
Tuesday Night, October 21

1

D.K. Greenwood, my police-officer friend from high school, looked up from the stolen-property report, shaking his head in disdain, disbelief, or maybe both. "You're kidding me. The haunted Velvet Elvis? *That's* what's missing?"

"Yuh huh," I said.

D.K. worked as a plain clothes cop in the special crimes unit and was here only as a favor to me. He'd been the shy, skinny kid who never dated in high school. But he'd blossomed over the years and was now a nice looking guy—blonde, lean, and he could easily pass for thirty, instead of thirty-nine. And unmarried. I made a mental note to fix him up with Molly if she and Elmer didn't work out.

If it weren't for the police Q&A, we might have been having a little soiree. We all sat in the parlor, D.K. on the pea-green couch. We all, being me, Bertram, Daddy, Martha Jane, and Molly. I'd made sure everyone had a hot beverage.

D.K. said, "And it went missing during the historic home tour?" as if asking for confirmation.

"Yes."

Boy, was I ever tired. We'd called the police around seven thirty, but D.K. hadn't arrived until a little past ten. I suppose a stolen Velvet Elvis ranked pretty low on the police priority scale.

Martha Jane piped up. "The fender bender and the girl selling ice cream drew everyone's attention, and when we came back in, the painting was gone."

"Anything else missing?"

"Not that I've noticed."

"But you did look?"

"Yeah." I sipped my hot cocoa.

Bertram was awfully quiet. He was nursing a cup of coffee, something he rarely did. I wondered how he was taking all of this. We hadn't had a chance to talk about it privately since the tour had continued after the accident, although the number of visitors had significantly decreased as word of the theft circulated. And when the thing was over at nine, Daddy and Martha Jane had helped me clean up.

"Was the painting insured?" D.K. sipped his own cup of coffee out of one of my kitty-cat mugs.

"No, not specifically," I said.

Daddy shook his head at that. With all the hoopla surrounding the Velvet Elvis, he thought we'd been idiots to not take out special insurance on it.

D.K. nodded and scribbled something on the form. "Do you know the value?"

Bertram spoke up for the first time since nine o'clock. "I paid my mother a thousand dollars for it."

I winced, and Daddy shook his head again. That was a lot of money for a black velvet painting. Of course, if it hadn't been stolen, we probably could have sold it for much more considering what a media darling it had become.

D.K. raised an eyebrow, but didn't say anything. I'm sure I knew what he thought of that. The Allister Police Department could barely afford to operate. People throwing thousands of dollars at tacky art was unconscionable.

"Do you know who took it?"

"No. There were so many people in the house at any given time. It could have been anyone."

"Anyone you suspect?"

Now *there* was an interesting question. I suspected a lot of people. Dupree Hardcastle and the Blue Shoe Loonies. Darlene. Aaron Vassals. The Ice Queen, who could have come through on the tour without ever saying a word to tip me off. One of several unknown Elvis kooks who had left wacky phone messages. Maybe Faye Eldritch. And even Elmer Inglebright. He said he'd top the highest bidder, but how did I know it hadn't all been a ruse to fool me?

Bertram spoke up again, so serious and solemn. "A guy on the tour did ask me to take it down from the wall so he could get a better picture of it." He frowned. "Certainly made it easier for the thief. Assuming he wasn't the thief."

"So where was the painting when everyone ran out to see the accident?"

"In the dining room." Bertram gestured in the general direction with his coffee mug. "I set it on the floor and propped it against the back of a chair by the table."

D.K. jotted notes.

"Did the painting have any serial numbers?"

Bertram and I glanced at each other before answering in unison. "No."

D.K. clicked his pen and slid it into the breast pocket of his shirt. "I'm not even going to ask for a description of it. It's not like people are stealing these right and left. If it turns up, we'll pretty much know it's yours."

"What's the likelihood of that happening?" I really wasn't sad to see the thing go, but I'd really been looking forward to the upgrade from economy to first class on our plane tickets to the Bahamas from selling it to Elmer. I guess we'd have to settle for a weekend at Molly's B&B.

"It's not good. I'll tell you that. There's only a ten percent chance of stolen property of any kind being recovered. But we'll send you the police report in a week, and you can file a claim with your insurance company. Do you folks have any other questions for me?"

Everyone was mum.

And then it hit me. *The Dead Speak* was coming on Saturday to do their show on the Velvet Elvis, and we no longer had the thing. Guess I was gonna have to call the whole thing off.

Surprisingly, I was a little disappointed. And not just about the money.

2

Maury and Cosmo slunk out from under the bed as I shucked off my clothes and slipped into one of Bertram's t-shirts. The shirt swallowed me up, but it was something of Bertram's and I loved it. The cats hopped up on the bed as I slid between the covers.

The bathroom light across the hall clicked off, and my he-man husband stepped out of the bathroom. He tossed his wadded up clothes at the laundry hamper in the corner and missed. Why is it that men can hold down jobs for money but can't seem to get their dirty clothes in the proper place at home? It's one of the mysteries of life.

He climbed into bed as if all were right with the universe, snugged the covers up to his bare waist, and said, "I can cure the common cold with my healing powers."

"Huh?" The cats scattered as if they'd never seen Bertram before.

"And say good-bye to Advil. I can cure aches and pains, too."

Oh, no. And just when I'd thought we were saying good-bye to kooky. My insides were all fluttery, and not in a good way.

"What healing powers are you talking about, Bertram?"

"I'm a regular pharmacopia, darlin'. Just ask me about any drug. I can tell you what it does and what the side effects are."

"Bertram, this is crazy talk. I'm calling Dr. Kerr tomorrow and scheduling an appointment for us.

Bertram's lip curled up in a sneer. "Who's Dr. Kerr?"

"A marriage counselor."

And that's when it dawned on me. The lip curl, the clean-shaven face, the hair that needed a good trim—Bertram angled his face in just the right way, and for an instant, in the dim light of the bedside lamps, he looked a hell of a lot like Elvis.

Then the moment was gone and Bertram was Bertram.

Weird.

Maybe I was the one going nutty. First I'd thought I'd seen the painting move. Now I thought my husband was Elvis?

Bertram clicked off the lamp on his side of the bed and rolled onto his side. I took the hint and turned off mine. I was just dozing off when Bertram said, "Good night, Priscilla, darlin'."

Oh, no.

The painting might be gone, but apparently Elvis had not left the building.

PART II:
SUSPICIOUS MINDS

CHAPTER EIGHT

A Few Days Later
Friday, October 24

1

The man atop the viewing tower was not my husband.

Oh, Bertram was somewhere underneath the white leisure suit with the high, stiff collar, flowery cravat, bell bottom trousers, mutton-chop sideburns, and mirrored sunglasses. And he was either wearing a wig or using some sort of miracle-grow hair tonic because his hair was a good two to three inches longer than it had been yesterday.

At least I wasn't the only one noticing the change in appearance. The entire marching band kept sneaking peeks Bertram's way as they warmed up on the practice field. I just hoped Bertram's boss didn't mosey on down anywhere near us. It was bad enough the homecoming court had to see him this way. Of course, they really didn't know Dr. Bertram Tidwell from any other ASU professor, but there was no mistaking the fashion warp from the early seventies. Bertram must have raided every vintage clothing shop in the area to come up with an outfit like that. Halloween wasn't that far away, so maybe I could tell people he was breaking in his costume. Yeah, like that was a believable story.

Bertram—or was it Elvis?—raised the bullhorn to his mouth. The sun glinted off the huge rings on his fingers. Why had men liked wearing so much gold jewelry in the early 70s? It made them look like pimps.

"All right, people," Bertram said, his deep drawl amplified. "Let's take it from the top. Homecoming court, that includes you."

Well, thank goodness he didn't *sound* like Elvis.

As Dr. Vin, our Assistant Director of Bands, escorted the beauty queens to the pink Caddy and the band ran across the field to the far sideline, I made the dreaded climb up the metal rungs to the top of the tower where a wooden platform and skimpy metal railing were all that stood between me and a twenty foot drop.

Now that Bertram had gone off the deep end, I really didn't like being around him. It was like waking up one day to find you were married to a complete stranger. But by God, I was going to do whatever it took to make this marriage last. I was done with chronic divorce syndrome.

As I reached the top, the drum major whistled off the opening tempo with slow, measured tweets. The percussion section kicked off the show with a tympani roll, followed by the majestic notes of "Also Sprach Zarathustra," the song Elvis had opened his 1973 Aloha from Hawaii concert with. I knew this because Bertram had regaled me with Elvis minutia in excruciating detail.

I stepped up beside Bertram at the rail. He smelled as if he'd been doused in Brut cologne. I had to slide a few steps to the right and hope a breeze came by soon. It was definitely not his usual soap-and-water clean scent.

"Why, hello, little darlin'." Bertram sneer-smiled at me, and it was all I could do not to fling myself down the ladder and run off to the nearest divorce lawyer. I was standing next to my husband, but it was Elvis who was lookin' at me through Bertram's eyes.

"I was talkin' to the Colonel about going back on tour. Being in charge of a college marching band is fine and well for some folks, but I miss being on stage and connecting with an audience. And I really miss getting to throw my sweat-soaked scarves to all my lady fans."

I bit the inside of my mouth. This was too much even for me, and I'd weathered three marriages. I was going to have to sleep on the couch tonight and every night until I could get Bertram some professional help.

Apparently undeterred by my silence, Bertram plowed ahead. "I was also thinkin' we should do some redecoratin' at home. I say we get rid of all that staid, old-fashioned furniture and bring in some bold animals prints, you know, leopard, zebra, tiger ... like a safari. We could call it the Jungle Room. And we could get one of them chimpanzees. It'd be like our baby. Whadaya think, Pris—Cleo?"

Well at least he hadn't totally forgotten my name.

"I think we should put any home improvements on hold until we've had a chance to have a nice long talk with Dr. Kerr about your new, uh, interests. That's what I think we should do."

"Well, you may be right about that. I was also thinkin' that we should give Dr. Vin and Danny Brown something nice for all the hard work they do for the marching ferrets."

Danny was a graduate student in music and the band's graduate teaching assistant, otherwise known as a GTA.

"Well, that's real sweet of you, Bertram. I'm sure they'd like a gift certificate to Hall's Music or maybe Throw Them Rolls Cafe."

Bertram knitted his brows. "I was thinkin' more like a gold ring with TCB on it."

"TCB?"

"Taking Care of Business."

Oh, boy. I needed to talk to Georgia. She knew all things Elvis. I had a feeling some of this newfound quirky stuff was Elvis related, like Bertram believing he could cure the common cold and this TCB stuff. Of course, everyone in the South knows that Graceland has got a Jungle Room. No mystery about that. Elvis liked each room to have a name and a theme.

"You know, I think a gift card will be thank you enough."

The band marched into their positions on the field, leaving a wide promenade down the fifty yard line, then finished the last few notes of "See See Rider." This was the part of the show where the homecoming court would ride onto the field in the pink Caddy to take their places in the center. The actual homecoming queen would be announced during tomorrow's half-time show.

Dr. Vin joined us atop the tower. Big sweat stains adorned his ASU Marching Ferrets polo shirt, and perspiration rolled down his face from underneath his ball cap. Rivulets of moisture trickled down my back to soak into the waistband of my khaki shorts. A swimming pool would have been nice at that moment.

Bertram passed the bullhorn off to Dr. Vin, then started climbing down the ladder.

"Where are you going?" I said, a bit alarmed. Band practice wasn't even half over yet.

"You'll see, darlin. You're gonna love it."

Dr. Vin made mock homecoming announcer noises over the bullhorn. ASU President Allen would have the honors tomorrow. Ergh! I just had to make sure Bertram dressed in his usual preppy attire for the game.

Down on the practice field, our GTA had set up a microphone where the fifty yard line met the sideline. The homecoming court piled back into the pink Caddy, and the Panhellenic president drove them off the field as the band played ASU's syrupy alma mater. It was the only non-Elvis tune in the entire show. Our majorette alternate prepped the fire batons by unwrapping the aluminum-foil covered wicks and lighting them as each majorette stepped forward to receive her now flaming baton. Bertram sauntered up to the mike, actually sauntered, instead of his usual athletic lope. From the rear I could have sworn I was looking at Elvis Presley. The GTA handed him the microphone, and Bertram stepped out on the field with his band.

Oh, no. Tell me he wasn't going to sing. Karaoke in front of my family was one thing. Singing during a half-time show when he wasn't a celebrity or a student was not good. Of course, if Bertram really thought he was Elvis, then I suppose in his mind he *was* a celebrity. Even if that celebrity had been dead thirty-something years.

The drum major blew out four energetic whistle blasts, and the band launched into a rousing rendition of "Burning Love" while the majorettes twirled fire. And Lord have mercy, Bertram sang. How he forced his voice into the tenor range is beyond me. But today he was singing tenor, and he actually sounded good. And he also sounded like Elvis. And not only that, he moved like a seasoned performer. Bertram has many talents and possesses the odd combination of athleticism and musical ability, but getting up and dancing and singing is not his thing. Maybe the game-goers tomorrow would think he was an Elvis impersonator. It wasn't farfetched, really. We were doing a half-time tribute to the King. It was just frowned upon for the faculty to take the spotlight away from student talent.

I leaned over to Dr. Vin. "Are you going to be announcing the show tomorrow?"

"Yeah." He couldn't seem to tear his gaze from his boss cavorting down on the field.

"Would you mind not mentioning who the Elvis impersonator is?" I did a sideways nod at Bertram.

"Wouldn't think of it."

Dr. Vin knew just as well as I did that what Bertram was doing just wasn't done, at least, not at ASU.

We had an appointment to see Dr. Kerr first thing on Monday morning. I hoped Bertram and I could make it through the weekend. I had no idea what other tricks he might have up his sleeve.

2

As soon as band practice was over, I whipped out my cell phone and speed dialed Georgia as I trudged up the pine-tree-studded hill to Goodwin Hall. Tailgaters were already lining the U-shaped drive around the outdoor amphitheater below the music building. The aroma of barbeque and burgers made my mouth water.

But all I got was her answering machine. "Hey, sugar. I'm off galavantin' like a young fool. So leave your name and number at the beep, and I'll call you back just as soon as I can. Bye, now."

"Georgia, it's Cleo. Please call me the very minute you get in. It's about Bertram, and it's urgent. Thanks."

Bertram caught up with me. "Hey, little darlin'. You almost got away from me there."

"When's your mother getting home? I really need to talk to her."

Suspicion flitted across my husband's face. "When have you ever needed to talk to Mama?"

"Oh, you know … she has this … recipe … for oatmeal coconut cookies that I want to make … for Halloween. I really think it's cheaper nowadays to make goodies instead of buy candy."

Bertram smiled, and it was the most beautiful thing. "Aw, well, she should be back sometime this afternoon. And speaking of Halloween, I found the perfect costume for you when I was at Goodwill donating all of my old clothes—"

All of his old clothes?

"—this morning."

Oh, no. What had Bertram done?

"Yep. And I got me some new clothes, too." He glanced down at the seventies duds he had on. "Well, not exactly new, but they feel more like me."

My stomach plummeted down to my toes. "Bertram, you kept your ASU polo shirts and khaki pants, didn't you?"

"Now why would I want to do that?" He sounded genuinely

puzzled.

"Because that's what you wear to the football games."

I wondered if I could take Bertram to the ER for acting nutty? I had a feeling the answer was no unless he was a menace to himself or others. And while a bad retro-fashion sense might make those of us with a lick of fashion savvy want to chortle like a chimp, it didn't exactly constitute a clear and present danger.

We'd reached the band hall, and Bertram held the door for me, Southern gentleman that he is. A blast of cool air bathed my face. Band members carrying percussion and large instruments like tubas and trombones scurried past us in the foyer of Goodwin Hall to the storage room where we kept all of the school-issued instruments.

"Okay, Cleo," Bertram said as we reached his office. "You've got to see this costume."

I have to admit I was a little curious. Okay, so I was a lot curious. I didn't even know what Bertram's costume was. Maybe he'd go as his old self?

"Sure, Bertram. I'd love to see it."

I mouthed *Have you seen it?* to Betty Lou as I passed her desk. She shook her head no with a wince as if she, too, were afraid of what Bertram might have scrounged up for me.

My goofy, Elvis look-alike husband waited at his door for me, then closed it once I was in, saying to Betty Lou, "I think I'll have her try it on." She was probably beyond being surprised by Bertram anymore, what with him thinking he could control the sprinklers by mind power, and dressing up like the King, and driving a pink Caddy to work. I wondered if I was beyond being surprised by him anymore.

And that's when I noticed the framed photograph on Bertram's desk. As Bertram fetched a big plastic bag from Goodwill, I picked up the picture. The photograph I held was a famous one of Elvis and President Nixon shaking hands in the Oval Office. Elvis is wearing a funky black suit with the jacket draped over his shoulders like a cape, a white shirt with the biggest collar I've ever seen, and a super-sized silver belt that belonged on a pro-wrestler. Nixon looks positively bland by contrast in his tweedy, light brown suit.

"Where did you get this?"

"Oh, that. I somehow lost the original. It was signed and everything. But I found a book at Goodwill with that in it, so I cut it out and framed it."

The plastic bag rustled as Bertram reached in for the costume. He pulled out a white button-down shirt, a tweedy light brown suit, a tie, and a Nixon mask and thrust them at me.

"Try it on, Cleo. I got the smallest men's suit they had. Hope it fits you. And you'll have to slick your hair back in a ponytail or something—"

If Bertram were his old self, I would have been laughing by now. But it was all too horrible for mirth. "I am not, I repeat, am not, wearing a Nixon costume."

Bertram ducked his head while making the peace sign with both hands. "I cannot tell a lie," he said in a pretty good imitation of Nixon.

"And who are you going as? Spiro Agnew?"

"Why no, darlin'. I'm going as myself." He took the frame from me and set it back on his desk.

"And who are you?"

Bertram actually seemed astonished that I'd even ask that. "Why, I'm the King."

"The king of what?"

"Of Rock and Roll."

Oh, dear Lord, Bertram was officially crazy. As if I hadn't been clued in enough already.

A new sheen of sweat broke out on my skin. It was suddenly hotter than seven hells in that office.

"Bertram, I have to go. I've got private lessons to teach this afternoon." Which was a flat-out lie, but he didn't seem to notice.

Another bad sign. My Bertram knew I didn't teach on Friday afternoons in the Fall. "And take that," I gestured at the suit and mask, too mad to say what it was, "back. Or burn it. I'm not wearing it." I grasped the door knob and turned it.

"Bertram?" he said, puzzled. "Why do you keep calling me Bertram?"

3

When I got home, I netted the Allister Gazette from the front porch. Once inside, I unrolled the paper. A big headline on the front page read:

The King Has Left the Building
See Talk About Town, 1D

"Talk About Town" was Bippy Barndale's weekly column. Having her own public access TV show wasn't enough. She had to write for the paper, too. Bippy didn't just report the news, she often fictionalized it. But since her daddy's money supported the paper, they pretty much let her write whatever she damn well pleased.

Talk About Town
by Bippy Barndale

This intrepid reporter participated in the well attended Haunted History of Allister Historical Home Tour, a fundraiser for the Allister Historical Society. The highlight of the tour was the McKay-James house owned by Dr. and Mrs. Bertram Tidwell on Founder's Row. The couple displayed a haunted velvet painting of Elvis Presley in their lovely Victorian dining room to the delight of the majority of tour-goers.

However, calamity struck, and the Velvet Elvis was stolen during the tour much to the dismay of ticket purchasers who had arrived at the Tidwell house after six p.m. Who would stoop to such a thing? Several possibilities come to mind. An opportunistic fan. A professional thief. A kleptomaniac with a penchant for kitschy art. A crazy kook. Or perhaps it was all a set-up for insurance money.

One thing I know for certain, the First Annual Haunted History of Allister will live long in our town's memory.

Oh, that Bippy. Insinuating that Bertram and I had stolen our own painting for the insurance. Apparently, our small town was still short on big news. If she'd just asked me, I'd have told her the painting wasn't insured. Sure, I could sue her for slander. But it would wind up costing us a fortune just to have a retraction printed.

I tossed the paper down in disgust and checked our phone messages. The answering machine was full. You'd think with the Velvet Elvis out of our life, we'd get a little peace and quiet and maybe a return to anonymity. But noooo.

So like the glutton for weird-ass punishment that I am, I hit play.

A man with a Southern accent so thick I could barely understand him said, "Yep. Got the Elvis. If you want it back, put a thousand dollars in unmarked bills in a baby stroller and leave it in the alley behind Walgreen's at two a.m. tomorrow night. And come alone or the Elvis gets it."

Beep.

Puh-lease! The Elvis could get it, and I wouldn't care a lick. As nutty as Bertram was, I really didn't want the painting in our life again. I don't know what part it played in his Elvis mania, and I really didn't want it back to find out. Whoever had it could keep it and good riddance!

The next message wasn't much better.

"I have some information about your stolen painting. I saw a couple of fellows loading it into the back of a moving van ... in an alley ... and they were wearing ... ski masks. Yeah, ski masks. And I followed them in my car. Yeah, and they parked at this house and took the painting inside. Uh, yeah, so my name is Tom Parker and my number is _____. There's a reward for this, right? 'Cuz I could really use the money. You know, there's this, like, restaurant I wanna take my girl to, but I'm flat broke right now 'cause I lost my job at Radio Shack—"

I punched forward.

A woman's voice this time. Darlene. "I have your black Velvet Elvis you snooty bitch. You know, Spike and me really thought we had a connection with you, but you blew us off like the bitch you really are—"

Okay, moving right along.

Another woman's voice. Not Darlene. "Yes, I hope I'm calling the right number. I'd like a refund on my ticket to the Historic Home Tour. I'd planned on going to the Tidwell house around eight o'clock, but the black Velvet Elvis had been stolen by then, so there wasn't anything worth seeing. I'd appreciate it if you call me back at _____, and tell me how I can get my money back. Oh, my name is Janet Dougal. D-O-U-G-A-L. Thank you."

Beep.

I jotted down her info to give to Marty.

The next caller's voice was all too familiar. "We done got the King, and he's in his rightful place now, you can be sure of that." The Ice Queen. I'd know that cold voice anywhere. "And don't come lookin' for him, neither. You'll just be in a world of hurt if you do."

As if I'd know where to look. I didn't even know who the Ice Queen was.

Beep.

"Mrs. Tidwell, this is Faye Eldritch again. I was just doing a Rainbow Stone reading on you, and I'm afraid you and your husband could still be in for a rough ride. That or your luck will change. I keep drawing the blue stone. It could mean one of several things. One: you'll have the blues. Two: a blueblood from England will come into your life. Three: Your husband will lose his current position and will have to get a blue collar job. Or Four: you'll win the blue ribbon at the state fair. Or Five: maybe all of the above.

"For only $14.95 you can find out which one applies to you—"

Beep.

Oh, for goodness sake. After Bertram's nutty episode during and after band practice today, my money was on number three. As if I needed a fortune teller for that.

"This is Sean Johnson with *The Dead Speak* just calling to remind you our crew will be at your house tomorrow at four o'clock to film the show."

Oh crap! I'd never called them to let them know the painting was gone. I jotted a note on a Post-it to call him ASAP.

The rest of the messages were from well meaning town folk calling to express their sympathy over our stolen painting or more kooks saying they'd stolen it and knew who'd stolen it or who wanted either a reward or ransom for supposedly having it. Yeesh! Didn't these people have a life?

The last message was from Georgia. "Cleo, honey, I got your message. I'm back from my trip now if you want to give me a ring."

Boy, did I ever. If anyone besides Dr. Kerr could shed some light on Bertram's behavior, it was his mother. It had been her Velvet Elvis that had started it all. It was her son who'd contracted Elvis mania. And she'd been about to tell me something on Monday afternoon, but I'd gotten snockered and passed out before she could. I had a feeling Georgia was the key to the puzzle that plagued my life.

But first, I had to disentangle us from *The Dead Speak*.

4

Sean Johnson, executive producer for the show, listened to me for about ten seconds, then said. "This'll still make a great show, Mrs.

Tidwell. Our psychic may even be able to tell you who took it. And Victorian houses are full of spooky ambiance. Besides, you're just one of three segments that make up one show, so if things don't play well tomorrow, we can always cut your airtime down and focus more on the other two."

Hmm. "Well, if you're sure …"

"Absolutely. Most of the stuff we investigate is enhanced with smoke and mirrors by Yours Truly. So, don't you worry. It'll be fun. And the check we give you won't be so bad, either."

He was right. The check would be great. But when the film crew arrived, was Bertram gonna be at my side or Elvis?

5

The iced tea Georgia gave me spiked my sinuses. I pinched the bridge of my nose, and set the sweating glass on a Jailhouse Rock coaster.

"Oh, dear," my mother-in-law said, pushing up from her cushy wingback chair. She had on an "I ♥ Hollywood" t-shirt and red denim shorts. "Everything you've described could be attributed to Elvis at some point in his life."

She retrieved several books from the mantel over the faux-fireplace and handed them to me. Elvis biographies all.

"Even controlling the sprinklers with telepathy?"

"Even that."

"And the Brut?"

"It was the King's favorite cologne." Georgia sighed, her chipper mood gone.

"And what's with the Taking-Care-of-Business ring?"

"That's what Elvis gave the men in his entourage, known as the Memphis Mafia. It was sorta like a fraternity ring. Those guys took care of Elvis's mundane business for him. He'd buy them cars, pay for their weddings, some of them even lived at Graceland. They became a very costly group to maintain after awhile." Georgia fixed me with a concerned look. "I was afraid this might happen."

"Why? What do you mean?"

Georgia sank back onto her chair and fixed me with an unreadable look. "Elvis might be Bertram's daddy."

Whoa! That was the news flash of the century.

"You don't know for sure?" On one hand it explained everything, and on the other, it explained nothing. Bertram acted more like he was possessed by Elvis than the son of. *There's a fine line between obsession and possession.* Who had told me that? It didn't matter. I didn't know if my husband was obsessed, possessed, or just exercising his DNA.

Georgia held her head high. "I was seeing several fellas at the same time. It could have been any of them. It was the sixties. I was an up and coming starlet. Or would have been if I hadn't gotten in the family way."

"So Fred Tidwell …?" All of this rang a distant bell.

"Isn't Bertram's father. Don't you remember the birth certificate I showed you?" She peered at my puzzled expression. "No, I guess you wouldn't. Bertram's birth certificate says: *father unknown.* I showed it to you Monday afternoon?"

And I'd thought I'd dreamed that. "I think that was right before I passed out."

"Undoubtedly. No, Fred always knew Bertram wasn't his. But we'd dated in high school, and when I came home from Hollywood with a bun in the oven, he did the noble thing and asked me to marry him. Of course, I said yes. I knew the reality of my situation. I wasn't so far along that Fred couldn't claim the baby as his own. A remarkable man, that Fred Tidwell. I do miss him so."

"But Bertram doesn't look anything like Elvis Presley." Well, he sorta did with all the paraphernalia, but he was no Lisa Marie. That gal was the spittin' image of her daddy.

"Do you look just like either of your parents?"

"Well, no." But I still wasn't convinced Bertram was following in his father's footsteps.

Georgia swirled her iced tea. "I saw in the paper the painting was stolen during the tour. For awhile there, I thought it was maybe haunting my son."

I nodded agreement. I'd entertained the same notion.

"But if it's gone," she said, "and he's getting worse, it's got to be something else. Either his parentage or …"

We both knew what she'd left unsaid. Or Bertram was going crazy.

"We have an appointment to see a therapist on Monday. I'm sure she'll be able to get to the bottom of all this."

"I hope so. You and Bertram make an adorable couple. I've never seen my son happier than when he married you. It would be a cryin' shame if something came between the two of you."

It would be a crying shame, all right. I didn't know if I could survive another broken heart. It might heal in time, but it still left scars. And mine was scarred up enough already.

6

Despite my protestations to the contrary, Bertram wanted to go out to dinner at Throw Them Rolls Cafe with Molly and Elmer. And when a six-foot-four hunk of a man wants his way, there is no stopping him. The restaurant was the happening place in town for both locals and ASU alumni. The plain wood booths and tables were packed with people wearing ASU's colors—orange and white.

Bertram hollered at a waitress clear across the barn-like room. "Hey, throw one of them rolls this way, darlin'."

She plucked a brick-sized yeast roll from the wicker basket on her hip and pitched it at my husband. His arm shot up to catch the thing, but he missed, and a bodacious hunk of bread hit the wall beside our booth and bounced onto a guy's head at the adjacent table. This was one of the liabilities of eating at the Throw Them Rolls Cafe. You never knew when you might get zinged with a rather substantial piece of bread.

"Try again," Bertram called out with good humor. "'Fraid I missed that last one."

"Sure thing, sugar!"

Bertram caught this one, slit it in half, and poured about half a bear of honey on it.

Elmer grinned from the other side of our booth. "Your man sure knows how to eat, Cleo."

"Yes, doesn't he?"

It was just the four of us. No parents. No kids. Molly couldn't seem to stop smiling. She and Elmer were sitting smooshed up against each other like a couple of teenagers. I guess with Elmer's magic touch, she was riding a wave of Big O's. Some girls get all the luck.

"Oh my God," a woman said over the din of table talk and clinking cutlery. "The King is alive after all and eating at Throw Them Rolls. Do you think I should go ask for his autograph?"

Another woman answered, "I bet he's just one of those impersonators."

We'd probably get home tonight to find a message on our answering machine about an Elvis sighting in Allister. If we were lucky that would be the only message.

Elmer sipped his beer, then said, "So, any news on your Velvet Elvis?"

Bertram said, "No," at the same time I said, "Nope and it's doubtful there'll be any."

"Why's that?"

"The police aren't very hopeful," I said. "Only a very small percentage of stolen property is ever recovered."

"Well, that's a shame. I was hoping it might turn up and I could still make you an offer."

Sounding like a schoolgirl with a crush, Molly said, "Elmer's extended his stay another week."

"You must want that painting really bad," I said.

"It goes with being a collector extraordinaire."

I hadn't really had a chance to give Elmer the third degree. Now seemed as good a time as any. "So where did you say you're from?"

"Don't think I ever did. But I don't mind tellin' you. I'm from Sarasota. Florida."

"That's quite a long way to come for a collectible."

"Not really," Elmer said, all good nature. I swear it was impossible to ruffle the guy. "I've been all over the country, all over the world, huntin' down oddities."

"Elmer has four daughters, too," Molly gushed. "Identical quadruplets."

"All red-heads like their daddy." Elmer laughed.

"Who stays with them while you're gone?" Geez, was I ever nosy. But when it came to my sister, I could be a pit bull.

"Well, they ain't so little anymore. Fourteen and in their first year of high school at the circus school in Sarasota. But their grandmother—my wife's mother—lives with us and keeps an eye on them when I have to travel."

"Circus school? They must be talented girls."

"You could say that. And you, Miss Cleo, would probably be interested to know that my girls are champion twirlers. One of them took first place at Nationals last year in the Junior Division, and the other three placed within the top ten."

Oh, be still my heart. Champion-level twirlers? Who might just happen to move to Allister if their daddy lost his heart to my sister? And who might just wind up going to ASU when they were older? I almost drooled with anticipation. Boy, the things I could do with four high-caliber majorettes.

Bertram cut in. "I made a movie—*Roustabout*—where my character was a carnie. That's sorta like the circus."

"Honey, you mean Elvis made a movie."

"What'd I say?"

"You said you."

"Is there a difference?"

Elmer caught my eye, shaking his head no almost imperceptibly. So I let it be. I'm not sure why. I guess I figured we could address all of this on Monday with Dr. Kerr.

"So, Elmer," I said, desperately trying to change the subject, "Inglebright. Is that German?"

"It might have been originally. Back in the 1800s many people couldn't write or read, let alone spell their surnames correctly. It might have been Ingelbert at one time."

Molly let out a little giggle. "As in Humperdinck?"

"Well, not in my family." Elmer smiled. "Besides, Engelbert was that Humperdinck fellow's *first* name."

I'd never known any Inglebrights or Engelberts. "So, what does it translate to?"

"Bright Angel."

"What a lovely name. Sounds so noble." Molly could use an angel in her life after being married to that devil Richard for way too many years. And she and Elmer were so taken with each other. Aaron might have been sexy as hell, but no real love connection.

Bertram shot up from his seat, bumping our table and spilling his beer. "'Scuse me y'all," he slurred. "Gotta go to the little boy's room."

He staggered off between the tables, quite the figure in his Elvis get-up.

Oh boy, what was up now? Bertram seemed a bit tipsy to me with the slurred speech and clumsiness, but he hadn't had any more beer than the rest of us. There was trouble brewing in Dixieland.

"Think I'll follow him and make sure he's okay." Elmer slid out of the booth and tailed my drunk husband. They managed to make it to the restroom without getting smacked by a roll.

I toyed with my bottle of beer. "Boy, Elmer's a keeper, huh?"

Molly let out a contented sigh, her elbows on the table. "Oh, yeah."

"And I take it Aaron has still not called?"

"That would be a pretty big no. And Brandie said he wasn't at school today. They had a substitute teacher."

"I think it's pretty freakin' weird that he bugged out on y'all's dinner date with the lame excuse that his brother was in town."

I heard my words and went *hmm*. I hadn't really thought about it until that very moment, but what if Aaron had stolen the Velvet Elvis? Of course, he'd been at Molly's during the tour, but he could have snuck over to my house during all the ruckus, come in the back door, taken the painting, and then skedaddled, no one the wiser. Boy, talk about an opportunist. And he was a Blue Shoe Loony, after all, and had asked all those questions about the painting when he'd come to dinner last Saturday. But why steal it? And from your girlfriend's sister? Or I guess ex-girlfriend now.

Molly made a clucking sound. "Aaron's from up north. He's not a Southern gentleman like Elmer." As if that excused his bad behavior.

"And speaking of gentlemen," I said. "You and Elmer haven't..." I waggled my eyebrows.

"No, but I think tonight's the night." She sighed with bliss, the corners of her mouth curling up ever so slightly.

She and Elmer really did make a cute couple. One blonde, one redhead, and both with freckles. They also seemed so at ease with each other.

"Oh, Cleo. It's just been so long since I had," she lowered her voice and leaned towards me, "S-E-X. Aaron and I never did, and Richard and I didn't for years before he left me. I just miss having a man around who loves me."

"Do you think you could date him long distance? Sarasota's pretty far away."

"I'm not even going to worry about that right now. It'll either work out or it won't. No use fretting about it at this point."

Bertram and Elmer were tottering back from the restroom. "Here they come," I told Molly.

Elmer had hold of Bertram's elbow and was steering him down the aisle. Every few tables Bertram stopped to sign autographs or shake hands as if he were walking down the red carpet. The two of them were quite a contrast since Bertram towered over just about everyone, and Elmer couldn't have been over five-foot-six and that was with Western boots on.

As they neared our booth, I heard Bertram say, "Thank you. Thankyouvery much," just like Elvis.

Elmer tugged on my husband's arm. "Right this way, big guy."

Bertram staggered to our table and plopped onto his seat, a goofy grin on his face. "Y'all are never going to guess what just happened to us."

I was afraid to hear this. "What?"

He glanced over at Elmer conspiratorially, just two partners in crime. "Elmer and I just went off in a spaceship."

"Oh, Bertram." It broke my heart to hear this. As much as Bertram irritated me with his Elvis obsession, I still loved the man underneath it with all my heart. What was I going to do if I lost him to it?

Cathy Godwin's snooty voice broke my pity party.

"Why look who it is. Cleo and Bubba. Or maybe I should say Elvis. And Cleo's sister, Clementine. With a little cowboy. How cozy."

Molly brewed a stormy expression. Oh, how she hated her given name. She'd been self-designated as Molly ever since middle school. But before that, we were known as little Clem and Cleo Kilgore.

Cathy Godwin smirked in her rich bitch sort of way. I gritted my teeth.

"Bertram. My husband's name is Bertram. And for your information, he's dressed up for a Halloween party we're attending later." It was a big fat lie, but I went ahead and put as much frosty indignation in my voice as possible.

"I don't see you in a costume. No, wait. You're a multiple divorcee."

I almost launched myself over the table at her.

Elmer made as if to shake hands with her. "Elmer Inglebright. Pleased to meet you."

Cathy Godwin stared at his extended hand as if it were a stinky fish. Then she actually showed some manners and grasped his hand.

"Cathy Godwin, wife of Dr. Godwin, the prominent plastic surgeon. Surely you've heard of—" She broke off with a squeak, clasping her other hand to her bosom. "Yes! Oh, yes! Oh, yes, yes, yes, yes, yes, YES, oh Jeeeeeezus, YES!"

All talk and cutlery-clinking ceased. Patrons paused in their dining to gape at her. For the first time in the history of the restaurant, no rolls were thrown anywhere. She thrashed about on the end of Elmer's hand like a fish on the line, her eyes rolling back in her head. Except I had a feeling it felt a hell of lot more pleasant that having a fish hook stuck through your mouth.

Raking a hand through her now mussed up hair, she finished with a chorus of, "Oh, God in heaven, YES!"

A moment of silence followed where she basked in the afterglow, still dangling from Elmer's hand. A pink flush spread across her bosom, neck, and face. She took a deep breath and went, "Mmmmm," licking her lips, her eyes closed.

When the restaurant broke out in applause, her eyes snapped open with a look of horror. She snatched her hand from Elmer's and clutched her shirt together where she'd unbuttoned it in the throes of passion, exposing fake boobs corralled in a pink, lacy bra.

"Been awhile since the good doctor banged you?" I asked sweetly.

With a shriek of indignation, she dashed out of the restaurant, her bibbitity, bobbity boobies bouncing in their bra. If ever there was an ad for plastic surgery, that was it.

Bertram had been quiet throughout the entire Cathy Godwin escapade—or should I say sex-capade? Now he turned to me and said, "Let's go home, Priscilla. I don't feel so good."

"Sure, Bertram. As soon as we pay the check."

"I'll take care of it, Cleo," Elmer said. "You and Bertram can head on out to the car. We'll meet up with you in a moment."

7

Bertram and I lurched across the asphalt toward the pink Caddy, Bertram from drinking too much beer and me from trying to hold him up. Business seemed to be booming at Throw Them Rolls. The parking lot was full, so full that some blockhead had decided to illegally park perpendicular to the Caddy's rear bumper.

"Damn it! Why do people do this? We're blocked in on all four sides."

"We could drive over 'em," Bertram said.

"I don't think that's an option. I'm going to have to leave you here while I go back in and ask them to tell the owner of a black Chevy pickup to come move his freakin' truck."

"Ohhh, such language, Priscilla." Bertram giggled. "Maybe we can get up to a little rumpus when we get home." He draped an arm around my collar bone and groped my breast right there in the parking lot.

"God, Bertram, you are so drunk. Or did you take something that's interacting with the alcohol?"

If Bertram thought he was Elvis, and Elvis took a variety of drugs, then didn't it stand to reason that Bertram might be popping pills?

"Not much. Just a couple of downers to take the edge off things."

"Well, are you too messed up to wait here for a moment? 'Cause you're kinda heavy, Bertram. You're a whole foot taller than me."

"Darlin', I'm all about waiting." And he saluted me.

Ay, chihuahua! "Okay. Stay put. I'll be right back."

And that's when chaos broke out.

An old Volkswagen van that might have been industrial green or might have been medium blue careened into the parking lot. I only caught a glimpse of Molly and Elmer stepping out of the restaurant arm in arm, all smiley and lovey-dovey, before the van screeched to a halt in front of me and Bertram. The side door rolled open with such force it made a smacking sound. A couple of men wearing Smiley Face masks and black sweat suits reached out and tried to grab me. A jolt of adrenalin flooded my system and I leapt back out of their reach, but bumped into Bertram who was unsteady on his feet as it was, and we went down in a heap on the asphalt.

Molly screamed, "Oh My God!"

Elmer raced over to the van, pulling a gun from somewhere on his person like a magician pulling the proverbial rabbit out of a hat. I mean, I'd had no idea he was packing heat.

"You'd best scoot," he shouted to the men in the van, "Or you'll answer to Mr. Smith and Mr. Wesson."

The van roared off, spewing smoke from its tailpipe. Elmer rushed to us, the gun now gone as if it had winked out of existence. It all happened kinda fast and even though the parking lot was lit, it wasn't exactly like being in bright sunshine.

"Are you hurt?" He helped me to my feet first.

"Just spooked." Yeah, liar, liar. I'd almost peed in my pants.

It took both me and Elmer to get Bertram off the pavement. My husband pointed at the Volkswagen van speeding off toward the interstate on-ramp. "Who were those guys?" he slurred.

"Someone up to no good," Elmer said.

Where had he stowed his gun? I saw no evidence of a piece.

Molly had reached us by then. "Oh my God, are you okay?"

"We're fine. They just scared the poop out of us." I glanced at Bertram. He was three sheets to the wind. "Well, maybe just me."

Elmer trotted around to the driver's side of the black Chevy, opened the door, which was apparently unlocked, stuck his head in the footwell, and fiddled around with something down there. The truck started, Elmer climbed in, and drove it around to the other side of the restaurant where he put it in park and left it running. Then we all piled into the pink Caddy. I really didn't want to wait around in the parking lot to file a police report with Bertram so messed up, so I drove us home, thinking I could call D.K. in the morning. It was really more a matter of getting it on record than hoping the police would actually apprehend the culprits.

But my hands were shaking on the steering wheel. Someone had just tried to abduct me. And they were still out there. Yikes!

CHAPTER NINE

Saturday, October 25

1

Bertram's side of the bed was empty at six forty-five the next morning. My eyes were as dry as raisins, my head still muddled from a restless sleep full of disturbing dreams, as I trudged into the bathroom. I would have slept on the couch, but Bertram had been so out of it, and I'd been so shaken from the abduction attempt that I'd gone ahead and climbed into bed.

A Post-in note was stuck on the bathroom mirror.

Priscilla darling
I've run to get us some doughnuts. Back in ten.
Love,
E.

Oh, no. Bertram was so confused. I wanted to cry over how sad it all was, but the Scarlett O'Hara in me said, "Chin up, no tears, big girls don't cry." So I threw on sweats and a t-shirt, and pulled my hair in a ponytail, and headed downstairs to have my ritual Diet Coke while I waited on him to return from Krispy Kreme. We have the same routine every game-day Saturday. We roll out of bed, dress very casually, eat something, then head over to ASU for eight o'clock band practice. Once that's over at nine thirty, we come home, shower, get gussied up for the game and have lunch, before heading back an hour and a half before kick-off.

I wanted to crawl back in bed, but today was going to be a busy, busy day with ASU's Homecoming Game this afternoon, and *The Dead Speak* afterwards. Even though we didn't have the Velvet Elvis any longer, maybe the show's psychic could pick up some ghostly vibes from the house. It was a hundred years old, after all.

I flipped through the newest issue of *Oprah Magazine*. Ah, here was an article I needed to read, "Eight Warning Signs That Your Man is Having a Mid-life Crisis."

Yeah, I was well on my way to writing my own piece on the subject:

1. He becomes enamored with a Velvet Elvis.
2. He puts on a Viva Las Vegas karaoke night during a dinner party.
3. He changes his personal style to reflect the early 70s.
4. He calls you Priscilla.
5. He impulsively buys a pink Caddy.
6. He wants to remodel the house like Graceland.
7. He suddenly has a hankering for fried peanut butter and banana sandwiches.
8. He says crazy things, like he can control the sprinkler system with his mind, cure the common cold, or has taken a ride in a spaceship.

Yep. All of this was pretty disturbing, but what I *really* didn't want to think about was why someone would want to kidnap me. The Velvet Elvis I could see. It had become famous and some kook just had to have it. But little ole me, a majorette coach in Allister, Alabama? It just didn't compute. My mind, of course, had to oblige with an instant replay of the vintage VW van zooming up, and the men in Smiley Face masks reaching out and trying to put their grubby mitts on me. I shuddered, and it wasn't because the house was cool. Thank God Elmer had been there with a gun.

And then, BOOM. An alternate memory of the previous night surfaced, superimposed over Elmer and his Smith & Wesson.

Elmer doesn't race to the van, but seems to travel instantaneously through space and time across the parking lot. And instead of pulling out a gun, he's holding a fiery sword. It just materializes in his hands. The guys in the van get one look at it, and they shove off yelling, "Let's get out of here!" to whoever's driving. The VW van burns rubber out of the parking lot. Elmer's fiery sword winks out of existence, and he asks us if we're okay. Then he snaps at the Chevy, the engine cranks, and the truck drives away by itself around the back of the restaurant to the other side where it parks and idles. Elmer says a strange word that sounds like some foreign language, only not one on Earth, and now the four of us are in the pink Caddy, and I'm driving us home.

Well, hol-lee hell! Where had *that* come from? Geez, maybe I was having my own mid-life crisis. I could see the bullet point in a magazine article:

* You see your sister's boyfriend do something that belongs in a Sci-Fi movie.

I shook my head. No, no, no, no, no. I was not allowed to lose it. *Pull it together, Cleo.*

And where was Bertram with those doughnuts? It was seven fifteen. I hadn't realized so much time had whizzed by. He should have been back twenty minutes ago. Krispy Kreme was only a few blocks away on the main drag.

So I called his cell phone. No answer. Odd. Bertram kept his cell on his person at all times on game days in case a band member called in ill. Of course, Bertram hadn't quite been himself lately. Maybe he'd …

1. Decided to stop at the gas station and fill up.
2. Gotten chatty with the Krispy Kreme employee and lost track of the time.
3. The hot and tasty doughnuts had been too tempting, and he'd sat down and eaten some at the restaurant.
4. Gotten distracted by thinking he'd gone off in a spaceship again.
5. Put on an impromptu concert in the Krispy Kreme parking lot.
6. High-tailed it to Graceland.

Okay, maybe, just maybe, Bertram had decided to head on to ASU for some unknown reason, one that involved not calling to let me know. I wrote my own Post-it to Bertram just in case he came home, then jumped in the PT Cruiser, and zoomed on over to the university with a stop at Krispy Kreme.

No Bertram. No pink Caddy.

By eight o'clock, everyone had shown up except Bertram. I hemmed and hawed, and finally said that Bertram was home sick and had hoped he'd feel well enough to make it to early morning rehearsal and left it at that. The homecoming court asked about the use of the pink Caddy. Damn! I'd forgotten about that. I told Dr. Vin he might want to find another antique car from the 50s for the game. I hated having to put him on the spot, but that's what he got paid to do. Besides, I had bigger things to do between the end of practice and the start of the game. Like finding my husband.

2

Georgia didn't know where Bertram was, either. I went through his phone list and called everyone on it. Absolutely no one had seen or heard from Bertram this morning. A finger of dread poked around in my stomach. Being a no-show for a game was unforgivable in Bertram's book. He'd kicked people out of the band for doing it, no explanations allowed. So for him to be a no-show was akin to committing a cardinal sin. Bertram would have to be chained down or dead to not show up for a game.

Chained down or dead.

I shivered at the thought. The previous night's adventure replayed in my mind again, and I had to ask myself: what if those men had been trying to abduct Bertram and not me? And what if they'd gotten him this morning?

Oh, my hands and feet went cold at that idea.

I finally put in that call to D.K.

"Oh, hey there, Cleo," he said. "We haven't found your Velvet Elvis yet."

I heard men laughing in the background.

"That's not why I'm calling." I took a deep breath, blew it out. "I think Bertram's been abducted."

"And what makes you think that?"

I relayed the abduction attempt at Throw Them Rolls and Bertram's note this morning about going out for doughnuts, but not showing up for work, and what a major no-no that was in Bertram's book.

D.K. was probably frowning as he said, "None of that sounds good. But I'd be hesitant to fill out a Missing Persons report on him just yet. Usually in cases like this, the husband comes home within twenty-four hours. Now and then one wigs out and takes off for parts unknown. Very rarely are men like your husband actually kidnapped in a town the size of Allister."

Somehow, none of that made me feel any better.

"It's probably best not to jump to any conclusions right now," D.K. said. "I'm sure Bertram will come home before the weekend is over."

"I'd be right there with you on that, D.K., if a couple of guys in

Smiley-Face masks hadn't tried to haul us into their van last night."

"Did you get a look at the license plate?"

"No," I said, crestfallen. "It all happened so fast."

"Look, here's what I can do for now. I'll put out a BOLO on the pink Caddy—"

"A bolo? What's that?"

"Be on the lookout. If we find the car, we might find Bertram. I think it's safe to say there's not another pink Caddy in all of Calooga County."

"I'm sure you're right about that." Boy, I didn't think the day could get any worse.

"Look, just sit tight and I'm sure Bertram will turn up."

Yeah, but when? That was the sixty-four thousand dollar question.

3

Twenty-one thousand ASU football fans wearing orange and white jumped up and down, sending a wave around the stadium. The crowd cheered wildly as air horns blasted and noisemakers clacked. The enticing smells of popcorn, hotdogs, and beer saturated the air.

The head cheerleader held a bullhorn to his mouth and shouted, "For-ward, Fer-rets, for-ward!"

Students and alumni joined in on the simple cheer, creating a massive chant as the percussion section pounded out a rhythm.

And I had never felt so utterly alone while surrounded by so many people.

Bertram was AWOL. I came clean with Dr. Vin in private, telling him the police were on it and to keep mum for the time being. He'd managed to scrounge up an old car at the last minute. It wasn't as eye catching as the pink Caddy, but then, so few cars were.

And what was I going to say to *The Dead Speak* people tonight? As much as I'd worried about Bertram masquerading as Elvis in front of

TV cameras, I was even more distressed that he was gone. Where was he? What had happened to him? Was he okay?

And I wasn't sure which was worse—the thought that he'd been kidnapped or the thought that he'd bugged out of our marriage.

So I sat up in the stands with the Marching Ferrets, totally numb to the game, the half-time show, and even my majorettes. Oh, I answered when spoken to and made appropriate noises at the right times, but it was a total act. Anything to just get through the damn game so that I could go home and cry my eyes out in private before turning on the charm for a TV crew.

My cell phone vibrated at the start of the fourth quarter. My heart leapt. Was it Bertram?

Nope. Molly.

"Hold on, Molly, I can't hear you. I'll call you back in five."

Dr. Vin said, "Bertram?"

"No," I said, disappointed. "My sister. I'm gonna go take it out by the restrooms."

The walkway round the outer part of the stadium was only half as noisy as the bleacher section. I leaned back against a cinder-block wall and called Molly.

"Cleo, there are a couple of guys moving stuff into your house."

My response was pure autopilot. "Oh, it's the TV crew for that psychic show." But what I was thinking was: *It's not Bertram calling.*

"Umm … it doesn't look like they're moving cameras or equipment. And I don't recognize the vehicle. Looks like a plumber's van, only without a logo."

Hmm. The TV crew didn't have a key to the house which was why they weren't setting up until four. I checked my watch. Three-thirty p.m. Only one person, besides Molly, had a key to the house. Bertram!

"Oh my God! I'm coming home. Do you see Bertram?"

"No, that's just it, Cleo. Neither of the guys is Bertram. Do you want me to call the police?"

"No. I'll call D.K. in route. Do me a favor and don't go over there. It could be those guys from last night. Do you recognize either one?"

"No. Not even with binoculars. But they're wearing baseball caps tugged low. Their faces are shadowed by the brim."

I was already jogging around the outer concourse to the nearest exit. Fortunately, I was parked over by the music department and by leaving early in the fourth quarter, could beat the post-game traffic jam.

"Before I hang up, I've got a question for Elmer. Did he get a look at that van's license plate last night?"

People were staring at me as I trotted past. I really didn't care. I wished I could just snap my fingers and instantaneously travel home.

I heard Molly conferring with Elmer.

"Cleo? He says he was so focused on scaring them off that he didn't look at the plates."

Oh, well. It was worth a shot. "Okay. I'll be home in a few."

I was exiting the stadium now and trotting up the hill to Goodwin Hall. Tailgate parties were in full swing. It amazed me that people would drive to the campus, park their vehicle and have a barbeque and picnic right outside the stadium while listening to the game on the radio or watching it on a flat-screen TV they'd brought along. And of course, booze was a huge component of the whole tailgate experience. Which was probably why grown men who should never go shirtless bared their upper torsos and painted themselves orange. Or stuck giant orange foam fingers on their hands. Or wore orange head bands. Head bands! Eek!

My first call was to Dr. Vin to let him know I wasn't coming back from the restroom, and my second call was to D.K. Greenwood.

"I'll send a car over," he said.

I was sweating pretty good by now, make-up running down my face, sweat stains spreading under my armpits. I was gonna stink to high heaven, but I was so galvanized by Molly's call that I didn't care if I looked like I'd been through boot camp or smelled as if I'd rolled around in cow patties. I just wanted to get home and find out what the hell was going on.

And of course, in my zeal to get to my car, who should I run in to but Cathy Godwin. And when I say run in to, I mean run into. As in plough over. As in knock down. Fortunately her fake boobs cushioned me from the fall like two giant air bags.

4

We went down in heap of orange and white on the edge what appeared to be the ASU tailgate party of the century: tents, campers, an RV, grills, smokers, hibachis, coolers, tables, brats, beer, banners, pendants, noisemakers, orange and white pompoms on a stick, and stuffed ferrets wearing tiny ASU caps. Oh, and drunk people. Lots of 'em. Not that I hadn't just left a stadium full of drunk people. Apparently ASU had just made a touchdown because the tailgaters did the wave.

Yeah. Wahoo. Go team. Whatever.

I pushed myself into a sitting position in the pine straw with a hotdog smushed against the bosom of my formerly white ASU polo, the ketchup, mustard and relish creating a modern art impression. Cathy's cup of beer now trickled down my bare legs and soaked into the edges of my khaki shorts. I wanted to slink on home. But noooo, I still had to run the gauntlet of tailgaters to get to my car, wearing food and drink on my clothes. Lovely. Just what I needed on top of everything else.

I don't think Cathy knew who'd knocked her down because the first thing she said was, "Damn it, Wes. Are you going to help me up or what?" Wes was her plastic surgeon husband who was busy refilling his plastic cup from the keg underneath the large tent.

Then she took a gander in my direction and went, "Oh, no, not you again."

"Yep, 'fraid so."

"You are so gauche, Cleo. Can you not live your life without continually embarrassing yourself and others?"

"I'm sure I don't know what you mean." Of course I knew what she meant. I wasn't going to admit it to Cathy, though.

"Look at yourself. You're a mess. Your family is a mess. Your husband is cuckoo. Everyone knows it."

Well, ho-lee hell! Them there was fightin' words.

"Leave my family out of this."

She laughed, an ugly mocking sound that reminded me of a chortling hyena, and picked herself up off the ground. I, of course, saw red.

Daddy always says, "All is fair in love and war." Well I was officially declaring war.

As Cathy turned her back to me, I sprang to my feet, grabbed the back of her shirt as if I were pulling on a slingshot, and unhooked her rather substantial bra. She shrieked, clutched her untethered boobies, and high-tailed it to the RV. Ladies of her social stature just did not go bra-less in public.

Yep, karma is a bitch all right.

5

Pure chaos was what I found at home.

A police car and two uniformed officers were frisking a bunch of guys with TV equipment against a couple of vans designated as *The Dead Speak* vehicles. Several cable-TV SUVs with matching reporters were trying to get sound bites from the neighborhood lookie loos who'd been drawn by the flashing police lights and growing crowd of people. My sister and Elmer were doing their best to convince the cops that they had the wrong suspects. More cameras than you could shake a stick at were snapping pictures of my house and the general mayhem out front. And the pink Caddy was parked so far down the driveway that ran beside our house that it was almost in the backyard.

The pink Caddy! Maybe Bertram was somewhere nearby after all. Molly might have missed him coming home. It wasn't like she'd had my house under surveillance or anything.

I couldn't even reach my own driveway with all the cars, vans, SUVs, and people in the way, so I parked in front of the big, vacant, white Victorian next door—the one with the big *For Sale* sign.

As soon as the news hounds realized who I was, they surrounded me in a rush, microphones and video cameras shoved in my face quite rudely. I crossed my arms trying to hide the ketchup, mustard and relish stains on my shirt without much success. Yeah, I look good in everything I eat. Even other people's food.

"How do you feel about the Velvet Elvis theft?"

"Is it true your husband is missing?"

"Can you substantiate rumors that your husband channels Elvis?"

"Do you think the thieves have come back for more?"

I waved the mikes out of my face as if they were pesky deer flies. "No comment."

I spotted D.K. just as he spotted me amid my own little traveling pod of reporters.

"Folks," he told the media people, "this is an official police scene. I'm going to have to ask you to keep your distance and remain on the sidewalk so that we can do our job."

D.K. grasped my elbow and escorted me to *The Dead Speak* people. He was dressed more casually today in a pair of trim, navy slacks and a white, button-down shirt.

"Having trouble staying clean today, Cleo?"

My lips zip-lined. "You could say that."

A middle-aged, accountant-looking guy with wire-rimmed glasses and wavy hair saw me and said, "Mrs. Tidwell! It's Sean Johnson from *The Dead Speak*. We spoke on the phone."

I told D.K., "These guys are supposed to be here. They're doing a show on us tonight."

Molly, quite fetching in her form-fitting, scooped-neck t-shirt, said, "I've been trying to tell them that. These aren't the guys I saw going in your house." She eyed my soiled shirt and beer-stained shorts, but had the good graces to keep her mouth shut.

Elmer nodded in agreement, just a good-ole-boy standin' by his woman. Instead of a western shirt, he had on a sky-blue t-shirt with the words *Guardian Angel* airbrushed across the front in white. The L in angel was a feather. What a cute shirt.

"Okay," D.K. told his men, "let 'em go. But keep these reporters back while me and Mrs. Tidwell go check the car and the house."

Molly gave me a little smile that said, "It's all gonna work out for the best."

I wished I could have been so sure.

As D.K. and I headed across the yard to the driveway, I caught sight of a heavily sequined Bippy Barndale among the reporters. Oh, great. Another busybody on the scene.

D.K. motioned to the front door. "House is locked, front and back. We wanted to wait for you before going in. And then we noticed the pink Caddy."

"Have you checked it out yet?"

"No, but it looks like someone's sitting in the driver's seat. I was heading down to take a look when I saw you coming."

"Maybe it's Bertram!" I wanted to do a mad dash down to the car, but restrained myself.

"Could be. We'll know very soon."

The driveway is only wide enough to accommodate a single car. It seems much more expansive near the front of the house with the yard on one side, and a small hedge and wrought-iron fence on the other. But as it wanders toward the rear of the property, the house looms close and the hedge has grown into a mini-forest giving it a closed in, almost claustrophobic feel. A two-room servants' cottage situated twenty feet behind the main house, and right smack dab alongside the drive, continues the feeling that you're entering a tunnel. And that's where the Caddy was parked.

As we neared the car, I could make out someone in the driver's seat, but was still too far away to tell who it was, especially with all the greenery shadowing the car. But my heart didn't want to listen.

"It's Bertram! I just know it's Bertram's in the car!" I lunged forward like a sprinter out of the blocks. D.K. pulled me up short.

He drew his gun. "Stay behind me, Cleo."

Uh oh, gun out. Okay, I was definitely staying behind him. We crept closer. Now that I had a better view, whoever was in the Caddy was too short to be Bertram unless he was slumped over.

D.K. said in his loud, official police voice, "You in the pink Caddy. Open the door slowly and come out with your hands up."

Nothing happened. My heart salsa danced in my chest. Maybe Bertram was in the Caddy sleeping. Yeah. That could be it. Or maybe he'd been knocked unconscious.

D.K. motioned for me to stay put. It was all I could do to hold myself back. I so desperately wanted to race to the car and yank open the driver's door.

"This is your second chance," D.K. said, projecting his voice. "I'm a police officer. Open the car door and come out slowly. Keep your hands where I can see them."

D.K. had almost reached the rear bumper.

I couldn't keep my mouth shut any longer. "Bertram? It's Cleo. Do what D.K. says and come on out. Okay?"

D.K. hushed me, shooting me a look of pure aggravation. He held his gun business-end up as he traveled along the driver's side of the pink Caddy. He was actually kinda graceful, creeping along the way he was. He reached his left hand for the door handle as if it were a sleeping dog he didn't want to wake.

And that's when a guy spoke up right beside me. "The man in that car is dead."

I think I leaped about three feet in the air.

6

"Holy crap! Don't do that!"

D.K. glared at us. "Who are you and what are you doing back here?"

But I recognized the guy beside me. He was none other than Don Rover, the host of *The Dead Speak*.

"I'm a professional psychic," Don said with what sounded like a tad of arrogance. "I do this sort of thing all the time."

And he did. I wasn't what you'd call a fan of the show, but I'd seen a few episodes. And I have to say, Mr. Rover was just as good lookin' in person as he was on the show. He had this whole rugged-blonde thing going on, as if he made his living diving for sunken treasure or going on safari, instead of being on TV. I assumed he wasn't dressed to do the show at the moment since he had on faded jeans and a yellow polo shirt. But he did fill them out nicely as if he worked out regularly.

D.K. was having none of it. "Well, you weren't invited in on this one, so stay where you are, keep your mouth shut, and let me do my job here."

He once again reached for the door handle and Don's words sank in. *The man in that car is dead.*

Dead. As in not alive. As in no more silly karaoke. No more calling me Priscilla. No more mutton-chop sideburns.

I bent forward at the waist, feeling like I was gonna throw up. Don Rover held my hair back. How sweet. If I weren't so busy freaking out, I'd have appreciated it.

D.K. opened the Caddy's door, jumped into a defensive stance, and pointed his gun at the person behind the wheel. The couple of seconds that ticked by felt more like hours.

"It's not Bertram," he said.

Relief washed over me.

D.K. holstered his gun, then reached in to check the guy's pulse.

"But the psychic's right. This guy is definitely dead."

Motioning me to come hither, he said, "Cleo, do you know this fellow?"

I didn't really want to see a dead body, but I was wondering what one was doing in Bertram's car.

So I took a look.

It was Aaron Vassals. A very dead Aaron Vassals.

I don't know where that phrase "dead sexy" comes from. Because let me tell you. Dead is *not* sexy. Not at all.

7

D.K. called in the dead body to police headquarters.

"There's no outward sign of trauma," he told the dispatcher. "Yeah. Tidwell house on Founder's Row. Pink Caddy."

What I couldn't get out of my mind were Aaron's glassy eyes and slack expression, if a dead body could be said to have an expression. How had he died? Oh! Did I even want to know? There wasn't any blood, at least not that I could see, and thank goodness for that or I'd be lying horizontal in the monkey grass lining the driveway right now.

D.K. put away his cell phone and turned to me. "So who is Aaron Vassals?"

"He was dating my sister. He teaches—" I caught myself. "Taught. He taught high school. And he was a member of The Church of the Blue Suede Shoes."

D.K.'s expression said I was pulling his leg. "That's a real church?"

"Yeah. Bertram and I attended a service at Aaron's invitation."

"When was that?"

"Last Sunday."

"When was the last time you saw Mr. Vassals?"

"Tuesday evening. During the historic home tour. He was helping my sister with the tour, and they popped over around five thirty to see how things were going." I frowned and went, "Hmmphf."

D.K. said, "What?" as though he were curious.

"He took off right before that fender bender when the painting disappeared. Said his brother had come into town unexpectedly." I shrugged. "It just seemed a little odd at the time. But if he stole the Velvet Elvis, what is he doing dead in my driveway in Bertram's car?"

Sirens whooped and hollered a few blocks away.

"That's the answer I'm gonna try to find out," D.K. said. "There could be several possibilities. He might have had a partner, double crossed him, and then the partner might have whacked him. Since he's in your car in your driveway, and your husband took this car to go get doughnuts this morning, but never came home, I'd say Mr. Vassals here is most likely connected with your husband's disappearance. We haven't gone through your house yet, so we need to do that next. No telling what we might find since you say your sister said she saw men carrying stuff into your house."

Don Rover stepped forward, all swaggering self-importance. "Your husband has disappeared, Mrs. Tidwell? And yet, I feel his presence nearby."

"Bertram's okay?"

"I didn't say that." Don looked off as if he were tuning in to a frequency we couldn't hear. "I didn't say that at all."

8

As we rounded the front corner of the house, reporters hurled questions like baseballs.

"What did you find in the car?"

"Is *The Dead Speak* here because someone died in your house?"

"Have the police recovered your Velvet Elvis yet?"

"Why is a professional psychic here?"

God, when would the questions stop? I was digging my house key out of my purse when a woman with a sweetsy-sweet Southern accent called out, "Yoohoo! Cleo. Cleo Tidwell. Won't you come join our fun little group?"

Oh, no. An entire contingent of Fried Okra Queens flocked like flamingoes out on the sidewalk in their pink wigs, rhinestone tiaras, and black outfits with feather boas. News people and sight-seers alike snapped pictures of them.

"I'm kinda busy right now," I hollered back. "Maybe later." *Maybe not.*

Molly jogged across the yard. "What'd you find around the side of the house?"

"Come up here to the porch." I'd forgotten Molly didn't know the Caddy was parked so far up the drive. From her angle she wouldn't have been able to see it since the houses were tall and the lots ran deep. I really didn't want to have to tell her about Aaron, but better she heard it from me now than later on the news.

A couple of reporters must have thought I was talkin' to them because they ran toward the porch, too.

"Not you!" I said. "Just my sister."

Boy, all we needed was a dog and pony show, and I'd have my very own circus.

Molly joined me, D.K., and Don on the spacious Victorian porch. I made introductions since Molly hadn't met Don Rover.

"I really should tell you inside," I told her, "but I don't know what we're gonna find there, so I'm gonna tell you out here. You might want to sit down." I indicated one of the wicker chairs.

"What, Cleo? You're scaring me now."

Just bite the bullet and do it, Cleo, I told myself.

"It's Aaron."

"What about Aaron?" Her expression was wide-eyed concern.

"We found him in the pink Caddy. Molly, he's dead."

"Oh my God, oh my God!" she said, hands on her freckled

cheeks.

"Yeah, it's quite a shock." My memory flashed an image of his glassy eyes, and I shivered.

"I know I wished that bastard dead on a number of occasions, but I didn't really mean it."

"Everyone says that about someone at least once in their life," I said, trying to signal her with my expression to shut up about that since we had a cop standing right beside us. "No one really means it. Except maybe psychopaths."

"But still. How awful." A tear ran down her face.

D.K. said, "Cleo," in his official cop voice. "We need to check your house."

"Yeah, okay." To Molly I said, "Are you going to be all right?"

She sniffled and tried to smile. "Uh huh."

Don stood next to D.K., arms crossed over his chest, as if here were going in, too. D.K. looked him up and down as if to say: *Pal, you aren't part of this investigation.*

"It's okay, D.K. I want him to come inside with us. He was right about Aaron."

D.K. frowned. "He had a fifty/fifty chance on that one. He just got lucky." To Don he said, "You can go in, but you have to follow my orders. Me first, then Cleo, then you. Got that?"

Don flipped an errant curl out of his eyes with a toss of his head. "Loud and clear."

D.K. held out his hand to me. "Give me your key, Cleo."

I did, and in we went.

At first glance nothing seemed amiss or out of place.

As D.K. checked the half bath under the stairs, Don said, "I'm inside the Tidwell house, home to a haunted painting of Elvis Presley on black velvet—"

I looked back at him, incredulous. "Are you *taping* this?"

He shrugged, totally nonchalant, a small recording device in one hand. "It's what I do."

D.K. headed into the butler's pantry."I didn't know you were going to do the show right this moment." I plucked at my nasty, sticky shirt and glared at him.

"Welcome to the world of tabloid TV, sweets."

Ergh! "Can you actually feel my husband's presence or was that just a load of crap?"

Don gazed off into space again as if consulting an internal Magic 8 Ball.

"Yes to the first. He's ..." He glanced at the grand staircase. "Upstairs. But there's something odd about him. I feel his presence, but he seems ... neither alive nor dead."

Saints preserve me. "I'm going upstairs!"

D.K. called out, "Not without me, you're not."

He re-emerged from the back of the house. "I've got to check the dining room."

As he disappeared through the French doors, Don and I left our post by the front door and waited at the foot of the stairs. From that vantage, I could see into the dining room, and everything seemed as I'd left it this morning. The box containing my good silverware was still on the buffet. Cobwebs were still strung from the chandelier. The wall above the fireplace was still bare where the Velvet Elvis had once resided.

D.K. removed the ornate but heavy iron fireplace cover and took a look up the flue. He then passed into the adjacent parlor where our entertainment center was set up. The TV was still there. So was all the furniture. Then he strode to the opposite end of the long double parlor and poked his head up that fireplace, too.

"Why are you looking in the fireplaces?" I asked, impatient to get upstairs.

"Just making sure there's nothing stuffed up there."

Ohhhhh, I so didn't want to know that.

"All right, "D.K. said, "The downstairs is all clear."

He led the way up, and every time a floor board creaked, it

seemed as loud as a gunshot. If Bertram was neither dead or alive, then just what was he? I held my breath, straining for the smallest telltale sound, but all I actually heard was blood pounding in my ears and our footsteps thumping up the stairwell.

As soon as we rounded the hair pin turn at the first landing, I noticed something different. The bedroom door was closed.

"That door up ahead was open when I left."

The dream I'd had almost a week ago flooded my memory. I heard my dream self telling a shape-shifting Monty Hall: *What's behind door number one?* A shudder wracked my shoulders.

Don put a hand on my arm. "Are you okay?"

"Not really."

We reached the top landing. D.K. drew his gun and stepped up to the bedroom door while motioning me and Don to wait beside the mirrored armoire that we use to store linens. He grasped the crystal doorknob, then opened the antique door and went in. If I held my breath any longer, I was going to pass out, so I sucked in some air. Every little noise seemed so amplified. Don could have been Darth Vader beside me. D.K. clomped across the hard-wood floor. We absolutely could not see into the bedroom from where we stood. I had a view straight ahead to what was once a sleeping porch. The wallpaper along the stairwell and the second floor landing was alternating stripes of burgundy and hunter green encased in stripes of gold, and so dark, the walls seem to be crowding in on me.

The clomping stopped. I held my breath again. Don must have been holding his breath, too, because I heard nothing but the ruckus from the crowd outside.

D.K. said, "Is this someone's idea of a sick joke?"

"What is it?" I suddenly didn't want to go in that room.

Don whispered, "Neither dead nor alive."

I wanted to elbow him in the ribs. He wasn't helping anything by saying stuff like that.

D.K. said, "You can come in … but be prepared."

Prepared for what? Okay, I was seriously creeped out. And I was chewing the inside of my mouth, something I do when I'm nervous.

I took one step, then another, feeling more like a wind-up toy than a real person, until I crossed the threshold and set eyes on what was hanging on the wall above the headboard.

The Velvet Elvis was back in all its House of Liberace glory, except instead of it being a painting of Elvis Presley, it was now a painting of Bertram—my Bertram! He was wearing the white, rhinestone spangled jumpsuit, but his hands pressed outward as if he were a mime trapped within invisible walls.

I soaked in the terror in my husband's brown eyes, noting the sweat glistening on his forehead, the rigid set of his shoulders, and the way his mouth stretched wide in a gaping O. That he was painted on black velvet made it all the worse. As if he were caught in some depthless, black void. I broke out in a sweat all of my own. It was a sick joke. It had to be a sick joke.

Don said, "Your husband's trapped in that painting."

CHAPTER TEN

Saturday Afternoon, October 25

1

"You have *got* to be kidding." D.K. looked from Don to the painting and back to Don again, frank skepticism all over his face.

I sucked in some air, but couldn't seem to catch my breath.

Don crossed his tan, sculpted arms over his chest. "I am absolutely not kidding, Detective …"

"Greenwood."

"Greenwood. The essence of this woman's husband is trapped within that painting."

I was breathing rapidly, almost panting.

D.K. shook his head. "Now I've heard everything. First a haunted painting, now a depository for someone's essence."

I sank my tushy down on the little upholstered seat that goes with my jewelry armoire. Air. I needed more air.

D.K. finally noticed me. "Cleo, you're hyperventilating." He came over to me. "Cup your hands over your nose and mouth and take deep breaths."

I did what he said and within a few inhalations, noticed an improvement.

"A paper bag works better, but who carries a paper bag around with 'em anymore?"

"God," I said through my cupped hands. "That looks like the same frame."

"Same frame?" D.K. said. "As the stolen painting?"

"Yeah."

"Like I said, sick joke. Listen, Cleo. I've got to go through the rest of the upstairs, and then I'll need to ask you some more questions. Do you think you'll be okay for a little bit?"

Oh, sure, everything was just A-OK. Either someone was playing a nasty trick on me or my missing husband was trapped inside a velvet painting. But I nodded anyway. I didn't need D.K. hovering over me.

"Good. Just sit tight. And neither one of you touch that painting. I want to have it dusted for prints."

Once he was out the door, Don said, "Do you feel sick again?"

I was clutching my gut and rocking back and forth on the little bench. "Sorta," I said through gritted teeth.

He left the room for a moment and returned with the trashcan from the bathroom. "Just in case," he said.

"Thanks. I can't stay in this room any longer." I stood up and my stomach lurched. "And I can't do the show. I ... just ... can't."

"Well, that's too bad, but I can certainly understand. Sean will be disappointed."

"Screw Sean. He didn't get a major shock today."

Don remained silent, giving first me, then the painting, an appraising look. Then he pushed the bedroom door closed with a quiet snick.

"What are you doing? I don't want to be closed up in here with that." I flapped a hand at the monstrosity on the wall.

Don speared me with an intense gaze. "Shh!"

He closed his eyes and held his hands out before him like a conductor before the first note of a symphony. His chest rose and fell slowly as though he were falling into a deep slumber.

"I'm seeing the color blue. It surrounds your husband's essence as well as Aaron Vassals'. And I'm seeing blood. Blood and paint mixed together. And a twin. Your husband has traded places with a twin. You've got to … oust the twin without destroying the body … before the mother returns."

He fell silent, and I wondered if that was it. Seconds ticked by. Trying not to look at the Velvet Bertram was like trying not to think about a purple cow. Virtually impossible. I fastened my gaze on the butterscotch-colored walls, but the Velvet Bertram called to me like a siren.

"The mother," Don said, startling me. "The mother holds the key."

"What mother? Whose mother? None of that makes much sense." I looked at Don's face, willing myself to look at nothing else.

Don opened his eyes, lowered his arms. "I don't interpret. Sometimes it's crystal clear and other times, like now, it's obscure. I'm merely a conduit."

"A conduit. Well, maybe it'll help somehow." I had no idea how but filed it away under potentially useful info.

Don held out his hand, and I clasped it. "It was nice meeting you, Mrs. Tidwell. I wish you the best. Now, if you'll excuse me, I have some bad news to break to my producer."

He opened the door and made it as far as the threshold before turning back to me. "That red-headed guy in the guardian angel t-shirt? He's hiding something from you."

"What? What's he hiding?"

"I don't know. He's like a closed door. Most people's minds are wide open to me. I have to filter out all the clatter-trap or I'd go insane. But that guy. When I passed by him outside, his mind was like a locked bank vault. I'd watch him if I were you."

2

Not wanting to spend another second with the tortured Velvet Bertram, I followed Don downstairs and showed him out.

What could Elmer be hiding? Was his dead wife actually alive and well? Was being a collector of oddities another way of saying he fenced stolen property? Could he even be the mastermind behind the whole Velvet Elvis thing and be playing us for suckers?

But then I thought about how good it felt to shake his hand, and how happy Molly was, and how he seemed equally taken with her. Maybe he was hiding something, but maybe it was something good, like he'd won the lottery, but given it all to charity, or maybe he'd saved a baby from a burning house. Or maybe … the alternate memory from last night resurfaced, and I saw him running towards the VW van with a fiery sword instead of a gun. Was Elmer …? No, it was too silly, too mystery-science theater. And yet, could he be … an alien from outer space? Or a traveler from a distant planet? The first made me think of E.T., while the second conjured up Buck Rogers. The fiery sword had sorta reminded me of a light saber. And his ability to give certain women orgasms with an innocent, or not so innocent, touch. That was definitely a talent most men didn't possess. At least, not men from the planet Earth.

I noticed the crowd outside had only grown larger since I'd gotten home. It really had become a circus, only instead of cotton candy and roasted peanuts, Girl Scouts were selling cookies, and an enterprising kid had set up a lemonade stand. Mr. Rigby from down the street was showing off all his surgery scars to the Birmingham news affiliate. Yeesh! Some people are so opportunistic! There were so many flashing red lights from police cars and an ambulance, I thought I was going to have an epileptic fit watching them.

D.K. tromped down the stairs. For a slim guy he had a heavy tread. "Does anyone have a key to your house besides you and your husband?"

"Just Molly." God, I sounded tired. Or defeated. Or both. "No, wait. I got it back from her last Sunday. So, no one besides me and Bertram."

D.K. grimaced as though he didn't like being the bearer of bad news. "There's no sign of forced entry. Doesn't necessarily mean your husband's key was used to open the door; a professional could pick these locks pretty easy. Does Bertram have any enemies?"

"Enemies? Mr. Happy-Go-Lucky? None that I know of."

"And how long have you known him?"

What was he implying?

"We dated in college. Then we went our separate ways, and I ran into him at an ASU Alumni Band reunion four years ago. We were married a year later.

"Look, D.K. I know my husband. He's a good egg."

"I hate to break this to you, but wives of known felons have been fooled before."

"Fooled? Just what are you getting at?"

"Cleo, we've known each other since high school. I'm going to be straight with you. I don't for an instant believe in paranormal explanations. Someone very dangerous is playing a bad joke on you, and that someone might even be your own husband. Men have disappeared and faked their deaths. There's even an urban myth that Elvis Presley faked his own death to get out of the limelight. What I'm saying is your husband may not be the victim in all of this. He may be the perpetrator."

"The perpetrator?" D.K. might as well have punched me, I was so blown away.

"Yeah, so prepare yourself. Do you have Aaron Vassals' address or the location of that Blue Suede Shoe Church?"

Geez, but I was having trouble thinking. "Talk to Molly for Aaron's address. The Church ... I've got their business card ... or rather, Bertram does. Or did. It's upstairs."

I didn't want to go in the bedroom again, not yet. But I would, for

Bertram.

I was halfway there when my cell phone rang. Martha Jane.

"Cleopatra, your father and I just saw the news. What's going on? Are you okay? And what happened to your shirt? It looks like you got in a food fight. Really, Cleo, if you're going to be on TV, you've got to make sure you're wearing clean clothes."

Count on Martha Jane to bring that up. She'd be more concerned with the state of my underwear if I were ever in an accident than my medical condition.

"Mom." Boy, I really was distracted if I was calling my mother mom instead of Martha Jane. "I'm glad you called, but I can't talk right now. There's a police investigation going on, and Bertram's been missing since this morning. I'll call you later."

I dashed the rest of the way, saying to myself, *I won't look at it, I won't look at it, I won't look at it.*

Once in the bedroom, I yanked open the nineteenth century armoire that nearly brushed the ten-foot ceiling and found the suit coat Bertram had worn last Sunday. I fished the business card from the inside breast pocket, all the while feeling the lure of the painting.

Don had said the color blue connected Bertram and Aaron. Was the Church of the Blue Suede Shoes somehow involved in this whole business? They'd certainly wanted the Velvet Elvis bad enough. But why would they kill one of their own or kidnap Bertram if they already had the painting? Unless Aaron had double-crossed them and taken the painting for himself. He'd been mighty enamored with it the night he came to dinner.

The Velvet Bertram's presence was like a laser beam boring into my back. I turned to it ever so slowly. My husband's silent scream rippled goose flesh across my arms. My stomach did a heave ho, but I managed to reach the trashcan in time. At least it broke my gaze.

How exactly did you get someone's essence in an inanimate object? And who would know how to do that? And why would they even want to? Assuming it was even possible.

Who and what did I believe? Don or D.K.? Paranormal versus rational explanation?

The one thing I did believe in was Bertram's innocence. I was not married to some criminal.

I pushed the heavy armoire door closed, then carried the trash can to the bathroom where I dumped the contents in the commode. I made a point of brushing my teeth and changing into some clean athletic shorts and a fresh t-shirt before heading downstairs.

D.K. was waiting for me by the front door. "I've got to go get a couple of search warrants. A CSI team is roping off the area around your Caddy, and I'll have someone go up and dust that painting for prints. As far as the inside of your house, we should be out of your hair in a couple of hours. However, I think it would be wise if you stayed with your sister tonight."

"What about the Caddy? How long will it be roped off?" It was always good to know these things.

"A day or two. In the meantime, try to stay out of trouble. Okay?"

"Sure, D.K. Absolutely."

It wasn't five minutes after he left that Faye Eldritch knocked on my back door.

"My goodness," she said, just barging right in as soon as I opened the door. "There are a lot of people out front."

Her owlish glasses lay askance across the bridge of her nose, half of her straight, blonde hair had come loose from its plait, and her bare arms were scratched up. Grass stains adorned the knees of her khakis.

"I had to go around to the alley and climb your fence. You should really think twice about clearing the stickers growing in the back of your yard."

"Yeah, I'll get right on that."

She straightened her glasses and smoothed back her hair. "The painting has been returned. But it's not quite Elvis anymore, is it?"

I shut the back door. "How do you know that? Only two people besides me have that information."

She tapped her temple. "It's a gift. I was meditating with my crystals, listening to Yanni, when BOOM! The psychic hotline rang. Your husband's in trouble, Mrs. Tidwell. And he doesn't have much time."

3

"It's worse than I thought," Faye said after returning downstairs from communing with the Velvet Bertram. "Your husband's spirit has been ousted from his body against his will and placed into the painting. If he isn't returned soon, he'll be trapped within that square of black velvet forever."

Well, that was just plain unacceptable. "So how much time does he have?"

"I'm not really sure. A week. Maybe less."

"Okaaaay. I'm sorta at a loss here, Faye. I don't know who did this to him or how to reverse it."

"Does the color blue ring a bell? I was doing a Rainbow Stone reading on you recently and I kept drawing the blue stone."

Blue again. As in maybe blue suede shoe? As in church of?

"I can see by your face," she said, "that blue means something to you."

"Yeah, it does. But if—I mean, *when*—I find Bertram, how do we switch him back?"

"I can consult my copy of *The Occult Made Easy: A-Z*. And there's always the internet."

Yowzah. The internet. But really, what options did I have? If the police found Bertram, he might be held as an accessory to Aaron's death. Maybe even as a prime suspect. I had to find him before the police did. And I had a lead. The Church of the Blue Suede Shoes.

"So how much is all this gonna cost me, Faye?"

"Well I'm running a special this week. Psychic investigation for only $99.99. Plus tax."

"Plus tax. Of course."

"But I'll only charge you if we're successful."

Why did I not find that reassuring?

4

Molly answered her cell immediately. "Speak of the devil. D.K. just finished giving me the third degree. How did the house check out?"

"That's what I'm calling about. We need to talk." I darted a glance at the police officers heading upstairs and lowered my voice. "In private. I'm coming over. Meet me at your back door … and wear good walking shoes."

"Good walking shoes?"

"See you in five," I said and hung up.

I gave the cops a spare house key and told them I was going next door and to lock up when they were done.

Molly was sitting on her back stoop, her knees drawn up toward her chest. The pink Keds on her feet matched her t-shirt.

"You're keeping me in suspense here," she said. "What'd you find in the house?"

"Grab your minivan keys. We're going for a ride. And don't tell Elmer."

She shot me an appraising look, but went inside and got the keys. Molly's Bed and Breakfast sits on the corner and her driveway exits on the cross street well out of view of the media circus in front of my house. I didn't want to alert anyone to where we were going.

As we climbed into her white minivan, Molly said, "Something's happened. I'm dying to know what."

"And you shall, verra, verra soon," I said, buckling up in the passenger seat.

Molly cranked the engine and was just about to shift into reverse when Elmer wrapped on my window.

Pow! Pow! Pow!

Geez! I thought I was going to rocket to the moon.

He flashed his good-old-boy grin and motioned me to roll down the window. I didn't really want to, but I did. A polite upbringing is sometimes hard to defy.

"Where are you ladies in such a sure-fire hurry to get to?"

I said the first thing that popped in my head. "Winn Dixie."

"Uh huh. Good try. I'm going with you."

Molly shifted into reverse and the doors automatically locked. The gear shift moved back to park on its own, and the doors unlocked with a pop. Elmer yanked on the rear sliding door behind me and jettisoned inside. The gear shift shot down by itself and the doors locked again.

Molly and I both twisted around in our seats and stared at Elmer. He nonchalantly fastened his seat belt.

"The Velvet Elvis came back, didn't it. Only it's not a Velvet Elvis anymore. Am I right?"

Molly's jaw dropped. I think mine did, too. How could he know that? Then I remembered Don saying *He's hiding something from you.* I thought of Elmer's magic touch, and the fiery sword in the parking lot of Throw Them Rolls, and how I'd wondered if he was from outer space or something.

I glanced down at Elmer's shirt. *Guardian Angel* with a feather for the L. *Bright angel* he had said. *Inglebright is German for bright angel.*

Elmer was hiding something, all right. And he was hiding it in plain sight.

"You're an angel, aren't you," I said with dawning wonder.

Yeesh, after dealing with Blue Shoe Loonies, psychics, and now a husband trapped in black velvet, an angel seemed pretty par for the course. That or I was as much of a fruit loop as Bertram and any moment now they'd take me away in a straight jacket.

"But angels have wings and halos and they play harps," Molly said. "They don't wear Wrangler jeans and have red hair and

Southern accents."

"Don't they?" Elmer said.

Molly and I stared at his guardian angel t-shirt. I could see a life of Sunday School lessons warring with this new revelation on Molly's cute face. As for me, I was just about resigned to this new life of the fantastic. I mean, it seemed like everywhere I turned these days some freaky new thing was invading my life. My whole world had been turned upside down, shaken but not stirred, and had left me with the put-upon attitude of *What next?*

Holy crap, I was becoming a cynic.

Elmer gave us an "aw, shucks" grin and said, "Ladies, you're looking at a bona fide, dyed-in-the-wool angel."

CHAPTER ELEVEN

Saturday Night, October 25

1

Well, I only had about a million questions running through my head. Had I finally lost it and gone bat-shit crazy like Great-aunt Pixie? And if I were really sane and there really was an angel sitting in my sister's minivan, what was he doing masquerading as a collector extraordinaire in Alabama and why did he want our haunted Velvet Elvis so bad? And was he really a widower and did he actually have four daughters who were all champion baton twirlers, or was that all part of his cover? And weren't angels all powerful?

Molly summed it up a little less eloquently. "Ho-lee shit!" Her eyes went wide as she clapped a hand over her mouth. "Oh! I probably shouldn't say that around you."

Elmer raked a hand through his red curls. "You don't have to monitor your mouth. Look, I can tell you gals have a hundred questions you'd like to ask me, but right now we need to get on over to the Church of the Blue Suede Shoes. I can fill you in on some of it as we drive over."

Molly stomped on the accelerator and we zoomed backwards to the end of her driveway. My forearms smacked against the dash as I doubled over from the force. "Whoa! Slow down there, Molly."

"Sure thing." Molly careened out into the street, then shifted to drive. "You know the way. Where to?"

"Take Tenth Street up to the mountain."

We circumvented the police and the paparazzi by heading away from Founder's Row. A few blocks down, we hooked a left at the country club onto High Street.

As we passed well-kept bungalows, Molly said, "Cleo, you've gotta tell me what you found in your house. What did Elmer mean by the Velvet Elvis came back, but it wasn't a Velvet Elvis anymore?"

I recounted finding the Velvet Bertram, Don Rover's psychic impressions, D.K.'s thoughts on the altered painting, and Faye Eldritch's unannounced visit and subsequent psychic reading. And how the Church of the Blue Suede Shoes seemed to be the common denominator between all the events, clues, and psychic readings.

Molly glanced at me. "Oh, my God. Cleo, I'm so sorry."

"Those bastards are not gonna win. I refuse to allow Bertram's soul to get trapped in black velvet for all eternity. And I can't count on the police. They might find Bertram, but they won't be able to transfer his spirit back to his body. If anything, they might arrest him and throw him in jail. Then what will I do?"

Elmer spoke up from the back seat. "The Church of the Blue Suede Shoes has been looking for that Velvet Elvis for about as long as I have. I don't want us to get bogged down in a tangential discussion, but for the sake of understanding the matter, forget what you learned in Sunday school about angels and angel powers. My job is to identify supernatural objects that pose a threat to the common good, locate and acquire them, and then keep them from falling into the wrong hands. Think of me as a divine Indiana Jones."

Ohhhhh, so that's why he'd wanted the Velvet Elvis so bad, and why he'd been willing to top the highest bidder. Which meant the thing really had been haunted. So Bertram hadn't been having a mid-life crisis and wasn't going crazy. He'd been *possessed*.

"I've been hunting for that particular Velvet Elvis," Elmer said, "ever since a rumor surfaced involving Elvis, an occult ritual gone bad, and a haunted Velvet Elvis painting."

I glanced at Molly, then back at Elmer. "I've never heard that rumor."

"I wouldn't think so," Elmer said. "More than half the stuff I hunt is not known to the general public. There's an entire underground of supernatural rumors, legends, and myths."

"Well, that's pleasant to know. So, are you telling me Elvis was actually haunting our painting?"

"That's *exactly* what I'm tellin' you. You see, what most people don't know is that Elvis was conductin' a secret, occult ritual the night he died. Elvis wanted to live forever, but he didn't exactly want to give up his pill-popping, gluttonous ways. So he and a swami friend of his cooked up this plan to transfer Elvis's vices into a painting so that his body would remain young and beautiful.

"But Elvis died unexpectedly. Instead of his vices going into the painting, his spirit wound up in it. But the swami and other members of his occult group didn't know that. At least, not right away. By the time they figured it out, the painting had disappeared in the hoopla concerning Elvis's death."

Molly had reached a red light at the intersection of High and Tenth Streets. The historic High Street cemetery was catty-corner to our right.

I rubbed my bare arms, suddenly cold. "So where's the painting been all this time?"

Elmer shrugged. "No one seems to know. It's one of those unsubstantiated rumors that I've been keeping tabs on for years. It resurfaced in your possession, at least as far as national media coverage is concerned."

The light turned green and Molly wheeled us onto Tenth Street. The houses over here were old instead of historic, most of them needing paint or roofing repairs. A banged-up washing machine squatted upon the front porch of one residence.

Molly darted a glance my way. "Well, we can trace it back to a road-side vendor at Graceland. Isn't that where Georgia bought it?"

I nodded. "Um hmm."

"I wonder if you could track down the artist?" Molly kept her eyes on the road. The van's engine chugged with strain as we headed up the steep, winding mountain pass. And to think, I'd walked down this very road in my Sunday best almost a week ago.

I said, "I don't think the painting's signed," at the same time Elmer said, "That's somethin' I might just look into for my own personal knowledge once we get Bertram back in his body. The artist was supposedly a member of Elvis's occult group. Although he might be in the dark about what happened to it just as much as anyone else."

"Do you know who painted it?" I was trying to imagine a fat, bloated Elvis trafficking with a bunch of black-robed folk right out of a Hammer film. The two images didn't mix, like peanut butter and asparagus.

"Nope. Sure don't. But you know, the frame might be hiding the artist's signature. If you remove it, you might find it in one of the lower corners."

Oh, I so didn't want to have to actually touch the Velvet Bertram or its frame. "Maybe y'all could help me with that later? On account of me not wanting to look at Bertram's tortured expression."

"No problem, Cleo," Elmer said. "All in a day's work for me."

Molly peered intently at the twisting road. "Tell me when to turn off, Cleo."

"It's not much further."

The houses had become more prosperous looking on the mountain, larger, newer, although by newer, built in the 60s and 70s. The yards were bigger and well kept, although sloping.

Molly smiled shyly. "So how are the Blue Suede Shoe people mixed up in all this? Why did they stick Bertram in the painting? Are they into the occult, too, or something?"

"Oh my God." The light bulb of realization was flaring in my head. "Last Sunday, Dupree Hardcastle said, 'And it is our mission, nay—our duty—to find the King and resurrect him to his former glory.' I thought he was referring to the urban myth about Elvis faking his death and living incognito in Albuquerque. But I think he had something else in mind. Like a haunted Velvet Elvis and a little soul swapping."

Elmer said, "I think you're right, Cleo. I've known they were lookin' for the painting, too, but hoped I could get it before they did. That's why I offered to outbid everyone. But I hadn't thought they might actually try to resurrect the spirit of Elvis into a living person."

I pointed up ahead to the left. "Turn left at the next street, Molly." Twisting around to look pointedly at Elmer, I said, "If you knew it was dangerous, why didn't you say so?"

"Would you have believed me?"

"No," I said morosely.

And I wouldn't have. I would have categorized him as a total kook, right up there with the Blue Shoe Loonies, Darlene, and the Ice Queen.

Twilight was creeping upon us as we drove along streets that wound about like a labyrinth on top of the mountain. But finding the right house was proving a bit more difficult. Without all the cars lining the curb to clue us in, all the houses looked the same.

And now that we were almost there, my fired-up enthusiasm for confronting the Blue Shoe Loonies about the whereabouts of my husband was quickly shifting to doubt. What had I thought we were gonna do? Storm their loony bin demanding answers? Yeah, and what reality did I live in? This wasn't the movies.

"Stop the van, I think this is it."

Molly pulled over to the opposite side of the street and let the engine idle. The house was just as I remembered it. Split level. Red brick with gray vinyl siding. White trim. Dark gray roof. Brick steps leading to a tiny front porch.

But there'd been one significant change since Bertram and I had been here last. A big *For Sale* sign jutted out of the rampant weeds sprouting from the lawn. Sun Realty.

"Well, ho-lee hell." I stomped out of the van and across the road, fixing that realty sign with a glare as if that would make it cough up all its secrets.

Molly followed close behind. "Maybe they haven't moved yet."

"Oh, I think they've vamoosed." I swept my arm like a game-show hostess, indicating the weed-eaten yard, the bare windows, and the lack of energy about the place. I was pretty sure the house was vacant.

Elmer was already peeking in the lower-level windows, a flashlight stuffed into the back pocket of his jeans. "You say they had a sanctuary in the basement?"

"Yeah. The windows were heavily draped."

"It's empty now."

I believed him, but had to see for myself. Cupping my hands around my face, I peered through the glass. Just your standard, finished basement. White walls, boring beige carpet.

"Let's go around back."

We tromped through crab grass and down the slope to the side of the house. The gate through the chain link fence gaped open, so we helped ourselves and went into the backyard. The yard sloped away rather steeply from a walk-in entrance at the rear of the house. I'd never even noticed that before; it had been well camouflaged from the inside. The three of us cupped our hands and looked through the glass panes of the French door, Elmer squatting, Molly leaning over him, and me on tiptoe. If anyone had been inside, we would have looked like three heads on a totem pole.

"Vacant."

"Bare."

"They're gone."

Steep stairs led up to a wood deck. "Just to make sure," I said, "let's go up and see if there's anything upstairs."

Elmer led the way and I brought up the rear. I had the strongest feeling that unseen eyes were watching us, which might have been neighbors or might've been my conscience telling me we were breaking the law.

The sliding glass door off the deck looked into the kitchen. Also empty.

"Well, crap," I said, turning in a half circle and looking out across the yard. A metal shed sat way back at the far reaches of the long, narrow, sloping lot. "They could be anywhere. For all we know, they moved across town."

God, I was so frustrated. I thought for sure we'd pull up and find Bertram tied up in the basement or maybe lounging around with his newfound pals. So much for getting my hopes up. "It's not exactly like they're in the phone book."

Elmer caught my eye, then looked to the back of the yard where the shed was. "My guess is now that they've got their prize, they've returned to the mothership."

"Mothership?" Molly said.

"Memphis."

"Well, that narrows it down." I was being sarcastic, but gee, Memphis wasn't exactly a small town, and The Church of the Blue Suede Shoes wasn't exactly advertising their presence. I sighed. Where was Bertram?

Elmer cracked his knuckles. "I say we head over to that shed down yonder while there's still a little daylight. It's probably vacant, too, but while we're here, we might as well check it out."

My gut clenched as a sudden image of Bertram, bound and gagged and very dead in that shed, popped into my head. *Stop it! Get a grip on yourself!*

"So, Molly," I said, "did Aaron tell you anything about the church? Anything that might help us now."

She thought about it as we tramped through the even taller backyard grass. "He did say once that he'd been chosen to be a special vessel for the living spirit because of his good looks and his name. Said it was a very special honor. A once in a lifetime kind of thing, actually. At the time, it sounded like typical churchy talk, you know. But in light of recent developments, I wonder if they were planning to use him for the transference before Bertram came along?"

"Aaron," I said. "Something about his name rings a bell."

"That's because Aaron was Elvis's middle name," Elmer said, "but his folks spelled it A-R-O-N. Although on his tombstone, it's spelled the traditional way. That's why some people think Elvis faked his own death."

"So," I said, trying to be careful not to slip and slide down the grassy slope on my ass, "I wonder if Aaron died from an attempted transference or if they killed him for some other reason? And if it was the former, why didn't it work? Why isn't Elvis in Aaron like they intended?"

And then I thought about what Georgia had revealed concerning Bertram's possible parentage. And Don Rover's words: *And I'm seeing blood. Blood and paint mixed together.* Was a blood tie the key to a successful soul swap? And how did we even know there'd been a successful swap? For all we knew Bertram could be dead somewhere, just like Aaron.

The corrugated metal shed loomed below us in the murky shadows of thickening twilight at the bottom of the slope, the door chained and padlocked.

Elmer pinched his nostrils shut. "Do y'all smell that?"

I caught a strong whiff of road kill. Oh, no. I had a bad feeling about this.

I was breathing out of my mouth. "Uh huh."

Molly made a face that said, "blech." I suddenly didn't want to go in that shed. And without bolt cutters we might not have to.

Elmer knelt in the weeds and fiddled with the lock. Molly tapped my arm, and I nearly somersaulted down the little bit of slope left. "What do you think is in there?"

"I hope to God it's full of dead rats."

"What if it's not?"

Oh, those four little words sent my imagination to a place it shouldn't have gone. I superimposed Bertram's face on Aaron's dead body. Tears pricked my eyes, and I bit my lip to keep from boo-hooing. Right. Let's just sob and alert any neighbors who might be home that someone was trespassing next door. Oh, that'd be great.

The padlock and chain hit the ground with a metallic clink. I mentally prepared myself for what we were going to see … and smell. Elmer glanced back at me and Molly. "Ready?"

"Sure." I didn't sound sure.

He pulled the flashlight from his back pocket and clicked it on. The beam of light made me realize just how dark it had gotten. He flung the shed door open and Aaron Vassals tumbled out, naked as a jaybird and as dead as Alabama road kill. Molly let out a shriek that scared the bejeezus out of me, and then I shrieked, and next thing I knew we were clutching each other like Hansel and Gretel lost in the woods.

Elmer said, "Well, I'll be damned."

2

Molly and I sat in the minivan with the doors open while police, CSI, curious neighbors, and media hounds swarmed about the Blue Shoe Loony house across the street. I shivered with a chill I couldn't shake even though the night was still fairly warm. D.K. had not been happy when I called to say we'd stumbled across a very dead Aaron Vassals look-alike while trespassing on private property. He'd flung a few choice words over the phone, then told me to stay put and try not to touch anything until he arrived. Now he and Elmer were speaking softly a short distance away amidst the flurry of activity, sound, and lights. From time to time D.K. would glance our way. It wasn't an endearing expression. But I didn't care. I was enormously relieved it hadn't been a dead Bertram in that shed, but I was also enormously disappointed that we'd found no trace of anyone else. Did the Blue Shoe Loonies have my husband? And if so, where'd they gotten themselves off to?

D.K. finished up with Elmer and stepped over to me and Molly. He looked pretty pissed off. "I oughta throw you both in jail. I was in the process of getting a search warrant for this place when you two junior detectives had to go and break the law."

"Well, in my defense, I was trying to find my husband."

D.K.'s expression soured even more, if that was possible. "Yeah, well next time stay out of it and let us do our job. That goes for the both of you."

Molly hugged her knees. She hadn't seen the first dead Aaron, and this one was freaking her out.

"Did you ladies know Aaron Vassals was a twin?" D.K. flipped open a small notepad. "Jared Vassals? From Witchawatchee, Florida?"

Your husband has traded places with a twin. A bodacious shiver overtook me, and I shuddered uncontrollably. Had Bertram become the sacred vessel for the spirit of Elvis? Holy crap! He had! I was sure of it. Aaron and/or his brother had been the original designees to become the vessel for the resurrected Elvis, but something must've gone wrong and they'd died. Bertram was most likely now walking around somewhere housing the King while Bertram's soul had been banished to gaudy black velvet. It was enough to make a person want to go all fetal and babble incoherently.

Faced with such a lovely option I said, "No, I didn't know."

Geez, I sounded guilty as hell. I always sounded guilty as hell. I could do absolutely nothing wrong, and I'd still feel guilty as hell.

"What about you, Molly?" But D.K. said it gently.

"No. He just said his brother had come into town unexpectedly. No mention of being a twin. How do you know which is which?"

D.K. pursed his lips. "We found clothes and ID in the back of that shed."

Molly said, "Oh," in a tiny little voice.

"So, any idea on where the church vanished to?" I said.

"Not yet. Checked with the realtor. Said this house was a rental, paid up till the end of the next month. Said she'd been instructed to put the For Sale sign out front this week. Renters didn't indicate they were moving so soon, nor did they leave a forwarding address. The house was rented to a Dupree Hardcastle."

I started at that name. Boy, ole Dupree had a track record of startling me.

"I take it you know this person?"

"Yeah, you could say that." I explained all the ways I knew Dupree.

"Well, maybe he's got a criminal file. I'll look into it." He flipped the notepad closed. "Okay, you ladies and Mr. Inglebright are free to go. But the next time you get a hankering to do a Nancy Drew, do me a favor and squelch it, okay?"

3

When life becomes overwhelming, my motto has always been: focus on the little things. Like organizing my DVD collection or pre-treating fabric stains or dusting ceiling fans. Mundane stuff that grounds me in everyday reality.

So as Elmer drove us home in Molly's van, my mind was preoccupied not with the escalating horror in my life, but with getting a shower. And feeding the cats. And calling Martha Jane back.

When we pulled up onto Molly's driveway behind her house, I said, "I don't want to go in the house by myself. But I'd really like to shower in my own bathroom."

See, focus on mundania and the big bad wolf will be held at bay. Plus, people in shock will often say strange things.

Elmer shut off the engine and reached back, handing Molly the keys. "I'll go in with you," he said. "Besides, I'd like to get a look at the painting."

The painting. Farthest thing from my mind right now.

Molly squeezed my hand. She'd ridden home next to me on the middle seat. But she had her own little shockwave going on after seeing Aaron's dead brother. "Let me run in and tell the girls where we'll be. And I insist that you stay over with us tonight, Cleo. You should not sleep in that house alone."

"I couldn't agree with you more." Each word seemed to have a fifty pound weight attached to it.

4

The message light on my answering machine blinked, taunting me to play back my missed calls. I could just imagine what I'd hear.

Did you kill them two fellers?

Can we get a sound bite with the woman who found two dead guys in one day?

I think I saw Elvis at Throw Them Rolls Friday night.

So, I let it blink. I had better things to do, like taking a long, hot shower. *And finding my husband.*

The three of us came in through my back door. The front door was locked, so the police must have finished up inside. I didn't see any activity out front although a couple of lookie loos were gawking at my house from the sidewalk across the street. No police vehicles. No sign of *The Dead Speak* van. Sean Johnson was probably having an executive-producer fit over me canceling at the last minute, but he was just gonna have to deal with it. Of course, they still might pull together some sort of half-assed segment from what was now public knowledge concerning a dead body in my driveway and Don's impressions of the house and painting. Honestly, I was too overwhelmed to give a fig about what people might think. I had a feeling the days of caring about that sort of thing were far behind me.

I trudged up the stairs to the first landing, Elmer and Molly on my heels, and peeked out the bay window overlooking the driveway. The pink Caddy was roped off with yellow crime-scene tape. Guess the cops were saving this for later tonight since they were currently searching the Blue Shoe Loony bin.

I let the curtain drop and faced my sister and her beau. "When we get upstairs, I'm heading straight to the shower." I leaned against the wall for a moment, trying to dredge up my last reserves of energy. "What you're going to see isn't pretty, so I'd appreciate it if you'd save your reaction until you hear the water running. Elmer, feel free to take your shoes off and step up on the bed to get the painting off the wall."

We trooped on up the rest of the stairs and I sequestered myself in the bathroom, showering in the claw-foot tub until the hot water ran out. When I was done, I slipped on my terry cloth robe, cracked the door, and poked my head out.

"Is the painting off the wall?" I called out.

Elmer answered from the bedroom. "Yep. It's face down on your bed."

"Okay, I'm coming in."

Elmer turned his back while I pulled out a drawer in my dresser and selected underwear for the night. I just wanted to be comfortable, so I opened another drawer and picked out sweats, a long-sleeved tee, and a faux-fleece sweatshirt. Then it was back to the bathroom to get dressed. At some point I was gonna have to find Cosmo and Maury. They were probably under the bed quaking in their cat suits.

And speak of the devil, as soon as I stepped back into the

bedroom, first Maury, and then Cosmo, streaked out from under the bed and zoomed down the stairs in a flash of orange fur to go hide somewhere else. I mentally checked *Finding Cats* off my "To Do" list.

"So," I said to Elmer. "Have you checked for the artist's signature?"

"Nope. Wanted to wait for you."

"Well, be my guest. Just don't expect me to watch you."

"No problem."

I plunked myself down on the bench at the end of the bed as Elmer worked on removing the gilded frame. I kept my eyes front and center, staring at the print of kittens playing with a ball of yarn hanging on the wall over my chest-of-drawers.

"So, this being a guardian angel thing," I said. "Do you have big, feathery wings?" Hey, I'd never met an angel before. All my notions on what they were like came from church and the movies.

"Naw. That's a myth. There aren't pearly gates, either, and we don't sit around on clouds playing harps. And the boss is more like a force field that envelops everything than a man with a snowy beard sittin' on a throne in the sky."

Wow, it was like everything you ever wanted to know about angels, but were afraid to ask.

Elmer let out a whistle. "Whew, this frame is being pesky."

Molly said, "Can you really marry and have children, or is that just a cover?"

"Those of us who are corporeal can marry and have children, although it's not encouraged."

"Why is that?" she asked. Molly was already looking down the road at the possibility of a serious future with Elmer.

"It's hard on the birth mother. Angels tend to father multiples, usually quadruplets or higher."

"Oh," Molly said, her voice full of empathy, "is that how your wife died?"

"Nope. But that's a story for another time. Ah, the frame's finally budging."

"Okay," I said, still focusing on kittens playing. "I have one more angel question for you. Are you guys exclusive to Judaism, Christianity, and Islam? I mean, what about those poor indigenous peoples around the world who just happened to be born into the wrong religion?"

"There is no wrong religion, Cleo. We're not a private club. I think the Buddhists say it perfectly: one mountain, many paths. The boss is the mountain and the paths are all the religions and even the non-religions. There is no discrimination of any kind. The boss made man, but man made religion."

Wow, I was getting a philosophy discussion, too. Kinda took my mind off of Bertram and where he and the Blue Shoe Loonies might be.

Elmer said, "Okay, Cleo, the frame is off, and I'm turning it over. Don't look."

"I'm not looking, either," Molly scootched next to me on the bench. "Once was enough!"

Elmer went, "Hmm."

"Who is it? Who's the artist?" I resisted the urge to see for myself.

Elmer sounded befuddled. "Lee Munford. Does that ring a bell?"

It did, but I couldn't recall where I'd heard that name. "I've heard that name sorta recently. But I don't remember where or when or who."

Molly shrugged. "You got me."

"Never heard of him, either," Elmer said. "But we can Google him later. Say, Cleo, do you have something I can wrap the painting in? The frame's pretty much shot. I'm not gonna get it back on without taking it to a frame shop."

"You angels, what good are you in a pinch?" But I smiled when I said it.

I fetched one of Great-aunt Trudy's antique quilts from the linen armoire out in the hall. My blood sugar plummeted at that moment and my knees buckled as I handed it to Molly. "I've gotta eat something."

"Me, too," she said. "Let's get a bucket of chicken."

While Elmer wrapped the Velvet Bertram, Molly and I decided to go get dinner in my car since I needed to move it off the street. Some hooligan had broken out the street light, shrouding the PT Cruiser in shadows. There was something off about the car. It seemed to be sitting lower than it should have.

"Uh, Cleo. Someone soaped your car again."

"Son of a biscuit!"

I stepped up on the curb. Someone had written: *Give up the ghost* on the passenger window.

And now I realized why the car was too low. All four tires were flat.

CHAPTER TWELVE

Saturday Night, Part II
&
Sunday, October 26

1

Turned out someone had seriously screwed with my car. Spark plugs missing, gas line cut, air hose sliced, and carburetor filled with sand. Whoever was messing with me did not want me going anywhere. At least, not anytime soon. I called a tow truck and sent Molly off to the Colonel to bring home a bucket of chicken.

After the car was towed, Elmer stowed the quilted Velvet Bertram in the butler's pantry. I fed the cats, grabbed my overnight bag, locked up the house, and headed next door to my sister's.

After dinner, a Google search on Lee Munford turned up diddly-squat. It was as if the guy didn't exist. And maybe he didn't. Anymore. And yet, something about that name seemed familiar. I just couldn't quite place it. The frustration was driving me bananas. So, what else was new? Life in general was making me nuts.

I emailed Faye with an update on Aaron's dead brother and discovering an artist's signature. Then I realized I hadn't called Martha Jane back. She picked up on the first ring.

"So, I see my daughter has been in the news again."

"Yep. Guilty as charged."

There was a long pause and I was just sure some sort of critical remark was going to follow it. But surprise, surprise, Martha Jane said, "Is there anything your dad or I can do for you?"

I almost fell over backward from shock. Gee, wave a magic wand and bring back Bertram? But since that sort of thing only existed in the land of fairy tales, I said, "No, but thanks. I'm staying over at Molly's tonight."

"That's what sisters are for. Are the girls still up? Can you put them on the phone?"

I tagged Brandie, my oldest niece, and let her deal with her grandmother.

Molly stage-whispered to me, "Have you told Georgia about Bertram yet?"

Oh Lord, Georgia.

"No, not yet," I said, keeping my voice low. Martha Jane didn't know Bertram was missing, either. "It's been one thing after another, bam, bam, bam. Besides, what am I going to say? Your son has been abducted by lunatics, but his soul resides in a velvet painting? She'll think I've flipped my lid."

"Well, you've gotta tell her something. She's going to notice that Bertram's not around."

I covered my forehead with one hand. "I know, I know. I'll have to think of something. But what, exactly, I don't know."

2

Bizarre dreams plagued me as I slept in Molly's Rose Room.

Bertram, Aaron, and Aaron's brother, all wearing Elvis jumpsuits, danced the Can-Can during a half-time show in front of the ASU marching band ... Bertram calling as if from a deep well. "Help me, Cleo. I'm lost and I can't find my way home." ... Don Rover the professional psychic wearing so much stage make-up he reminded me of a blonde Rudolph Valentino. "Oust the twin without destroying the body before the mother returns." ... Georgia, very Donna Reed in a full-skirted dress from the 50s and white pumps, pushed through a swinging kitchen door with a bowl of cooked greens, saying, "Would anyone like some polk salad?"and Dupree Hardcastle jumping up off a sofa covered in plastic, shouting, "Amen, Sister Gladys. The King's mama makes a hell of a mess of greens." ... and Faye Eldritch dressed head to toe in blue, even wearing blue eye shadow, whispering in my ear, "Does the color blue ring a bell?"

3

I woke from my troubled dreams like a deep sea diver bursting to the surface. For a moment I forgot where I was. The antique clock on the draped night stand said eight o'clock. Time to rise and shine and get a game plan going.

I schlumped out of bed, the mauve-colored carpet so soft under my bare feet. Molly was going to have to re-think the decor in this room. The rose-patterned wallpaper made the room seem much smaller than it was. It hurt my eyes to look at it. If I had to stay here long, I think I'd be crawling along the baseboard like that woman in "The Yellow Wallpaper." I wondered if any of her guests had complained about it, or if it was just me. Thank goodness, the bathroom was done in a pristine white. No wallpaper here. Just white, white, white. And more white.

After a quick shower, I joined Molly downstairs in her kitchen. Her four girls were still asleep at this early hour. But someone else was missing.

"Where's Elmer? Still asleep?"

She gestured for me to have a seat at her kitchen table. "He left about ten minutes ago. Said he had some business to attend to in Florida."

I sat. Molly set a bowl and spoon in front of me and passed me a box of Lucky Charms and then fetched me a Diet Coke from the fridge.

"He left? But I thought he was going to help me find Bertram."

"Yeah, I thought so, too." She sounded sad.

"You miss him already, don't you?" I lit into my pre-sweetened cereal. Sugar and Diet Coke are must-haves during times of crisis.

Molly wiped away a little tear. She was wearing a really cute fuzzy pink robe that went perfectly with her complexion. "Yeah, I do. Funny, isn't it? I've only known him a week, but it feels like I've known him forever."

I got out of my chair and gave her a hug. "He'll be back. I just know it. He's not an Aaron."

"No, he's an angel. He's got bigger stuff to deal with than a divorcee with four kids in Alabama."

"I think he's smitten with you." I took my seat. "I haven't seen a man look at a woman like that since I ran into Bertram at the alumni-band reunion four years ago."

Molly sniffed, plucked a tissue from the box on the table, and dried her eyes. "Well, my problem is small potatoes compared to yours. Maybe we can figure out something between the two of us."

"Let's see. We know the Blue Shoe Loonies have gone … somewhere. Maybe Memphis. Maybe not. We know there's nothing on Google about Lee Munford. We know Bertram's soul is trapped in a velvet painting. We know he'll be stuck there forever if he's not returned to his body soon. We know someone involved in all of this killed two men. We know D.K. thinks there's a rational explanation for what's going on and that Bertram might even be a suspect! And we know Georgia bought the Velvet Elvis from a roadside vendor at Graceland. So, basically, we really don't know a whole lot. Some Nancy Drew I am."

"Well, maybe you should focus on what you *can* do until we get more information."

"And what's that?"

"Maybe you should call Georgia and tell her Bertram's missing."

"I think I'd rather spend a week at a polka convention."

"So let me see if I have this straight," Georgia said at Noon over a burger and fries at the Bama Burger Shack. "My son was almost kidnapped Friday night, disappeared Saturday morning, returned later that day trapped inside the velvet painting, and then that good looking fella …"

"Aaron."

"Lordy, how could I forget? He's got Elvis's middle name. And then Aaron turns up in your pink Caddy, deader than a flattened possum on the roadside, and you find his twin brother in a likewise situation in a shed behind the house where you said that Church of the Blue Suede Shoes was meetin'."

"That pretty much sums it up." I picked at my French fries.

"Well, bless your heart, haven't you had a time of it?" Georgia shook her head and her blonde flip swayed back and forth as a unit.

"That's the understatement of the year."

ASU students filled every single outdoor table at the verra, verra popular campus hole-in-the-wall. Even though we were surrounded by scads of people, I felt like we had a lot of privacy, especially since each table sat underneath a large, rainbow-colored umbrella.

A college-aged waitress in short shorts, a red tank top, and inline skates, rolled over to us. "Hey y'all. More sweet tea?"

"We're good, thanks," I said.

As soon as she moved on to another table, I told Georgia, "I thought you'd be more upset."

"Honey, when you get to be my age, you realize that if you want to keep your looks, you can't let worry and stress wear you down. How do you think I stay so young? It's from having a level head. It doesn't mean I'm not concerned for my boy. I am. But we've got to use the ole noggin instead of losing our heads over this." She tapped her temple as she said this.

She polished off the last bit of her burger, then reached out and patted my hand as I went for my iced tea. And here I'd had no idea what a steel magnolia my mother-in-law was.

"Don't you fret, Cleo. We'll figure this out and find Bertram. Where there's a will, there's a way."

"Georgia, have you ever heard of Lee Munford?" It seemed like a long shot to ask her, but I was willing to take a chance.

My mother-in-law looked at me with surprise. "Why, sugar, that's the fella who was posing with me and Elvis in my *Fun in Acapulco* photo. I showed it to you when we were cleaning out my house a few weeks ago."

Bingo! "I knew I'd heard that name recently."

Georgia's eyes sparkled with excitement. I think she sensed intrigue. "How did his name come up?"

"He painted the Velvet Elvis."

"Are you sure?"

"Yep. The frame was hiding his signature."

"Well, goodness gracious. What a small world. I remember he did art design for movie sets back in the day, but I had no idea he'd gone the Velvet Elvis route. Makes sense in a way, though."

A pesky fly buzzed around our food and I shooed it away. "If he was out in Hollywood, how did one of his paintings wind up at a roadside vendor outside Graceland?"

Georgia graced me with a million dollar smile. "No mystery about that. After I left Hollywood in the family way, I continued to keep in touch with folks for awhile. Lee followed Elvis's entourage back to Memphis."

A ray of hope bloomed in my heart. "What are the chances he's still in Memphis?"

Georgia wadded up her napkin and stuffed it in her empty drink cup. "There's only one way to tell."

"And what's that?"

"Call 'em up and see if he knows anything about these Blue Suede Shoe people."

I stared at her in amazement. "You've got his phone number?"

She plucked a shiny new cell phone from her Elvis purse. "I've got his old number. It's worth a shot." She flipped open the phone. "And don't look so surprised. I finally decided to join the twenty-first century and transferred my Rolodex into this little gadget. Although a few people didn't make the cut on account of them being dead."

"Like who?"

"Rock Hudson."

"You had *Rock Hudson's* phone number?"

"Sure. I had a small part in one of his movies with Doris Day. I'm telling you, shug, the man was quite an actor. I had no idea he was of a different persuasion. Too bad he's gone now."

Georgia's phone went beep-beep-beep as she scrolled through her contacts list. "Okay, here we go. Lee Munford. Let's hope he still lives in Memphis." She held the phone to her ear. "It's ringing," she stage-whispered to me.

Her face perked up like she'd hit pay dirt. Maybe he'd answered the phone.

She listened for a moment, then said, "Hey, Lee, it's Georgia Jeffries. You and I were in Hollywood together in the early sixties. We both had Elvis in common. Listen, hon, I happened to buy a painting of yours recently, a Velvet Elvis—"

She broke off and mouthed: *He picked up.*

"Uh huh, Georgia Jeffries. The sexy blonde from the South? That's me, shug, ... uh huh, the one's that's been in the press lately." She nodded even though Lee couldn't see her. "My daughter-in-law owns it now. Or did until someone stole it ... that's right, Cleo Tidwell ..."

Georgia winked at me, listened some more, then said, "Uh huh. I sure would. That'd be real nice, like old times ... okay, then. Thank you, darlin' ... buh-bye."

She snapped her phone shut and smiled triumphantly.

"Pack your bags, Cleo. We're heading to Graceland."

PART III:
HEARTBREAK HOTEL

CHAPTER THIRTEEN

Sunday, October 26

1

Wind roared through the open windows of the pink Caddy, whipping Georgia's hair about her head and face, as we zoomed west on I-20 toward Memphis. The Caddy didn't have air conditioning. Nor a CD or cassette player, not that we'd be able to hear any music above the maelstrom of the wind and road.

Georgia shouted, "We're just like Thelma and Louise! Woohoo!"

"What?"

"Thelma and Louise!"

Except we hadn't done anything illegal, at least, not yet. And we had a freaky Velvet Bertram in the trunk.

The police had released the Caddy back to my custody an hour ago. It seemed fitting with the PT Cruiser out of commission that we should drive Bertram's car to Graceland. Of course, I kept picturing Aaron Vassals slumped deader than a door knob right where I was sitting. And when I did, I'd shiver even though the afternoon was warm.

We rumbled along the ribbon of interstate past mile after rural mile of evergreens mixed with oak, hickory, birch, and beech that had yet to turn color. Trying to hold a conversation was useless. It'd be like talking in a tornado. But by golly, that car was roomy. The thing really was built like a boat.

Once we passed Birmingham, the scenery turned deadly dull. At least from Allister to Birmingham there are little towns along the way and even a mountain pass. But the rest of the route to Memphis—all four tremendously long hours of it—had little of viewing interest to break the monotony. And we had the sun in our eyes the whole way. Goody. Now I was debating the wisdom of bringing the Caddy. It might have plenty of leg room, but hearing nothing but the wind storm through the car was like a mini-version of hell.

Georgia had done the smart thing and was taking a nap. That wasn't exactly an option for me, not if we wanted to arrive alive.

I glanced in the rearview mirror, more for something to do than a need to see how many cars might be behind us.

A jolt of terror lanced my gut. An industrial-green hippie-mobile, eerily like the one that had careened into the Throw Them Rolls parking lot, was trundling up the interstate only a few hundred yards back. And the nearest exit was more than thirty miles up the road. Crap! Nowhere to go but forward.

I stepped on the accelerator and got up to a shaky 55 mph. Yeah, like we were going to outrun them in a fossil of a car.

Another peek in the rearview confirmed the VW van seemed to be maintaining its distance from our bumper. But was it the same VW van from Friday night?

I drove in a sweat, my stomach churning with anxiety. They already had Bertram. Why were they following us? Or were we somehow on the right track heading to Memphis? Elmer *had* said he thought the Blue Shoe Loonies might have returned to their mothership.

A billboard thirty miles later advertised gas pumps, home cooking, and clean restrooms. We needed to fill up, anyway. I sure as hell didn't want to run out of gas on this desolate stretch of highway with that creepy van on our tail.

So, when the exit came up, I waited until the last minute to take it, wrenching the steering wheel to the right. The Caddy swerved across the dotted line and up the ramp a little too fast. My maneuver toppled Georgia across the seat and jostled her awake.

"Whoa! What's happening?" she said as though disoriented. "Are we there yet?"

Now that we'd slowed, the wind wasn't whipping through the car. Georgia smoothed down her wild hair.

I looked over my left shoulder out the driver's window. The van shot past the exit ramp. "I think we're being followed."

Georgia peered out the rear window. "I don't see anyone."

"Green VW van. I think it might be the one from Friday night."

We'd careened to a stop at the top of the ramp by then. I turned right and drove the fifty yards to Lulu's Diner and Pit Stop, home of the deep-fried turkey leg. Georgia ran in to the restroom while I filled up the gas tank and wiped the bugs off the windshield with a squeegee.

"Can I get you anything, shug?" she said, pausing at the screen door. The restaurant reminded me more of a ramshackle cabin in the woods than a legitimate business. The corrugated metal roof had gone to rust, the siding was weathered wood that hadn't seen the business-end of a paint brush in an awful long time, and the windows needed a date with some Windex.

I thought for a moment. "A Coke, a pecan log, and maybe some Fig Newtons? And Doritos. A big bag." We were on a road trip after all. Road trips required junk food. It was in the handbook, for God's sake.

Georgia clucked at me. "How you eat like that and keep your figure, I'll never know."

"Nervous energy. Runs in the family."

My mother-in-law nodded as if that answer satisfied her, then disappeared into Lulu's.

I whipped out my cell phone. Twilight time was upon us out in the boondocks of north-western Alabama, and we had a suspicious VW van in the vicinity. Time to touch base with Molly … just in case things went south from here.

My sister picked up on the first ring. "Where are you?"

"Right smack dab in the middle of No Place, Alabama." I eyed the rickety screen door Georgia had disappeared through. "Actually, I think we're near the state line. At Lulu's Diner and Pit Stop, home of the fried turkey leg."

"So, how's it going so far?"

"I think that Volkswagen van is following us." I filled her in on the past half hour.

"But it didn't pull off when y'all did?"

"Nope. Didn't give it a chance."

"Well, maybe it's a coincidence, but you're right to play it safe. Better paranoid than dead."

"My thoughts, exactly."

Georgia pushed the screen door open and barreled out with a bag of goodies.

"Here comes Georgia. I'll call you when we get to a hotel."

2

After a quick trip to the restroom, I started up the pink Caddy, turned on the headlights, and hand-cranked my window up. Georgia had already rolled hers up and was chowing down on a fried turkey leg.

"Here's your Coke." She handed me a 16-ounce bottle that I stuck between my legs. No built-in drink holders in the Caddy, unless you counted the inside of the glove compartment door where you could set your drinks when you were at the drive-in … back in 1956. Not very practical for liquids while zooming down a highway in the present.

Georgia patted the plastic bag on the seat between us. "Junk food's in the middle. You should try this turkey leg. It's good."

Hmm … it did look good, but I didn't want to get grease all over the steering wheel.

"Thanks, Georgia, but I think I'll stick with the other stuff."

We got back on the interstate.

Now that we'd left the comforting glow of Lulu's lights far behind, the phrase "blacker than pitch" took on a whole new meaning. Night pressed in around us on all sides. I could only see as far as the headlights. The rest of the world ceased to exist. There was just me, Georgia, the Caddy, and a short leash of road perpetually running ahead of us. Were we really going somewhere, or were we traveling the same, small loop of gray highway over and over, forever and ever, never arriving, continually driving? This sorta thing could drive a person insane.

I clicked on the radio and got nothing but static. So I clicked it off.

Georgia finished her drumstick and cranked her window down a couple of inches, letting in the roar of the road again. She tossed out the bone, then rolled the window up, sealing out the wind.

"It's biodegradable." She shrugged, the green glow of the dash lights bathing her in soft color.

I really couldn't argue with that.

"So," I said, "what was it like being in Hollywood in the early 60s with Elvis?"

"Oh, honey, it was a magical time. People said I had the potential to be a Connie Stephens or an Ann Margaret. I even might have been if my little bundle of joy hadn't come along. And Elvis was always such a gentleman. Very respectful and courteous. Did you know he was into the occult?"

I glanced over at her. A little bird named Elmer had told me, but he hadn't elaborated.

"What exactly do you mean by the occult?"

"Elvis was very interested in Numerology and life after death and all manner of odd subjects—"

Georgia tended to get very enthusiastic when speaking about her two favorite subjects: Hollywood and Elvis. She also often repeated herself, but in this situation there wasn't anything else to listen to.

"—and my, what a voracious reader. Lordy, but he had stacks and stacks of books all over his Hollywood home written by yogis and swamis and gurus. Elvis wanted to live forever. And he had a fascination with things that come in threes. Like the Holy Trinity. And did you know the date he died adds up to a three in Numerology—August 16, 1977—oh, what a sad day that was. I loved that man so. It was hard not to. He had a way about him. Guess you could call it personal magnetism. Or good old-fashioned charm."

"So, did you and Elvis stay in touch after you left Hollywood?"

"He wrote me a couple of times. But you have to remember, his life was like a beehive. So many women wanted his attention, and he was always surrounded by the Memphis Mafia. So, I fell by the wayside. But that's okay, honey, because I had my little Bertram, and I had Fred who treated me like a queen. Can't ask for more than that. Men like Elvis, they're bright stars who'll burn you up if you get too close for too long."

The beam of our headlights illuminated a car parked on the right shoulder. A green VW van.

I had enough time to register this, say, "Crap!" and then we were zooming past it. "That's the van!" I checked the rearview mirror. Twin headlights burned behind us. "They're following us again. Crap, crap, crap!"

Georgia twisted around to look out the rear window. "Maybe it's a coincidence."

"Damn! I can't get the Caddy past fifty-five."

"Maybe Bertram's in that van."

I almost swerved off the road. Hope welled up in my heart to the point I thought it might burst. *Bertram.*

Of course, he might already be in Memphis with the rest of the Blue Shoe Loonies, but what if he wasn't?

We were passing another entrance-ramp. A second set of headlights from a merging car ran parallel to us. I had an idea.

"Georgia, do you have a pen and anything to write on?"

"I do in my purse."

"Can you find it and be ready to take down a license plate number?"

"I most surely can."

"Wait until I say okay."

"All right."

I steered the Caddy over to the left lane to allow the new car onto the road. The VW van kept pace, but remained in the right lane behind the merging vehicle. I eased off the gas until the merger car was neck and neck with the Caddy, then pressed down hard on the accelerator as the car beside us picked up speed. The Caddy shook like it was having spasms, but I managed to get her to sixty without falling apart.

"Are you ready, Georgia?"

"Ready."

"Brace yourself."

As the car, a four-door something or other, nosed ahead of us, I stomped on the brake, not enough to stop, but enough that the four-door and the van seemed to zoom forward ahead of us in the right lane.

"Okay!"

The van's license plate was visible in our headlights for a couple of seconds.

"KNG333! KNG333! Tennessee plates."

"Got it!" Georgia cried triumphantly.

I dug my cell phone out of my pocket, and with one hand on the wheel, speed-dialed D.K.

"Hey D.K., I've got a license plate number for you. I think that

VW van that was in the Throw Them Rolls parking lot has been following me. Bertram might be inside."

"Where are you?"

"Um … I'm on my way to Graceland."

Silence. Then, D.K. said, "*The* Graceland in Memphis?" He sounded incredulous. I couldn't blame him.

"Uh huh." I winced. It sounded pretty strange even to me when I heard it that way. Hmm … my husband was missing, a dead guy I knew was found on my property in our car, another was found while I'd been trespassing on private property, and here I was heading out of state to the house of a dead rock and roll idol. Yep, sounded kinda fishy.

"Cleo, is there something you're not telling me?"

"I'm just trying to help my husband."

"By going to Graceland?"

"It's a long story."

Another silence. For a moment I thought I'd entered a dead zone. Then D.K. said, "I'll run the number and put a BOLO out on it."

I gave him the tag number.

"Where are you now?"

"We just crossed into Mississippi. We're not far from Tupelo. Maybe thirty miles."

"Okay. I've driven that stretch before. There's no safe place to pull over. Keep driving until you reach Tupelo. If the van is still following you, or they do something threatening, then you can contact state troopers or police from a well lighted, public place."

"So, what you're telling me is basically we're on our own for awhile."

"That's what I'm telling you. We can't apprehend someone for following you on the interstate. I'll run the tag and see what turns up. But right now there's no proof that it's the same van as the one from Friday night."

Great. Just what I wanted to hear. "All right."

"Where's the van now?"

"It's ahead of us."

"Try to keep it that way."

"D.K.?"

"Yeah?"

"What if they do try something threatening?"

"Then gun the engine and get out of there."

"I'm in the pink Cadillac. It won't go over sixty without shaking apart."

I heard muffled cussing. And D.K. had always been such a nice, quiet boy in high school. Guess twenty years of living will harden a fellow.

He came back on the line. "Then pray they don't make a move against you and dial *77 for state troopers if they do. Is that clear?"

"Crystal." I hung up.

The van's tail lights flared red ahead of us.

I eased my foot off the accelerator. And eased off. And eased off as the tail lights up ahead continued to flash each time we slowed down.

"Any ideas?" I asked Georgia. We were practically at a dead stop.

"I think we're in what you call a Mexican stand-off, sugar."

Oh, this so didn't feel good at all. "Do we have anything we can use as a weapon?"

"I've got a bodacious can of Aqua-net. That stuff'll blind someone if you spray it in their eyes."

Death by hairspray. That was a good one.

I continued to inch us up the interstate in the inky night. Thank goodness this stretch of road was pretty dead. On second thought, that didn't sound so good. The dead part, I mean. We were going to have to gun it. We were getting way too close.

Georgia rifled through her purse. "I've got a lighter. Course, you know I don't smoke anymore, Cleo. But now and then I like to light one up for old time's sake."

Hmm. What were we going to do? Singe them if they attacked us?

"Um, Georgia, I'm glad you're getting in the spirit of our potential defense, but I'm not sure a lighter and a can of hairspray are going to save our butts if we get in trouble."

The van up ahead had pretty much come to a halt on the interstate. I braked completely and there we were like sitting ducks on a desolate stretch of road in the deep dark of rural night. The driver's side door of the hippie-mobile swung open in the wash of the Caddy's headlights and a big fella clutching a baseball bat slid out. He looked nothing like a hippie. More like a steel worker. Or a road-crew guy. His arms rippled with muscle. He could probably swing that bat real good. It wasn't something I wanted to experience.

I glanced in the rearview mirror, very much aware of our jeopardy should another car come along behind us. I hitched a breath as twin beams pierced the dark way, way, way back. So someone was going to get creamed in a few minutes by the vehicle goin' most likely seventy-plus mph. But someone, namely us, was going to get smashed by a baseball bat sooner than that. What great options.

Georgia was rolling down her window.

"What are you doing!"

"Get ready to hit it, Cleo." She released the window crank, grabbed the Aqua-net in one hand and the lighter in the other, and held them out the window.

"I hope this works," she said. "Saw it in the movies."

I heard the whoosh of hairspray and then a whoompf when she flicked the lighter into its path. A blow torch flamed out the window. Holy hell! Who knew my Hollywood-starlet mother-in-law had it in her.

"Hit it, Cleo!"

I stepped on the gas, hoping this baby could burn some rubber.

The Caddy screeched forward and we swerved onto the left shoulder, dodging the man with the bat as Georgia kept up a steady stream of fire.

"God damned crazy women!" He leapt back against the side of the van as the impromptu blow torch flared his way. The torch had done its job and kept him at a distance long enough to get past him. Whether he was singed or scorched, I had no idea. We were ahead of the van and the plan at the moment was to keep it that way. As to how, I was gonna have to make it up as we went along.

"Wooooohooooo!" Georgia chortled. "Take that, you sucker! Teach you to mess with the Tidwell women!"

The Caddy shuddered as it gained momentum. I swerved us across the left lane and back over into the right. A quick glance in the rearview told me two things. One: the van had its high beams on because I was nearly blinded when I looked in the mirror. And two: the vehicle coming up from behind in the left lane was not only almost upon us, but was most likely a big ole truck considering how high its headlights rode.

Georgia had shut off her make-shift torch and was rolling her window up.

"I have an idea," I said. "I can't get the Caddy past sixty on its own. But a Mac Truck is about to whiz by. We're going to hitch a ride in its wake."

I kept the pedal to the metal as I tried to watch the road and the rearview mirror at the same time ... all without going blind. The truck's headlights were sweeping past us. The Caddy rocked on its chassis as a sleek bus, rather than a truck, zoomed past. I shot over to the left lane, right on its tail, and it gave us the giddy-up we needed—all the way to Memphis.

3

A couple hours later, the bus turned in to the Love Me Tender Motel on Elvis Presley Boulevard. Two intertwined hearts on the sign out front flashed and blinked and shimmered in colorful neon. Reminded me of Las Vegas. The rest of the motel reminded me of the little travel lodges from the 50s. One story, L-shaped, with a small pool out front enclosed in chain link. A Denny's next door. And down the street—Graceland in all its touristy glory.

We were going to have to wait in line to get a room with a busload of people ahead of us, but I felt safer staying around a lot of people.

And it didn't look awfully expensive, either.

Georgia got out of the Caddy, her hair a windblown mess. I slid out on my side, scanning the E.P. Blvd. for the VW van. Maybe we'd lost them. No one had seemed to be tailing us ever since we'd followed the bus.

"Oh, my, how sweet." Georgia eyed the same-sex couples exiting the bus. "That must be a Graceland tour for brothers and sisters."

"Uh, sure, Georgia" I said.

We waited our turn in the surprisingly spacious lobby. The red shag carpet and gold wallpaper could have used some updating. But then I thought of all the times Georgia had told me how Graceland was like a time capsule from the 70s, so why should a motel that catered to Elvis lovers be any different?

We were almost to the front desk when Georgia decided to strike up a conversation with the two men behind us.

"I'll bet your parents are proud of you," she told them.

The two guys, who didn't look remotely related, glanced at each other in puzzlement. The stockier of the two said, "Actually, they don't know."

"Don't know? Well, bless their hearts. They should."

The same guy said, "Really, you think so? I've been telling Rodney that we should tell them for months now, but he said they wouldn't understand."

"Wouldn't understand? What, did the two of you fight when you were little?"

Rodney, who about as average as they come, said, "We didn't know each other when we were little."

"Oh, what a shame," Georgia said. "Parents divorced? Had to live apart? What an awful thing for broth—"

I nudged her with my elbow. "Georgia, I'll cover our room tonight."

That pulled her attention to me. "I wouldn't hear of it, sugar. It's my boy we're looking for. And you drove and bought gas." She was opening her purse and pulling out her wallet. "In fact, I absolutely insist."

"Okay." I glanced away at the super-sparkly chandelier to hide my smile.

The lesbian couple ahead of us, both wearing matching denim jackets, stepped away with their room key. We were next in line to get a room.

The motel clerk, an obsequious little guy who barely looked old enough to shave, said, "Welcome to Love Me Tender. How many nights?"

Georgia looked at me. "You want to book two, just in case?"

"Sure. Two nights is good." I really had no idea how long we'd stay in Memphis. We were going to meet Lee Munford tomorrow and try to track down the vendor who'd sold Georgia the Velvet Elvis. After that, who knew? It all depended on whether we got any more leads to investigate or not.

Georgia had set her sequined Elvis purse up on the counter, resting her wrists on the clasp. Even though Fred Tidwell had died three years ago, Georgia still wore the gorgeous diamond wedding ring he'd given her.

I was feeling lazy, so I propped my elbows on the counter beside her. My wedding ring was much more modest, but the light from the chandelier really picked up the sparkle from our diamonds.

The clerk glanced at our hands, a benign smile touching his lips. "Oh, I have just the room for you two—the King's suite. You'll love it." He tapped on a keyboard the way the ticket agents at the airport used to. "That'll be $228 with tax."

So much for inexpensive. The Graceland area was like the International Drive in Orlando, Florida, of Memphis. One big tourist trap.

The clerk ran Georgia's credit card, she signed the receipt, and he gave us our magnetic key card. At least they'd updated something around here in the last thirty years.

"Room Two," the clerk said. "Enjoy your stay."

4

I backed the Caddy into the parking space right outside Room Two. As Georgia and I collected our bags and the quilt-wrapped Velvet Bertram from the trunk, the sleek, silver bus we'd followed—Transcontinental Tours emblazoned in turquoise across the side—rumbled off to find a bus-sized parking space for the night.

I slid the key card, pushed open the hot pink door, and flicked on the light.

"My gracious," Georgia said right behind me. "I think we have the wrong room."

A round bed took center stage. Two red roses lay crossed on the red coverlet. Red shag carpet—the color of congealed blood—covered the floor.

And there were mirrors everywhere. On the ceiling over the bed, on the wall behind the bed, on the walls on either side of the bed. The only place there weren't mirrors was the outer wall which featured the same gold wallpaper I'd seen in the lobby, and a window draped in deep red velvet.

The single chair in the room was covered with gold, synthetic plush, like a giant teddy bear that had morphed into a piece of furniture. A couple of chocolate-dipped strawberries and an ice bucket holding a bottle of champagne awaited us on the small table in the little alcove to our left.

Remembering the way the motel clerk had noticed our wedding

rings, I was pretty sure we were in the right room, at least in his mind.

Georgia said, "I wonder what this does?" and flipped a switch on the light plate. The bed revolved lethargically while "Love Me Tender" played from a hidden speaker.

At least it was a large bed. "I think we're in the honeymoon suite."

Georgia looked perplexed. "Now why would they put us ..." Her expression changed to one of understanding. "Ohhhh. That's not a brother-sister tour." Then her eyes grew round. "That hotel clerk thinks we're—"

"Pretty much."

Georgia barked out one of her contagious laughs. I was soon laughing, too. We laughed and laughed and laughed.

"Oh, my," Georgia said, wiping tears from her eyes. "What would Fred Tidwell think of this?" She smiled ruefully. "When I was out in Hollywood, the homosexuals, as they were called back then, were careful to keep their secret hidden. I'm glad they can be themselves nowadays."

"We could try to switch rooms if you want, but I have a feeling this motel is going to be booked up from that tour."

"And miss out on these strawberries and champagne?" She picked one up and took a bite. "Yum. I'm okay with it if you're okay with it."

"No problems here. As long as you're not a cover hog."

"That was Fred's domain. I sleep like the dead."

I shivered. It reminded me all too much of Aaron Vassals and his twin brother, Jared.

"I'm gonna call Molly and let her know where we are before it gets any later." It was close to eleven and I'm sure she wanted to go to bed, if she hadn't already.

"Okay, hon. You do that and I'll open the bottle of bubbly."

Molly's answering machine picked up. I left the name of our hotel along with the address and phone number.

Georgia handed me a cheap, plastic champagne glass brimming with Brut. She raised hers, tapped it against mine, and said, "Here's to finding Bertram."

"I'll drink to that."

5

A bottle of bubbly later, Georgia said, "I think I'm ready to see my boy." She gestured with the hand holding the plastic glass and sloshed champagne on the shag carpet. "Oops."

"You mean …the velvet painting?" Elmer might not be around, but I felt good. And nicely buzzed. Bertram didn't call me a light weight for nothing. A couple of drinks and I was snockered.

"Yep. Ready to see him." She stumbled toward the closet where I'd stashed the Velvet Bertram.

"Well, I don't wanna see him."

"Suit yourself, hon." Georgia slid open the mirrored closet door.

"I'm not looking," I sang out. I kept my eye on the cheap, plastic glass in my hand. It probably cost all of ten cents.

I heard something thump, like the sound of a stack of folded up towels dropped onto a bed.

"I'm still not looking," I sang again.

"And I still know that." Georgia sang back.

I drained the rest of my drink. Boy, was I ever relaxed. And happy. A good combination in my book.

Georgia gasped.

"Not pretty, is it?" I said, slurring my words a little. My tongue did not want to fully participate in the activity of speech.

"Oh, my dear Lord! Oh, this is horrible! Oh, Bertram, honey."

"The first time is the worst."

"I think one time is enough."

I heard the closet door slide closed. I risked a look. The painting wasn't in sight.

Georgia said, "Well, honey, I believed you, but I didn't think it would be all that bad. But you were right. That thing is just awful."

"Let's try not to look at it again." I twirled the cheap glass back and forth by the stem. Little drops of champagne sprinkled me.

"I agree wholeheartedly. I'm goin' ta take a shower now. My hair looks like a rat's nest."

"Are you okay to do that?"

Georgia had her suitcase open and was pulling out her toiletries bag. "I'm a little buzzed, as you young people like to say, but I'm not falling down drunk."

"Just checking. Don't want you to fall in the shower."

Georgia gave me a genuine smile full of love. "I'll be fine, Cleo."

While she showered, I checked for the fifth time that the door was locked, the dead bolt drawn, and the chain in place. Then I peeked out the window. Parking lot was dead. And the pink Caddy was like a neon sign under the wash of the parking lot lights. I wished there was a way to camouflage the thing. And then I got an idea. But I was going to have to wait till Georgia was out of the shower. Which would give me some time to sober up a bit.

When I heard the water shut off, I waited five minutes, then knocked on the bathroom door. "Hey Georgia, can I have a bar of soap?"

She cracked open the door and passed it to me, eyebrows raised with an unspoken question.

"Thanks," I said. "I'm doing a little camouflage."

"Okay, hon."

I nabbed a pack of dental floss and nail scissors from my make-up kit, then grabbed the motel and car keys and went out to do a little dumpster diving.

6

At midnight I stepped back and admired my handy work.

I'd soaped *Just Married* in big letters on the side and rear windows of the pink Caddy, and tied empty aluminum cans to the bumper with dental floss. It wasn't the greatest camouflage, but in Memphis with all the people who get married at Graceland, it would raise reasonable doubt as to whether it was my pink Caddy or someone else's, even with Alabama plates.

I went back into the room. Georgia was already asleep. She'd left the bathroom light on and just cracked the door so I wouldn't have to stumble around in total darkness or flick on the light and wake her up. Or flick on the revolving bed by mistake.

I washed my face, took off my shoes and socks, shimmied out of my skinny jeans, and climbed into bed in my shirt and underwear.

And was zonked out in about five seconds.

7

Sometime during the night, I surfaced close to waking, thinking I heard the deep-throated, sultry sound of a bass clarinet. Bertram's instrument. The tune sounded familiar, but was something I hadn't heard in awhile.

Then it came to me. It was my favorite country-western song from the early 90s.

"Cleopatra, Queen of Denial."

CHAPTER FOURTEEN

Monday, October 27

1

Bertram was hogging the covers again. And snoring. I tugged the pillow over my ears hoping to drown him out. And gave the comforter a good yank toward my half of the bed. Bertram rolled toward me and we spooned, his arm draped over me as if I were his teddy bear.

And all was right with the world. Until I opened my peepers. Ack! Where was I?

Then it all came rushing back. Mainly from seeing my reflection in the tacky mirrors over the bed. The Love Me Tender Motel. The round bed with the red coverlet, said coverlet clutched in my hands at the moment. Mirrors everywhere. And my mother-in-law lying snuggled up beside me, curlers in her hair, snoring like a bulldog.

I pried her hand from my waist and rolled her over to her side of the bed. Cover hog, indeed. But at least she wasn't snoring again. I called dibs on the bathroom, not that anyone was awake to lay claim to it.

When I got out of the shower, Georgia was up and dressed, curlers gone, make-up done, bed made. She was wearing the cutest pair of white Capri's, a pink sweater set, and a matching pink scarf, and she'd tamed her hair into a blonde 60s flip again.

She handed me a Diet Coke. "Here you go, shug. I trotted down to the vending machines while you were in the bathroom. I know how you like a Co-Cola first thing in the morning."

I was touched. I really was. "Boy, aren't you on the ball." I wasn't quite human until I'd had my morning Coke, which I proceeded to guzzle while I put on my make-up and pony-tailed my hair. That done, I threw on some jeans, a t-shirt and a zippered sweatshirt.

She smiled wryly. "I like what you did with the car. I'm assuming that's what you wanted the soap for."

"Yep. Thanks. It's kinda hard to hide a pink Caddy in plain sight."

"Well, you did a good job with it."

I wadded up my clothes from yesterday and stuffed them in my travel bag.

"So," Georgia said, "you 'bout ready for some breakfast? I can call Lee from Denny's and see what time he wants us to come by."

"I'm famished. Let's go eat."

Dazzling sunlight nearly blinded me as we stepped out of the room. But the morning was cool and I had to zip up my sweatshirt against the chill. A lesbian couple a few doors down were heading our way, probably off to Denny's, too.

They spotted the car with its newlywed camouflage and smiled as if we were all sorority sisters. "You ladies rock!"

Georgia blasted them with her million-dollar smile. "You got that right, sugar. This here's my love muffin."

I guess you can take a girl out of Hollywood, but you can't take Hollywood out of the girl.

Denny's was apparently the happening place on Elvis Presley Blvd. The restaurant was packed. I recognized some of the same-sex couples I'd seen in the hotel lobby. Guess we'd fit right in, at least as far as keeping up appearances went.

As I opened the door for Georgia, I noticed a missing-persons flyer taped on the glass beside it. Ruth Gruber, age 61, last seen at this very Denny's on Saturday. A happy woman smiled out at me from the photocopied picture. How little we know of our future. Ruth might not have been so happy if she'd known she was going to wind up as a missing person. I thought of all the things I'd said to Bertram recently that I wished I could take back now. Georgia and I *were* going to find him and bring him home, by golly. I still didn't know how, but we'd find a way from sheer determination.

The hostess seated us at a booth and a waitress appeared with menus. I ordered bacon, biscuits, and cantaloupe. Georgia had grapefruit, an English muffin, and coffee. We didn't waste any time devouring our food when it came.

As soon as we were done, Georgia gave Lee a ring at the table.

"Hey, Lee, it's Georgia Jeffries again … yes, we're both here in Memphis … The Love Me Tender Motel on E.P. Blvd." She was smiling as she spoke, and I could see why men would have fallen all over themselves to go out with her when she'd been a starlet.

"Two-thirty?" Georgia said. "Why, that sounds just peachy. What's your address, hon?"

She made writing motions and spread out her paper napkin. I quickly rummaged through my purse and found a pen. She practically snatched it out of my hand and jotted down directions.

"Okay, we'll see you this afternoon at two-thirty. Thank you, shug … yes, it'll be like old times. Bye, now."

Georgia closed her phone. "He's invited us to his house." She waved the napkin like a flag.

"At two-thirty."

"Uh huh." She glanced at the directions before placing the napkin in her tote. "You ready to hit the road and see if we can find that vendor who sold me the painting?"

"Absolutely. Let's do it."

2

Once behind the wheel of the Caddy, I put on my sunglasses, gave the fuzzy dice hanging from the rearview a nice smack that set them to swinging, and cranked the engine. Georgia pulled her legs into the car and slammed her door closed. She really did look like a movie star from the early 60s sitting in the passenger seat with her sunglasses on and the pink silk scarf tied over her perfect hair.

"I'm not taking any chances today," she said, patting her curl. "I haven't see Lee in forty years, and I am not showing up like the wild woman of Borneo."

"Hey, I don't blame you a bit." I put the car in drive. "Okay, Georgia, point the way."

"Turn left out of the parking lot and head towards the interstate. Last time I was here, he was selling Elvis stuff from the back of his station wagon not too far from Graceland."

She leaned forward and peered through the windshield, checking out the sky. "I was afraid it might rain or be too cool, and we wouldn't find him. But it's a beautiful day."

"Amen to that." I gripped the white-leather steering wheel, eased off the brake, and rolled us out of the Love Me Tender parking lot and onto Elvis Presley Boulevard, empty Coke cans clanking behind us.

We passed a number of Elvis souvenir shops, the Graceland Visitor Center, several Elvis museums (including one for his car collection and another for his jumpsuits), an Elvis souvenir outlet, Elvis's two airplanes, the Rock-n-Roll Cafe, Heartbreak Hotel, and Graceland itself. The stately home was sequestered behind a tall stone fence and wrought-iron gates that only the tour shuttle bus, private personnel, and members of the Presley family had access to. The entire area had a retro Panama City Beach feel to it, all bright lights and gaudy exteriors. What would the King have thought of the tourist trap that had grown up around his house? A house that would have been out in the country, well away from the city of Memphis, when he'd bought it in 1957.

He was probably rolling over in his grave. Or in my husband. Ick.

Georgia reminded me of a hound dog on a scent. "It's not much further," she said. "Up here to the right, I think."

We'd passed the mansion a few blocks back. All I saw up ahead was a vacant gas station ... and a dented faux-wood paneled station wagon parked on concrete broken up by weeds and grass. The tailgate was down, displaying an array of velvet Elvii. T-shirts sporting the King's likeness dangled from clothes hangers on a length of laundry line strung across the back of the car.

"That's it! That's him!" Georgia tapped her finger on the passenger window.

I stomped on the brake and swerved the car off the road before we missed it altogether. The white-walled tires bumped up over the curb, cans banging like a noisemaker, and then we bounced to a stop.

A wiry fellow, his skin tan and leathery from the sun, emerged from the station wagon. He wore rumpled green fatigues, an Elvis t-shirt, a gray, zip-up sweatshirt, and a brown ball cap. A couple of days stubble lined his thin jaw.

"Good mornin', ladies." His snaggletooth grin revealed an abundance of color: yellow, brown, and green. I think I'd seen better teeth in a dog's mouth.

"See what you like, like what you see. Everything's for sale, and I mean *everything*. Make me an offer you can't refuse."

Every inch of the back of the station wagon was jam packed with every sort of Elvis doodad imaginable. Mugs, collectible plates, watches, notepads, calendars, board games, records, tapes, CDs, postcards, and more, as well as the t-shirts and velvet paintings we'd seen from the road. And the prices were all over the place from dirt cheap to outrageously expensive.

"My special today is a genuine—" he pronounced it gin-you-wine "—lock of the King's hair. An old Indian woman told me it has the power to heal you of dandruff, dry skin, baldness, psoriasis, and lying. Just sleep with it inside your pillowcase every night between the full and new moons, and you'll be cured. And for the bargain price of only fifty dollars. What do you say? It's a small price for such miracle healing."

Oh, Lordy. I knew this guy was a scam artist when he suckered Georgia out of a thousand bucks for her haunted Velvet Elvis. But this was taking con work to new levels. Of course, the painting had turned out to actually be haunted, in which case the thing was more liability than asset. Considering how our lives had been turned upside down, he should have paid *us* a grand to take it off his hands.

Georgia was starting to look googly-eyed, so before she went on a shopping spree, I figured we'd better get down to business.

"We're researching the history of a painting we bought from you a few weeks ago. A Velvet Elvis. I was wondering if you could tell me where you acquired it and if you know anything about the artist. I've got a picture of it in my purse."

As I tugged the photo from *Snazzy Magazine* (the one with Bertram holding the painting up in front of his face and torso), Mr. Scam Artist said, "I sell the work of several artists. Don't reckon I'd know offhand which one did it. Did you check to see if maybe it was signed?"

Georgia said, "Lee Munford. It was signed Lee Munford." She had her hands on a pair of Elvis earmuffs.

I handed Mr. Scammer the magazine photo. "You might remember this one. It was a haunted Velvet Elvis."

He smacked his forehead. "Oh, right. The haunted one." He gave me a look that said *Lady, are you kidding?* "No, I don't remember. And I don't know any Lee Munford. You sure that's the name."

"Yeah, we're sure."

"Nope, don't recall anyone like that. I did find a painting behind a warehouse a few months ago. Could be the one you're talking about. Don't know how it wound up there. But finders, keepers. That's what I always say."

I decided to try a different line of questioning. "Have you ever heard of The Church of the Blue Suede Shoes?"

He shrugged. "Sure. Who hasn't? It's Memphis, home of all manner of Elvis nuts. You can take your pick. The First Church of Elvis. The Blue Shoe group. The Cult of Elvis. Yonder Elvis Presley Enterprises with their Heartbreak Hotel and mansion tours."

I felt a prickle of excitement. Maybe he knew where their home base was.

"What can you tell me about them?"

He squinted at me in the piercing morning light. "That they're a little cuckoo? That they worship Elvis? That you have to be invited to attend one of their services? They've come sniffing around here a time or two, always looking at the Velvet Elvii, sometimes buying them."

"Have you ever been to one of their services?" Maybe he knew where they met. Was it too much to hope for?

"No," he said a little too offhand, as if he'd been about to say yes.

Hmm. I had a hunch.

"But they gave you their card." It wasn't a question.

"Maybe." His expression turned crafty. "For the right amount of greenbacks I might be able to remember where I put the darned thing."

Yeesh. "How many greenbacks are we talking?"

He eyed me, eyed Georgia, eyed the pink Caddy. "A hundred dollars."

"A hundred dollars to jog your memory? That's crazy."

Georgia popped up beside me. "Twenty dollars. No more."

Yeesh! Why hadn't she dickered him down when she blew a grand on the Velvet Elvis? Then I had a horrible thought. What if that *was* the haggle price?

Mr. Scammer narrowed his eyes. "Thirty."

Georgia crossed her arms over her bosom. "Fifteen and we don't call the cops on your questionable business practices."

He pursed his lips, thought about it. "Oh, all right, lady."

She extracted three five dollar bills from her wallet and handed them over. He peered at the cash, then stuffed it in his pants pocket.

"Just one minute, ladies." He ducked into the front seat for what was more like several minutes, but when he was done, he handed me a business card very much like the one Aaron had given Bertram, except with a Memphis address.

"Here you go. And don't never come back."

I tucked the card into my purse. "We wouldn't think of it."

3

The red message light on the hotel phone was blinking when we returned to our room.

"Maybe Molly called." I shrugged. "Nobody else knows we're here."

"Except Lee Munford." Georgia plopped onto the red coverlet like a sixty-something Gidget or Sandra Dee. "Well, let's find out, shug."

"I don't think it plays them out loud like an answering machine." I poised my finger over the message button.

Georgia rolled onto her back and admired herself in the overhead mirror. "That's okay, darlin'. You can tell me after you listen to it."

I put the receiver to my ear and punched messages.

A woman's voice as cold as an Artic blast and as Southern as sorghum syrup said, "You won't find the King in his castle. And you won't find the answers you seek. Go home, before someone paints *you* in a corner."

The Ice Queen! I scribbled her words on the hotel note pad. How had she known where we were? Then I realized I'd just learned another life lesson: Don't drive a pink Caddy if you want to be inconspicuous. Even one pseudo-camouflaged.

I passed the note pad to Georgia. She flopped onto her belly and read what I'd written.

"More clues," she said. "We've got to be detectives, like Cagney and Lacey."

"Yeah, you're right." I flopped on the round bed beside her. Just us two gals, having a pillow party at ten in the morning. "I think I know what the first line means."

"Uh huh?" Georgia said expectantly.

"Bertram's not at Graceland."

"Oh, Cleo, I think you're right. 'You won't find the King in his castle.'"

"And, I think we're on to something, or why else would they be warning us off. 'You won't find the answers you seek.' I think that might mean Lee Munford. Especially because of that last line, 'before someone paints you in a corner.'"

"Oh, that could be a double entendre, meaning to get into trouble and to literally be painted into a corner." Georgia's green eyes widened. "They're threatening to do to us what they did to Bertram."

That was a little scary. Could they really do that?

I put in a call to Faye.

"Ah, Mrs. Tidwell. I knew you were about to call. I could sense it with my psychic antennae. So, what may I do for you today?"

"You know that thing that was done to my husband?"

"Ye-es."

"Could it be done to me if I weren't present?"

She laughed and it reminded me of Glinda the Good Witch from *The Wizard of Oz*.

"Oh, goodness me, no. That's why your husband was abducted. He had to be physically present for it to work."

"Okay. Good to know." Relief swept over me. At least I didn't have to add the fear of being captured in a tacky painting at any given moment to my list of worries.

Faye said, "Where are you calling from? I sense you're far away."

"Memphis. Specifically, the Love Me Tender Motel." I filled her in on what all had occurred since my email update from Saturday evening which now seemed like a million years ago.

"Well, be careful. I have a feeling you have more obstacles ahead of you."

Oh, great. More obstacles. Something to look forward to. Uh huh.

"Faye, have you come up with a counter-ritual for Bertram yet?"

"Oh, golly. I was hoping you wouldn't bring that up."

"Why?" Creeping tendrils of dread threaded through my stomach. Getting Bertram back depended on Faye's counter-ritual. I certainly wasn't a witch or a Wiccan or a ceremonial magician. "What's wrong, Faye?"

"Oh, deary me." I could just picture her wringing her hands with nervous energy. "Working out a counter-transference ritual is proving tougher than I thought. There's absolutely nothing about it in *The Occult Made Easy: A-Z*, and I haven't had any success on the internet, either. I'm afraid this whole affair smacks of black magic. And finding either practitioners or published works of that sort of thing is proving to be a bit of a challenge. These people don't tend to publicize what they do."

I closed my eyes and counted to ten. A headache like tiny silver hammers banging in my brain bloomed behind my eyes.

"Faye, is this about money?" Because I was prepared to throw some her way if it would help. Whatever was within my resources to get Bertram back.

"No. This would be one of those obstacles I mentioned."

I told myself to keep it in check. Faye was doing the best she could. It wasn't every day someone hired her to hunt down that ole black magic. "Okay. Keep trying."

"I will, Mrs. Tidwell. I know there's a lot at stake. I have one more avenue to check out that might yield results."

I hung up. Georgia was over at the little table with my laptop. She waved a motel note pad page in the air.

"I Googled directions for the Blue Shoe Loony address. It's about fifteen minutes from here."

"Great. I'll be ready in a few. Gotta make some calls first."

I called Bertram's boss—the head of the music department at ASU—and gave him some cock and bull story about me and Bertram coming down with a highly contagious virus and not being able to come to work for a week. Doctor's orders. Yeah, that was me, Dr. Cleo. Then I canceled our marriage counseling session with Dr. Kerr, recycling the same reason.

Her receptionist told me, "You know, getting sick is a sign of resistance to dealing with emotional issues."

I told her, "I'm sure you're right," and hung up.

My last few calls were to cancel my twirling lessons for the rest of the week.

Then Georgia and I hit the road again to do a little reconnaissance.

4

I'm not sure what I'd been expecting. Another split-level. A Graceland knock-off. An old farmhouse.

What I hadn't been expecting was a Mexican restaurant. Los Tres Hermanos. The Three Brothers. And it appeared to be a fully functioning restaurant. There were even a few cars in the parking lot already. A neon sign—Corona Beer—blazed in the front window.

"Is it too early for lunch yet?" Georgia peered over her shades at Los Tres Hermanos.

"Georgia, this is the place. The Blue Shoe Loony gathering spot." I hated to ask, but I didn't see any way around it. "Did you Google the right address?"

She handed me both the business card and the directions she'd written down. If she'd copied them correctly, they matched up. Well, this was a puzzler.

"Maybe they meet here at night," Georgia said.

"Maybe. Seems like they'd have to meet awfully late. I'll bet this place stays open till ten or eleven. Hmm. I wonder what time they open? I'd really like to have a look."

"I'll go check." Georgia got out of the car and trotted to the front door. I figured it was a good time to call Molly.

"Cleo, I was just about to call you."

"Yeah? Any news?" Georgia was peering through the window of the restaurant's front door.

"Actually, yes."

I perked up at that.

"Elmer called. He found the location of the Blue Shoe people in Memphis."

"Wait a minute. Is it—" and I read off the address for Los Tres Hermanos.

"That's right." She sounded amazed. "How did you know that?"

Georgia was trotting back to the Caddy, happy about something.

"Long story. Georgia and I are meeting with Lee Munford this afternoon at two-thirty."

"Call me afterwards and let me know what you find out."

"Will do. Bye."

Georgia opened the passenger door and climbed into the Caddy. "They open at eleven."

It was 10:45.

"I think we need to check it out. Elmer called Molly and told her this is where they meet."

"We can get some tacos while we're here." Georgia patted her slim belly.

Something occurred to me. "Say, did Lee give you his actual address? Because I was thinking we might want to Google directions just to be on the safe side."

"He sure did. I have it here in my purse." She rummaged around, pulled out the crumpled napkin from Denny's, handed it to me.

She'd written down his full address, zip code and everything, as well as directions. But like most folks who live out in the country or who've lived somewhere a long time, he'd used landmarks that no longer existed.

Go about 10 miles down EPB, turn L where Tastee Freeze used to be. Then make a R about a mile after you pass the tree that lightning hit. If you pass railroad tracks, you've gone too far …

"Uh … yeah," I said. "I think we should Google directions. Mind if I keep this until we return to the motel?"

"You go right ahead."

I folded the napkin and tucked it in my purse.

Georgia eyed the clock on the dash. "Five more minutes. I wonder if they have real *sopapillas* here. When I was out in Hollywood, you could get some of the best Mexican food. And margaritas. When we find my son and get him out of that painting, we should have a margarita night to celebrate."

"Okay, Georgia. I'm putting you in charge of organizing it. So, tell me a little about this Lee Munford fella."

"When I knew him from Elvis's entourage in Hollywood, he didn't paint on velvet, I can tell you that. Elvis got him work painting and decorating sets in his movies. Like most artists during the early sixties, he was something of a Bohemian. Wore his hair long before it became fashionable. He and Elvis would stay up late talking about life after death, and occult mysteries, and numerology. They both liked to read. I think Lee's favorite author was Oscar Wilde. He used to say Wilde was a Bohemian before that word had even been invented."

"Sounds like an interesting guy."

"Yes, but that was Lee forty years ago. No tellin' what time will do to a man."

Several more cars had pulled into the restaurant parking lot.

"It's eleven o'clock," I said. "They should be open now."

5

A plump Latina woman showed us to a booth. The restaurant had a new-ish feel. Bright paint and spanking-clean, terra cotta floor. Big straw *sombreros* on the walls and colorful *piñatas* hanging from the ceiling. The booth seats seemed newly upholstered. No rips or tears. A couple of small TVs were mounted in opposite corners, so no matter where you sat, you could see a TV.

The news was on, a familiar woman's face on the screen in a side bar. I realized she was the woman from the missing-person's flyer at Denny's just as the reporter said, "Ruth Gruber, age 61, was found dead this morning in a ditch in West Memphis. She was last seen Saturday night at a Denny's on Elvis Presley Boulevard."

A good looking, young Latino man blocked my view of the TV. "*Buenos dias*," he said, his Spanish accent thick. "What would you like to drink?"

I ordered water. Georgia ordered tea. When he left to get our drinks, I said, "That poor woman from the Denny's flyer was found."

"What woman, Cleo?"

"The missing-persons flyer at Denny's this morning?"

Georgia looked blank.

"On the door? Ruth Gruber? Age 61?"

"Sorry, hon. I didn't notice it."

"Oh. I just saw on the TV she was found dead this morning."

"Isn't that a shame? Why can't they report some good news for a change? Like family dog saves kids from fire?"

Mr. Hot Tamale arrived with our drinks and took our order. A couple more people came into the restaurant. I just couldn't see the Blue Shoe Loonies meeting here. There was no room with all the booths and tables.

Geez. Another dead end. I wanted to rip up a bunch of napkins in frustration. Maybe this was another of those obstacles Faye had mentioned.

The food came pronto. I didn't want to admit it, but I was feeling like a second grader who'd been given a ninth grade assignment. In other words, I was in over my head. But who else was going to find Bertram? And the clock was ticking. I hoped to God we got a lead when we spoke to Lee Munford this afternoon. If not …

I wasn't going to indulge myself in "if not." It wasn't even an option. I tossed it into the recesses of my mind and left it there.

Georgia sat back in her booth seat. "Oh my, that was good. And I think I still have room for dessert."

"Great. Why don't you order us some? I'm going to head to the ladies room."

On the way there, I asked the hostess, "Have y'all been here long?"

Like our waiter, she, too, spoke with a thick Spanish accent. "No. We no here long. Open six month ago."

"Do you know what was here before?"

"I sorry. Do not know. Come from Texas." Except she pronounced it *Tay-has.*

"*Gracious, Senora. Donde esta el baño?*" Wow, I was actually getting to use my high school Spanish in the real world. Fancy that.

She pointed to the opposite end of the restaurant. When I reached the door marked *Senoritas,* I couldn't even see our booth or Georgia. I still didn't know where the Blue Shoe Loonies might meet in this place unless it was the kitchen. And I highly doubted that. My intuition was telling me they'd changed meeting locations since that card had been printed.

I took care of business, washed my hands, and dabbed on a bit of opalescent-pink lipstick. All the recent stress wasn't sitting well with my skin. I counted two new wrinkles near my mouth I'd never noticed before and a fresh zit on my chin. Great. Not quite thirty-nine and I still had acne.

I was starting to wish I was psychic. Then I'd know exactly where to find my husband. Although, if it were so damn easy, Faye would have found Bertram already without Georgia and me having to gallivant across three states.

I put on my best I'm-handling-it face and marched out of the restroom. But when I reached our booth, Georgia was gone. A couple of *sopapillas* and a pot of honey awaited us on the table. But no Georgia.

I looked around the restaurant. Business had picked up since we'd entered. Half the tables and booths were filled.

I said, "Georgia?" projecting my voice like I was on stage.

Everyone looked at me. Everyone, except Georgia.

The waiter appeared at my side. "Is problem?"

"My friend is gone."

He looked at the empty booth as if to confirm that yes, she was indeed no longer sitting there. "*El baño?*"

"I just came from there. She stayed here."

He shrugged. I wanted to smack him. But of course, it wasn't *his* problem.

"Can you bring the check?"

Then I saw that he'd already brought it and placed it next to Georgia's glass of tea. I snatched it up, and walked through the restaurant, checking every booth and table. No Georgia. Ditto the restroom. I asked the hostess if I could check the kitchen. Still no Georgia. I paid for lunch and headed out into the sunny parking lot. Maybe Georgia had gone ahead to the car. I didn't know why she'd do that, but hey, ya never know.

Nope. The Caddy was empty.

Now I had a horrible feeling, as if the world was spinning while my guts did a free fall down to the pavement. I staggered against the Caddy's pink hood. Oh, my God. First Bertram. Now his mother. Even though the day was warming up nicely, my hands were snowman cold, and I thought I heard music in my mind. I bent over quickly to get some blood in my brain before I threw up or passed out.

Once that crisis had been averted, I managed to drag myself into the Caddy and start the engine. I was going to have to go out to Lee Munford's by my lonesome. Thank God I had the address. Otherwise, I really would be up shit creek.

Scratch that.

I'd be further up shit creek.

Without a paddle.

Without a freakin' boat even.

CHAPTER FIFTEEN

Monday, October 27, Part II

1

I drove down the street. No Georgia.

Around the block. No Georgia.

Shit! Shit! Shit! Shit! Shit! Someone must have nabbed her like Ruth Gruber who'd disappeared from Denny's. The question was: Were these two disappearances connected? I didn't know. Crapola! I made a lousy detective.

As I drove back to the motel, I called D.K. and told him what had happened along with the news story about Ruth Gruber. He echoed his earlier advice about Bertram's disappearance.

"Look, Cleo. Adults have the right to be missing. It isn't like she has Alzheimer's and disappeared from a nursing home or assisted living."

"But she disappeared under fishy circumstances."

"Let me repeat. Adults have the right to be missing. When you get back to your motel room you can contact the local police station about filling out a missing persons report. Don't dial 911. The police do not want to waste their time zooming out to you for a non-emergency. Real life isn't like the movies."

"But—"

"No buts, Cleo."

"Any news on the VW van?"

"Not yet." D.K. sounded irritated. I was not making his day. Not in the least. "Try to stay out of trouble, Cleo."

"Okay, I will, D.K. I promise."

I thought I heard him say, "Yeah, when pigs fly," as I ended the call.

I speed dialed Molly next and filled her in.

"That settles it," she said. "I'm comin' to Memphis."

"God, no. What if you were to disappear? I couldn't bear it."

"Yeah, but Cleo, what if *you* were to disappear?"

I didn't say anything to that.

Molly said, "Add me to your room at the Love Me Tender. I'll be there in five hours—four, if I don't get stopped for speeding."

"Okay." There was no use arguing with my sister. When she made up her mind, she was like a tenacious bulldog.

"Are you sure you should be goin' out to see that artist all by yourself?"

"What choice do I have? Georgia had the phone number with her, so I can't reschedule. And I've got to do everything in my power to find Bertram. I'm just going to have to chance it."

"Okay, but if you feel the least bit hinky while you're there, leave. Even if it feels impolite."

"Yes, *Mom*."

"Just watchin' your back, Cleo. I'll be there as soon as I can."

Once at the motel, I went into the lobby and added Molly to the room and told the desk clerk to give her a key when she arrived. That done, I headed to Room Two. The message light on the phone was flashing. Maybe Georgia had called. Of course, Georgia had my cell number, but maybe her phone had been confiscated or lost in her misadventure.

But it wasn't Georgia.

A man with a kindly voice said, "Hey, Georgia. Lee Munford.

Something's come up and I was wondering if you and your daughter-in-law could come out to the house a little earlier? Say, one o'clock? I'm looking forward to seeing you after all these years."

What time was it now?

12:15.

Okay, I needed to Google directions and find out how long it would take to get there. I pulled the napkin with Lee's address on it out of my purse and entered the info on my computer. Thank God for free internet access and the providence to have gotten that napkin from Georgia before she'd gone poof! Since I didn't have a printer, I wrote the directions on the motel note pad. The pen was so crappy, I had to bear down hard to get it to write.

According to MapQuest, it was gonna take me at least half an hour to drive out to Lee's. And it was now 12:23. I had just enough time to brush my teeth and put on some fresh lipstick. Filing a missing person's report was just going to have to wait until I got back.

2

Lee Munford was nothing like I imagined he would be. I'd envisioned him as an aged Bohemian, long white hair pulled back in a ponytail, wearing a colorful Florida shirt, Bermuda shorts, and sandals with socks, living in some artist's commune in the wilds of Tennessee.

The only detail I got right was the white hair. But it was cut stylishly short and he was dressed like a retired preppy. Polo shirt tucked neatly into a pair of pressed khaki slacks, and deck shoes—no socks—on his feet. He reminded me of a kindly Grandpa who loved puppies and children and crossword puzzles.

He did live out in the country, a goodly jaunt south of Graceland, practically to the Mississippi state line. But there was no artist's commune. Just Lee, his golden retriever, Picasso, and a modest house built some time during the 80s on several acres of land with a swimming pool and barn out back. He said the previous owners had kept horses, but he used the barn to store his pool and yard equipment.

All in all it was a picturesque setting. His nearest neighbors were at least a quarter mile away on all sides. Perfect solitude for an artist.

He and I sat in rocking chairs on his front porch, glasses of sweet tea in our hands, Picasso lying at our feet, a jack-o-lantern on the front porch step. I'd carried the Velvet Bertram with me to the porch, but it was still wrapped in the quilt.

"I appreciate you seeing me on such short notice. I'm afraid Georgia became ill after some bad Mexican food at lunch, and she's resting at our motel." I really didn't want to go into the whole missing persons spiel, so I figured a white lie was acceptable.

Lee smiled kindly. "Is she now?"

"Uh huh. She told me to give you her regrets."

"I'm sure I'll see her soon."

There were a lot of pine trees on his property and I was struck by how clean and fresh the air smelled.

"Yeah, maybe when she feels better we can come back to see you before we go home."

God, where was Georgia? Had the Blue Shoe Loonies nabbed her, too? But why? Or was it the same person who'd snatched Ruth Gruber and then killed her? I had way more questions than answers. But maybe I'd get some answers from Lee, or at least some understanding.

Lee Munford gestured at the quilt wrapped painting I'd brought. "So, is that my painting?"

"Yes and no."

He raised his eyebrows at that.

"Let's just say it started out as your painting," I said.

"Ah. What a teaser." He settled back in the rocker, crossing his khaki-clad legs. "May I see the painting?"

"Yes, but not quite yet."

"Oh?" He sipped his iced tea. Picasso watched us as if we were a ping-pong match. "And why is that?"

"Because I have a story to tell you first. And then I hope you'll tell me one."

3

I started at the beginning. Of course, he knew some of it from the media coverage. But I didn't want to make any assumptions. And there was something about Lee Munford that made me want to spill out my whole sad story as if I were in confessional or talking with my beneficent grandpa. He just had this aura of goodness about him.

When I reached the part about Bertram possibly being the King's illegitimate son, Lee said a bit wryly, "Oh, isn't that a splendid little detail. Makes things all the more interesting."

I continued, wondering if he thought I was deranged to be telling such a crazy story. But he listened, a thoughtful look on his face. I finished with lunch at Los Tres Hermanos, but left out the part about Georgia disappearing since I'd already lied about that.

"And then I came out here to talk to you," I said, feeling a little sheepish. I knew my story was true, but hearing it out loud, it came across as a bit outlandish.

"May I see the painting now, the Velvet Bertram as you call it?"

"Yes, but answer one question for me first. Did you know it was haunted when you painted it?"

"Not at first."

It was my turn to raise a brow.

"But remember, I have my own story to tell."

I nodded, removing the quilt. Picasso whined, then jumped up and dashed off the porch. I turned away, not wanting to see my husband in such a state.

After what seemed like a long moment, Lee said, "That's my

signature, all right. But I never painted this particular subject."

I was about to protest when he added, "I believe you, Mrs. Tidwell. No need to get yourself into a tizzy. I saw the photographs of my painting in newspapers, magazines, the internet, and TV a few weeks ago. It's definitely one of mine.

"You can cover it again."

I wrapped my great-aunt Trudy's quilt around Bertram's tortured portrait. "Cleo," I said. "Please, call me Cleo."

"All right, then. Cleo. Did you know you can paint in blood?"

4

Lee smiled wryly, then took a long draught of his tea, the ice cubes clinking in his glass.

"I first met Georgia," he said, "out in Hollywood in 1962. She was a beautiful young woman. There were many who thought she might be the next Stella Stevens. Elvis was certainly taken with her, for a short while at least. He had many ladies at his beck and call, and for a time, Georgia was one of his beck-and-call girls. Which is how I met her. I'd become part of Elvis's entourage. We'd all sit around his rented Hollywood house, drink beer, watch television, shoot the shit, talk philosophy, talk books. It was like living in a fraternity house.

"Now fast forward fifteen years. 1977. I get a call from Elvis and a very strange request. He wanted me to come out to Graceland and paint a portrait of him. But a portrait of him in his prime as he had been, and I was to mix a pint of his blood into my paints."

And gee, I thought my story had sounded kooky. But hey, was there really anything that could surprise me at this point?

Lee must have noticed my expression. "Sounds fantastical, doesn't it? I'd heard the rumors, read the tabloids. I figured it was his drug-addled mind at work. But drug-addled or not, he offered me a ridiculous sum of money. You've heard the term starving artist, no doubt? Yes, well, I was still one of those. Who was I to turn down such a commission, even if it seemed more in line with *The Twilight Zone.*

"So, of course, I said yes. I wasn't a total fool. Elvis flew me out to Memphis, and I stayed as his guest at Graceland. He was up all hours of the night and slept a good part of the day from his concert schedule. It was an amazing time, but I was saddened to see my old friend in such poor health.

"One night as I'm painting, he says, 'Lee, do you ever wish you could live forever? But young, virile, and healthy?'

"Well, who hasn't entertained that fantasy at one time or another? But alas, reality just doesn't allow for such a flight of fancy to become reality.

"Or so I thought.

"Elvis says, 'What if I told you it was possible?'

"I told him, 'I'd say someone sold you a bill of goods.'

"'It's true,' he said. 'I know a swami who's going to make it happen for me. That's why you're painting this here portrait of me in my prime. He's going to do some kind of occult ritual so that all my vices go into the painting. That's why I had you mix my blood in the paint. It's part of the ritual, to create a magical connection. The me in the painting will get fat and sick and old, but as long as it exists, I'll be young and handsome again, man, like I used to be.'

"Being that Oscar Wilde was one of my favorite authors, I said, 'Elvis, that sounds like the plot from *The Picture of Dorian Gray.*'

"He nodded. 'That's right, Lee. That's right. Art inspires life. Life inspires art. You know what I mean?'

"I kept on painting. You couldn't argue with Elvis. Once he set his mind on a thing, he was hell bent on making it happen. And it also sounded like another of his wacky ideas. Like going off in spaceships, and hearing Christ speak in a bird's song, and thinking he could turn the sprinklers on and off with his mind."

Gee, that all sounded so familiar.

"I finished the painting and signed it. He'd wanted it done on velvet, maybe so people would think it was a piece of crap and not mess with it. But something must have gone wrong with the ritual, because he wound up dead on the toilet, and the painting ... the painting disappeared from Graceland.

"This is my guess," Lee said. "I'm no occultist, but I'm thinking that when things went wrong and Elvis died, his spirit was pulled into the painting due to the blood link. And if your husband really is his son, then that same blood link allowed the possession."

5

Don Rover's words flooded back to me. *And I'm seeing blood. Blood and paint mixed together.* Without even hearing Don Rover's prediction, Lee had just confirmed it with his story.

"So, what do you think happened to the painting after Elvis died?" I said.

Lee gazed out across his well-tended lawn. "Most likely someone took it as a souvenir. One of the household staff. Or a friend or family member. Probably thought it was a trinket that wouldn't be missed. It was a Velvet Elvis, after all."

"Have you painted any more Velvet Elvii since then?" Boy, it was so peaceful out here. And quiet. No neighbor sounds. Just birdsong.

"Not a one. I can show you some of my work, if you'd like."

"Sure," I said, curious to see his serious artwork. "How do you think it turned up with a roadside vendor?"

"Not a clue."

I had pretty much run out of questions for Lee Munford. His tale had cleared up the why of things, but what I really needed to know now was where the Blue Shoe Loonies had taken Bertram, and of course, I needed to find Georgia, but I didn't know if the two abductions were related or not.

"So, my dear," he stood up and proffered me his arm like a Southern gentleman. "Shall I show you my studio?"

He escorted me inside. His studio occupied a sun room at the back of the house. I was impressed by the variety of media he worked in: painting, sketching, sculpting, ceramics. It all seemed like regular art to me. Like something you'd see for sale in a fancy-schmancy gift shop.

The row of windows along the back wall gave a lovely view of his backyard and closed-up pool. Picasso was running around outside like a greyhound. He dashed along the dirt driveway that continued past the house and on down to the barn. Lee had said he kept pool and yard equipment in the barn, but he must have kept his car there, too, because no weeds grew up between the twin tire tracks. Someone drove along it pretty regular. Of course, maybe Lee kept a tractor in the barn for mowing the large yard.

Picasso disappeared inside the barn. The barn door didn't appear to be open, but from this distance it might have been cracked enough for the dog to get through.

I realized I had one more question for Lee.

"Do you know anything about The Church of the Blue Suede Shoes?"

"They pop up in the newspaper from time to time as a local interest story."

"But you've never had any dealings with them?"

The look he gave me for a brief moment was one of intense scrutiny. Then his beloved-grandpa face resurfaced. "Do you think they're connected to Elvis's occult dealings?"

"I'm asking you."

Boy, was I ballsy. I mean, Georgia might've known this guy a million years ago, but he was a stranger to me and I was in his house, just me and him, alone. No one knew where I was exactly. Geez, if I'd have been a puppy I would have whacked myself on the nose.

He glanced at his watch. "As much as I've enjoyed talking to you, I must bid you adieu. I'll show you to the door."

That's the polite Southern way of giving someone the bum's rush.

He escorted me to the front porch. We shook hands and I marched off to the pink Caddy with my quilt-wrapped Velvet Bertram. I'd cut the cans from the bumper before driving over, but the *Just Married* was still soaped on the windows. Amusing, I'm sure.

Lee stood on his porch, arms crossed over his chest, as if waiting to make sure I actually drove away, although many Southern folk will stand outside and wave as you leave their house. He watched as I stowed the painting in the front seat, and frankly, I was getting bad vibes from him. I glanced at my watch. Wow, three o'clock. Had I been here two hours? I'd really lost track of the time.

I went around to the driver's side and was about to slide my butt onto the car seat when Picasso came bounding across the yard, something pink and silky clamped in his mouth. Lee whistled for his dog, but the golden retriever galloped up within reaching distance of me. I reached down to grab his prize, but the wily dog turned on a dime and loped across the grass in yet a new direction. It was all just a big game to him. But I'd gotten a good look at what he'd been carrying.

Georgia's pink silk scarf.

6

God, I felt sick. I'd been alone with the enemy for the past two hours.

Hoping Lee hadn't seen the scarf in Picasso's mouth—the man had to be past seventy—I tumbled into the car, slammed the door, then waved out the open window as if I didn't know I'd just been talking to the lying bastard who'd kidnapped Georgia.

"Thanks for your help, Lee!" I hollered, all cheery. What I really wanted to do was spin a doughnut on his lawn and get the hell out of there as fast as the pink Caddy would go. Which wasn't that fast.

If Lee knew what his dog was running around with, he didn't give any sign. Just waved back, all Southern Gentleman-like. Which freaked me out even more. Was he toying with me, or did he truly not comprehend yet? Well, I wanted to make tracks and get to the police before he figured it out.

Stomping on the gas, I revved down the winding driveway in reverse, plowing right into the brick pillar holding Lee's mailbox. Crapadoodle! Talk about a rude awakening. I was okay, but the Caddy's poor rear had a serious dent.

I gave the steering wheel a sharp twist to the right, then stepped on the gas once more, spinning gravel as the Caddy darted onto the rural highway in front of Lee's house. I thought I'd feel safe once I got back on the road, but my hands were shaking, my legs were quivery, and I felt like I'd just drunk about ten diet colas all at once.

Here's another life lesson: don't try to navigate a curvy country road while fumbling in your purse for your cell phone.

The Caddy was all over the place, weaving as if a drunk were behind the wheel doing fifty. I finally hit pay dirt, wrapped my fingers around the phone, then glanced at the road. Adrenaline shot through me in a jolting rush as I stared at the oncoming car—an ancient VW van—before jerking the wheel to the right again, just narrowly missing a head-on collision. I think we might've had an inch to spare.

"Shit!" The roar of the wind through the open windows carried my expletive off to Oz. Yes, it is unladylike to cuss, but in certain situations it's warranted. Like barely avoiding death.

I spared the phone a glance and speed-dialed Molly. Trees, mailboxes, and farm houses flew by as I raced along the most curvaceous ribbon of asphalt I think I've ever driven on. I hoped to God I'd actually be able to hear her if she answered, because at the speed I was going, with the Caddy's windows rolled down, it was like being in a wind tunnel.

The phone rang and rang then went to voice mail. I think. Hard to tell with all the noise.

"Oh my God!" I shouted, as if Molly were the person who

couldn't hear. "It's Lee Munford. He has Georgia and he might have Bertram. He lives out in the country south of Graceland. I have his address here on the seat."

I reached for the page from the motel note pad, trying to steer one-handed while holding the cell phone, and my fanny bounced about half a foot into the air as the Caddy bumped off the road onto the gravel shoulder. The car jounced like an amusement park ride before I was able to steer back onto the tarmac.

When I was finally able to sneak a peek at the phone, all the little bars were gone. I was in a dead zone.

And if I wasn't careful, I was gonna be in a dead zone, too, just like Aaron, his brother, and Bertram and Georgia.

I had a feeling I should check the rearview mirror.

The industrial-green VW van was on my ass and closing.

BAM!

My cell phone went flying as I slammed against the steering wheel—no shoulder harness seat belt in a '56 Caddy. No seat belt at all, for that matter. The right tires rumbled onto the shoulder again. Damn! Where was that phone? Somewhere in the footwell.

I wrenched the Caddy back on the road. The van rammed me again, and my mouth hit the steering wheel, busting my lip in a bright wash of sharp pain. I swallowed a mouthful of coppery blood. Oh, God, I hope I hadn't broken a tooth. I didn't want to die, but I also didn't want caps on my teeth.

I needed that cell phone, and I couldn't grope around and drive at the same time. So I kicked off the platform shoe on my left foot as I zoomed down a country road at fifty-five miles per hour and let my toes do a search and rescue as the right foot bore down hard on the accelerator. Thank God for ambidexterity!

I peeped in the rearview again like the glutton for torture that I am. The VW van was about to ram me again. The Caddy was built like a boat, but it was also more than fifty years old. I didn't know how much more of this it could take.

The Caddy flew over a rise, passing a crossroads sign. My toes came across the phone and I pinned it down to the floor with that foot as I took the other off the gas and cranked the wheel hard to the right, hoping I didn't flip the car over.

I couldn't hold the tight turn. The Caddy bounced off the road onto the left shoulder, but the VW van overshot the junction, just like it had done on the interstate. I tapped the brake and prayed that I wouldn't veer off the shoulder or run into a ditch or swipe another brick mailbox. Not that there were any mailboxes on this stretch of road. Nope. Just me, the road, and a bunch of trees.

We jounced along for a bit until I could get the Caddy under control. Then I swerved up onto the asphalt and zipped into the right lane, just narrowly missing an oncoming truck. The driver leaned on his horn, as if I didn't know we'd almost had a fiery crash. I barreled on down the road, hoping another turn off would come up soon. It wouldn't take long for the van to hang a U and follow me again. If I could make a few turns before they got me in sight, I might be able to shake them.

The phone was still pinned down with my bare toes. I rounded a curve and came upon another crossroad.

Right or left?

I chose left.

And as the Caddy careened in that direction, I saw the VW van in my peripheral vision, swooping around the curve on the road I'd just been on. I lost my focus and shot over onto the right shoulder, swiping a mailbox, but at least it wasn't made of brick. The Caddy jounced like a carnival ride, and it was all I could do to keep the phone from sliding all over God's creation. The phone was still open, so I plucked it from the footwell, my toes like a crab claw. I was probably dialing Sweden with my foot, but that couldn't be helped. I'd just have to explain it to the cell phone company later. If I survived to call them.

Now, if I could just lift my knee and nab the phone before I dropped it again, I'd have a fighting chance of calling for help. So, with one hand on the wheel, one foot on the gas, my eye on the road, and the VW van on my ass, I hoisted my knee up, cell phone clamped between my first and second toes, and made a blind grab at it.

Bingo! I snapped it shut and crammed it down the front of my pants.

The houses along this stretch of the road were mostly ranch-style from the sixties, with large yards and fields with crops or cattle. And quite a few of them were now missing their mailboxes, thanks to moi.

The van pulled into the oncoming lane as if it were going to pass me. For a moment blind panic overtook me. I felt like a rat before the cat pounces.

It came up beside me and ran parallel. My right tires were still bumping along on the shoulder. I glanced over at the van. Big mistake. An Elvis impersonator sneered back at me from the van's passenger window.

I had about half a second to think *Bertram!* before the van rammed me again in a violent sideswipe.

I lost control of the Caddy and lurched completely off the road, rocketing across someone's yard as my insides got vigorously shaken, but not stirred. The car flattened several saplings, knocked down a Halloween scarecrow, and plowed up turf like nobody's business. But when I saw the swimming pool looming up ahead, I let out a holler and tried to stomp on the brake. It was like trying to thread a needle in a motorboat on rough seas. I just couldn't quite get my foot in the right place. And the Caddy was racing down a slope.

My foot finally made contact with the brake, but all it did was slow the Caddy down a little and deepen the furrow in my wake. I pumped the brakes again and again just like Daddy had taught me all those years ago when he gave me driving lessons out on the back roads.

The Caddy busted right through a picket fence surrounding the pool, and when the front tires hit the concrete deck, I did stamp on the brake for all it was worth, squeezing my eyes shut and turning my head away. The front end of the car pitched forward into the pool with a mighty splash that sounded like a big SPLOOSH in my ears as I smacked into the steering wheel, bruising my boobs and knocking the wind out of me. My purse, the painting, and the directions to Lee's slid off the seat with a crash. I felt like I was on the up side of a seesaw with no way to get down. And my throbbing lip was swelling up like an inflatable raft on my face.

But I was alive, at least for the moment.

I opened my eyes, wondering if I had time to get the cell phone out of my pants, call my sister, and give her the directions that had crashed to the floor and were out of reach. My intuition said, *go for it.* So I stuck my hand down the front of my hip huggers, but since I was sorta in a standing position now, the phone had slid down in my jeans to where the hip meets the thigh.

And that's when Bertram, who was now for all practical purposes Elvis, said from the pool deck, "Cleo Tidwell, look at what you've done to Mama's car. And what are you doing with your hand down your pants?"

CHAPTER SIXTEEN

Monday, October 27, Part III

1

Being tied up is bad. You develop maddening itches in places that up to this point were perfectly fine and you weren't even aware of. And of course, you can't reach them. And try riding in a vehicle with your hands behind your back. You can't sit back, you have to lean forward, your shoulders are uncomfortably rotated, and you can't balance worth a damn on curves or sudden stops. Add a seat belt to this mix and you can include claustrophobia to your list of why your day turned to shit. Then throw in a busted lip, bruised boobs—oh, and a gun pointed at your head, and you can see why I would have been in a mood worthy of one of my worst PMS days.

Bertram, or rather, Elvis in Bertram's body, twisted around in the front passenger seat of the VW van to look at me.

"Cleo, why'd you have to go poking your nose where it doesn't belong?"

I summoned my iciest voice. "Maybe because I love my husband?"

"He no longer exists, darlin'."

Oh, that was like a spear to my heart. But I knew it wasn't altogether true. Faye had said Bertram's spirit was in the velvet painting. I was going to choose to believe she was right, otherwise, there was no hope.

And there had to be hope.

Bertram was not lost to me.

He wasn't.

"Then who are you, exactly?" Talk about identity theft.

He gave me a thoughtful look. After a moment he said, "Jesse. I think I'll go by Jesse Garon."

"Okaaaaay. Where in tarnation did that name come from?"

"It's Bubba's name."

"Who the hell is Bubba?"

The gal sitting next to me with the gun in her hand smacked me upside the head.

"Ow!"

"The King's brother, you Jezebel."

I'd recognize that voice anywhere. The Ice Queen!

Well, now I knew which team she played for. And realized I'd seen her before. She'd been the female Elvis impersonator at the Blue Shoe Loony bin. She was actually pretty without the Elvis get-up.

"The King has a brother?" News to me. Or was it? I couldn't keep all the trivia straight between those in the know such as Georgia, Elmer, and now, Jesse.

"*Had*, Jezebel." The Ice Queen was waving the gun around which didn't do much for my already shot nerves. "A twin. Jesse Garon. Died at birth."

And the TV psychic's prediction echoed in my head: *a twin. Your husband has traded places with a twin. You've got to oust the twin without destroying the body before the mother returns."*

Elvis had been a twin. No wonder the Blue Shoe Loonies had tried to reincarnate the spirit of Elvis via the Vassal twins. And I didn't know what the last part meant. *Before the mother returns.* What mother? Whose mother? Of course, the whole body/spirit switcharoo mumbo jumbo thing still didn't make a whole lotta sense to me, but then I wasn't a certified occult cuckoo, either.

"Does she really have to point that thing at me?" I said. "What if it goes off by mistake?"

The newly minted Jesse Garon said, "You can lower your weapon, Ruby."

"You sure, boss?" she said in the thickest hick accent, her tone like a frosty wind. "What if she pulls somethin'?"

"She won't be pullin' anything." Jesse Garon glared at me. "Will you, Cleo?"

I shook my head no.

The Ice Queen lowered her gun. Which gave me one less thing to be bitchy about.

"So, did you kill Aaron Vassals?" My back was aching already from having to lean forward. The curvy, winding road was killing me ergonomically. I made a mental note to never allow myself to be taken hostage ever again.

"No, darlin'. That was the work of the Blue Suede Shoe members. They didn't realize at that point that I was inhabiting your husband and had vacated the painting. So when they tried to do a soul swap with Aaron, it killed him. Ditto for his twin brother. Don't ask me to tell you how. I never did understand that hocus pocus stuff.

"But they figured things out and came and got me. A little presto, chango, and next thing I knew, I was the only tenant in this here body. And your husband's soul was in the paintin'."

The painting! There'd been no way come hell or high water that I was leavin' the painting to sink with the Caddy. Without it, there'd be absolutely zero chance of ever getting my husband back. But Bertram—or rather, Jesse—had taken it from me as I'd been rudely escorted to the van. It lay on the floor between the front seats. So close and yet so far. But at least it wasn't in the bottom of a swimming pool.

"You're sure Bertram's totally gone?"

Jesse Garon smirked. "Absolutely. Ain't no one home but me."

Well, wasn't that just spiffy? I was so not in the mood for this. However, being that my bitch quotient was still pretty high, I just couldn't pass up the opportunity to pick at things.

"Lee told me about mixing your blood with his paints. That's what allowed you to possess my husband, wasn't it?"

Jesse Garon said, "Lee always had an eye for the pretty girls. And speakin' of pretty girls, is that one of them new-fangled mobile phones in your pants leg or are you just happy to see me?"

Well, damn! So much for keeping that a secret until a crucial moment.

Jesse gave me his trademark sneer. "Think I wouldn't notice? A gal with a behind as nice as yours? Funny how it's been twenty-six years since I died and women are still wearing hip huggers."

"You know what I find funny? You're nothing like I expected you'd be."

"And how's that, darlin'? Genteel? Kindly? Try getting stuck in a painting for a quarter century and see how nice you are once you get out. I do have to say your husband has a great body. Hard to believe he's forty. I was considered a washed up has-been at that age. Took about fifty different kinds of pills. Couldn't keep the weight off. But this body is fit and healthy. Your husband's a good lookin' fellow, too. And virile."

He had the nerve to leer at me. He was probably remembering our love making from when he'd shared a body with Bertram.

"So what happens now?" My hands were going numb. If I had to stay in this position much longer, I was going to lose it.

"You'll see. Wouldn't want to spoil the fun by telling you."

Ruby the Ice Queen smirked at that. I clamped my mouth on a smart-ass reply and we drove the rest of the way in silence. The old VW van didn't have any side windows, so I couldn't see much of where we were going. But I had a suspicion we were heading back to Lee Munford's place.

And I was right.

We turned into Lee's winding driveway, passed the house, and wound our way to the barn. A garage had been added to the side of the barn, and we pulled into it. I blinked back tears. I would not cry in front of these people. No matter that I was in the middle of nowhere, that nobody knew quite where I was, that no one but the bad guys would be able to hear me scream or call for help, that my cell phone was about to be confiscated, and that my beloved husband had been taken over by a dead icon. I was a steel magnolia. I did not break down in times of crisis.

Yeah, right. Who was I kidding? I was a wuss if I didn't have a diet cola every few hours or forgot to take a lipstick with me when I went shopping. And I was a major wuss if the power went out and I couldn't take a warm shower, or wash my hair, or shave my legs.

I had a feeling my days of being a major wuss were just beginning, assuming that I even had any more days left in my life.

"Okay, Miss Priss," Jesse Garon said. "End of the line. This is where we get out."

The Ice Queen gripped my arm so hard, I thought she was going to cut off the blood flow. Damn, but she was strong. I wondered if she wrestled gators in her spare time.

She hauled me across the seat and out of the van. My phone was still wedged in my jeans where my hip met my thigh. Yes, my jeans were that tight.

The driver got out and crossed in front of the van to join the three of us. I recognized him as the guy with the baseball bat on the way to Memphis.

Jesse Garon came up so close to me, we were almost touching. I looked up into his face, so like Bertram's, yet so not like Bertram's. The person behind the eyes was definitely not Bertram. But my body didn't know that. All it knew was I had tremendous sexual chemistry with the person standing before me. My pulse quickened and my breathing deepened. My eyes were probably dilating, but I couldn't help that. Nor could I help the trembling. If I was lucky, he'd mistake it for fear.

Jesse told his lackeys, "Leave us for a moment."

The Ice Queen said, "Are you sure that's a good idea?"

Jesse just glared at them. They backed out of the garage, exiting through a side door that led into the barn.

When we were alone, he grasped my arms and pulled me against his chest. It surprised me and I gasped.

"You're a pretty gal," he said. "And a nice piece of ass. Don't think I haven't forgotten making love to you."

He's not Bertram, he's not Bertram, he's not Bertram, I repeated to myself like a mantra.

A single tear rolled down my face. Traitor! No crying allowed in front of the enemy.

Jesse tilted my chin up. Pressed against him as I was, it was hard not to notice his Mr. Pop Up and Say Hello.

"I'm not such a bad guy—"

"Don't. Don't even go there. You're not Bertram. You might have his body, but you're not him."

"But I could be him if I wanted." He leaned down and brushed his lips against mine. Damnation! A jolt of pleasure shot straight to my hoo-ha. I couldn't control my trembling now. My body wanted him so much, but my mind said no. *Fight it!*

He brushed my hair away from my face. "I was always a good actor. I could become him." He nodded toward the door to the barn. "Those guys think I'm their savior returned from the dead. They think I'll pick up the yoke of the King and resume my glory days."

My body ached so badly for Bertram's, I wanted to cry out from the tension.

Jesse caressed me with exquisite slowness from my jaw down past my collar bone, brushing a breast, trailing along my abs all the way to my hip. He might not be Bertram in spirit, but his body remembered. I shivered with desire. I really couldn't help it. Bertram's hands knew exactly how to play me, and I was practically thrumming from his attentions.

"When I was famous," he said, "I often yearned to be a regular man again, to live a regular life. Anonymity is a gift. You don't realize it until you've lost it. I could live a regular life again. I could be Bertram Tidwell, regular man."

"But I'd always know you weren't. And I don't love you. I love Bertram."

"I beg to differ with you, darlin', but your body says differently." He cupped my breast, and honest to God, I sighed with pleasure.

I wanted him to stop.

I didn't want him to stop.

He kissed me again, deep, passionate. With my eyes closed, I couldn't tell it wasn't Bertram. He smelled like Bertram, a musky, manly smell that reminded me of gym socks, but in a good way. He kissed like Bertram, all sultry smokiness that stoked my fire.

When he broke the kiss, I was breathless. Absolutely breathless. And confused.

And my panties were wet. And wouldn't you know it, I didn't have any spare underwear with me. Isn't that the way things work out sometimes?

He kissed my chin, then nuzzled my neck, sending a little thrill shooting through me with each touch. He worked his way south, leaving a trail of delicious pulsations that had me all in a tizzy. He rucked up my shirt and pressed his lips to my belly button, and I thought, *If he doesn't stop, we're going to have sex, right here, right now, in this garage.*

He didn't stop.

I moaned. This was so wrong. And soooo confusing.

But my hoo-ha disagreed.

She thought it was right, so very right.

He unbuttoned the top of my jeans and unzipped them as every nerve cell in my skin sizzled with anticipation. He peeled the tight jeans from my hips with such agonizing slowness, I wanted to shout at him to just throw me down and have his way with me already.

My cell phone fell out of my pants and hit the floor. At that point I didn't care. A nuclear bomb could have gone off, and I wouldn't have cared. My hoo-ha was quivering with need. Quivering! And God knows, we had to keep my hoo-ha happy.

I was barefoot. Jesse … Bertram … whoever he was, slid my jeans down my legs and tugged them free.

"Untie me," I whispered.

"You might escape," his voice was husky with need. He almost sounded like Bertram.

"Would that be so terrible?"

He seized me, kissing me so hard my busted lip wanted to scream. He was still fully dressed, but I could tell he wanted me bad.

Sex was the only weapon I had. My choices were commit quasi-adultery and stay alive, or be a good girl and wind up dead in a ditch somewhere. Gee, that's what I call a no brainer.

So I said, "I can't touch you the way you like if my hands are tied."

He spun me roughly, yanking off the bonds around my wrists. I heard him undo his zipper, and as I pulled my arms to my chest, he pushed me forward so that I had to brace myself against the van. But at least my arms were now free.

My panties were heading south under his guidance when a door knob rattled and a pair of thirsty hinges screeched.

Then Lee Munford said, "Some things just never change, I see."

2

Yikes! Talk about getting caught with your pants down. I yanked my panties back up, absolutely mortified.

Jesse zipped up. "Lee, don't you know you should knock before opening a closed door? And turn your back so the lady can have a moment of privacy, man."

"I had no idea you'd turned the garage into a love shack."

"Just wanted one last time with the little wife."

Was he acting or sincere? A few moments ago he'd expressed doubts about being these people's savior. Maybe I could use that to my advantage until the cavalry arrived.

Oh, wait. There would be no cavalry. No one knew where I was. I was going to have to depend on myself.

I wasn't off to a very good start.

Jesse handed me my jeans and I shimmied into them. When I faced the two men, my face flamed with embarrassment. It wasn't every day I got felt up in a garage and then caught with my bare bum hanging in the breeze. I'd sunk to an all-time low. Martha Jane would be appalled.

"She's decent," Jesse said. "You can turn around now."

Lee was holding my cell phone, checking my call log. "You called your sister. Who else knows you're here?"

Well, I could have said Georgia, but the jig was up, and he knew I knew that he knew she wasn't sick back at the hotel. I'd bet my great-aunt Trudy's inheritance she was somewhere nearby.

So I fibbed. "A whole lotta people know I'm here. My sister, her boyfriend, my parents, the police, the Marines ..." Okay, maybe I was stretching it with the Marines. But damn it, I was pissed off with this guy and his loony associates.

"You're a bad liar, Mrs. Tidwell." Lee snapped my cell phone shut with a rude flourish. "It'll be awhile before anyone realizes what has happened to you, and by then, it'll be too late. For you, of course," he added, in case I didn't get that.

Ergh!

"The way I see it, Mrs. Tidwell," Lee said. "You have a choice. We can either tie you up again—"

I shook my head vigorously. *NO!*

"Or you can accompany us peacefully, and we'll delay restraining you."

I didn't like the way he'd said delay. But at least I didn't have to be tied up at the moment.

"I'll come peacefully."

I glanced at Jesse but couldn't read his expression. He seemed to be considering something, but whether it had to do with my plight, or his, or something else altogether, I had no idea.

So I followed Lee through the door I figured led to the barn. But rather than a storage area for yard equipment or the ghosts of horses past, the barn had been converted into what seemed like a replica of our room at the Love Me Tender Motel where shag carpet, overhead mirrors, and gaudy taste ruled. Georgia was gagged and tied to one of the gold plush armchairs. And a metal coffin, caked with dirt and red clay, balanced across a set of sawhorses smack dab in the middle of guadyland.

3

I glimpsed a bathroom, floored in marble, through an open doorway to the right of the round bed. The porcelain throne was fit for a king. There was another door opposite the one we'd just come through, but it was closed. Stacks of books on the occult, religion, and pharmacology rose in teetering towers from the dresser tops and on the floor beside the bed. Someone who had known Elvis very well had designed this room. And I guessed that someone was Lee.

I rushed to Georgia, happy to find her alive, and removed the gag.

"Thank you, Cleo, darlin'!" She fixed our host with her most forbidding look. "Lee Munford, I declare. What harum-scarum notion are you entertaining? Abducting an old friend. You should be ashamed."

I wanted to add a hearty, *Yeah!*, but held my tongue. We weren't exactly guests.

But Lee was far from shamed. "If you untie her, Mrs. Tidwell, I will have you shot."

I prayed a wee part of Bertram still remained in his body, and then took a leap of faith.

"Bertram," I said, in my most chastising Martha Jane voice. "This is your mother sitting here! How can you stand to let her be treated like this?"

A look of confusion flitted across his face. "That's not my mama." But he didn't sound so sure.

Lee waved me off. "We haven't time for this," he said, addressing Jesse Garon. "If we're going to transfer Gladys to this living receptacle, we need to do it now."

"Gladys?" I said. "Who's Gladys?"

"The King's mother, rest her soul," Georgia said. "Lee Munford, I cannot believe you dug up her body. And from the Meditation Garden at Graceland. Of all the low down skunkery. Disturbin' a poor woman's rest. Someone oughta paddle your backside."

I now understood the rest of Don Rover's psychic revelation. *You've got to oust the twin without destroying the body before the mother returns."* Elvis had to be expelled from Bertram without killing Bertram's body before Gladys was transferred into Georgia. Then I'd have my husband back.

Oh, sure. No sweat. Easy as pie.

Riiiiight.

Georgia piped up again. "Oh, Lee, you have got to be kidding. This is the last thing Gladys Presley would have wanted. She'd roll over in her grave if she knew what you were up to."

All four of us looked at the coffin. I had this image of a severely decomposed woman rolling over within its confines. It wasn't a pretty picture.

That look of confusion crossed Jesse's face again. "She's right, Lee. Mama would want to rest in peace. She died almost fifty years ago. The world now would confuse her. Hell, it confuses me. All these gadgets and computers. She wouldn't be happy."

But Lee was not to be deterred. "Our mission all along has been to resurrect you and your sainted mother into the flesh, so that your hallowed work might be finished. We've accomplished one miracle so far and are only moments from accomplishing another."

"But what about what I want?" Jesse smacked his hand on a bit of bare space on the dresser beside him. "I have no desire to be worshipped again. I just want to be a regular man."

Lee gave Jesse a no-nonsense look. Why had I ever thought this guy was a kindly grandpa type?

"I didn't ask your opinion, now did I?"

I recognized the storm clouds brewing on Jesse's expressions. They were Bertram's storm clouds. He glanced at me and Georgia, then at Lee, indecision warring on his face.

"The whole reason we started this thing, Lee, was so that I could transfer my vices to that trashy paintin' of yours and then do a disappearing act and go live out my life in good health and anonymity. I don't care a toot about what you or the church members want from me and Mama. I get to choose how I live my life."

"I'm afraid you don't. You're an icon; you belong to the world. We have plans for you, my friend. Big plans. A permanent Church of the Blue Suede Shoes tabernacle dedicated to you and your sainted mother in Salt Lake City. A World's Greatest Impersonator show in Vegas. And when the time is right, a run for the Presidency! If the Gipper could do it, so can you. What are a couple of nobodies," he gestured at me and Georgia, "compared to all of that?"

A couple of nobodies! Who did he think he was?

Oh, wait. A crazy cuckoo. There's just no talking logic with a kook.

It was good to know that Jesse didn't want to take up his former cross, so to speak, and pick things up where he left off. Fame is what had ruined him the first time.

"You are your own man, Jesse," I said. "You don't have to do what he says."

Georgia added her two cents. "Sugar, you had a lot of vices, but stealin' was not one of them. Do you really want to be part of a group that steals other people's bodies? Their lives?"

Lee smirked. "Don't listen to them. They're about to die and they're desperate." He strode to the louvered closet door on the wall opposite the bed and removed what appeared to be a black choir robe from a hanger. "It's time to call in the inner circle. Come get into your robe like we rehearsed."

Jesse pierced me with an anguished look, then took a couple of steps toward the closet.

Crapazoid! The sands of our hour glass had just about run out.

I glanced over at the casket again. "Jessie, what will your mama say when she finds out what you've been up to?"

The man that had my husband's body stopped in his tracks as if he were playing statue. His head swiveled our way again and this time, a determined light gleamed in his eyes. He sneer smiled at us, but it was one of compatriotism, not condescension. Lee missed out on this whole interchange as he dropped a black robe over his head.

Jesse reared into motion again and stalked to the closet like a bull moose. He definitely had a height advantage going on. Before the robe could clear Lee's head, Jesse balled up his fist and knocked the older man's lights out. Kapowie! I almost cheered.

"Get my phone," I stage whispered to Jesse while I fiddled with Georgia's knots. I didn't know how close the rest of the inner circle might be.

Jesse Garon gingerly fished my phone from Lee's pants pocket, probably concerned the man would regain consciousness. But he was out cold. I spotted a letter opener on the desk near Georgia's chair and snatched it to cut through her bonds. The rest of the Blue Shoe Loonies were likely to show up any moment now and I was all thumbs from nervous tension.

Jesse came over and helped me, and we freed Georgia in no time.

The funny thing was, I was thinking of him as Bertram again. This was the kind of thing Bertram would have done.

As if reading my thoughts, he said in a voice that was all Elvis, "My mama wouldn't have been happy in this woman's body."

"The King loved his mother dearly." Georgia rubbed her wrists and flexed her feet. I helped her stand.

"What now?" I asked.

"The keys are still in the van," Jesse said. "Let's high-tail it out of here before they defile Mama and put me in Vegas impersonator hell."

As the three of us trundled through the adjoining door to the garage, the bedroom door on the opposite side of the room smacked open, and a gaggle of Blue Shoe Loonies in full Elvis regalia burst in. One of them pulled a gun and fired at us. The gunshots were deafening. I now understood why people wear ear protection at an indoor shooting range.

I think someone yelled, "Cease fire, you big dummy! You might hit the King and the receptacle for his sainted mother." But it was kinda hard to tell because my ears were ringing so bad.

I kicked the door we'd just gone through shut and then locked it. Not that it would hold for long with all those Blue Shoe people putting some muscle to it, but it would buy us a little time.

Georgia and I practically dove into the van as Jesse ran around to the driver's side. I never thought I'd actually be happy to be inside the Volkswagen. Jesse cranked the engine as I banged the sliding door shut.

He shouted, "The garage door is closed! Hold on!"

Since there was zero time to fasten our seat belts, Georgia and I clung to the back of the seat, but as the van shot backwards, we were both flung forward, slamming into the front seats. The Blue Shoe Loonies must have breached the locked door because someone fired at us. A couple of shots zinged through the windshield with ear-splitting cracks, splintering the glass into a spider web of fissures.

We crashed through the garage door with a screech of metal and rocketed out of the barn, arcing a half-circle through the tall grass. Jesse stomped on the brake to put the van in drive, and Georgia and I smacked against the seat we'd been trying to sit on just a few seconds earlier. Lordy, our bruises were going to have bruises. I made a mental note to never take a job as a crash dummy.

Georgia smiled wanly. "When can we get off the ride?"

Good question. I'd been wanting off ever since dead Aaron and the Velvet Bertram had shown up at my house. But sometimes you don't have a choice.

I braced for Jesse to full-throttle it down Lee's driveway, but he shifted into park and said, "Well, I'll be a monkey's uncle."

An amplified voice outside the van said, "This is the police. We have you surrounded. Put down your weapons and come out with your hands up."

I slumped down on the floor, squeezing one of Georgia's hands. The cavalry *had* arrived.

Jesse opened the driver's door and eased out of the van. I heard Molly shout, "That's my missing brother-in-law!"

"Molly's here!" I said to Georgia with the excitement of a three-year-old. My sister must have burned some serious rubber getting to Memphis.

Georgia flashed her dazzling Hollywood smile at me, one that would have been right at home on the red carpet. "Well then, let's not waste any more time, shug."

There was no way I was going to leave the Velvet Bertram behind, so I grabbed it, and we crawled out of the van. Georgia had both of her hands in the air, but I could only get one up with the painting under my arm. Didn't want the police to think we were Blue Shoe Loonies. But as soon as Molly saw us she shrieked. If Elmer hadn't held her back, she would have broken the police line and dashed to us. So she had to settle for shouting, "That's my sister and her mother-in-law!"

Everything was happening so fast, it took me a moment to process that Elmer Inglebright was here in Tennessee, when a few hours ago, he'd supposedly been down in Sarasota, Florida. Course, he *was* a guardian angel. Maybe he took the Angel Express and poofed himself across four states to be with his honey in her time of need. I don't know. I was still gettin' used to the idea that angels didn't have white, feathery wings and play harps up in the clouds.

Anyway, me, Georgia, and Jesse tromped across Lee's yard toward the police line. Lee hadn't cut his grass back here in awhile, and it had gone to seed, looking more like a wheat field than a lawn. I felt like Dorothy and friends in *The Wizard of Oz* as they run through a meadow of poppies to get to the Emerald City. Only instead of Toto, I was lugging the Velvet Bertram. I hoped no one asked to see the painting. I wasn't sure how I was going to explain it.

The Blue Shoe Loonies were emerging from the barn and garage, their hands in the air, too. There had to be fifty to sixty of them. They looked like a bunch of certified wackos in their Elvis impersonator outfits. I spotted Dupree Hardcastle and Mavis Mathews amongst them as well as the Ice Queen. She supported Lee Munford as he limped out of the barn. I guess Jesse Garon had really rung his bell. Served him right for deciding to foist my husband's soul into a tacky ole velvet painting while stealing his body for a long dead pop icon to inhabit. I hoped he spent the rest of his life in jail.

Everything was going well. The sun was setting behind us, and I was walking behind and slightly to the right of Bertram, with Georgia a couple of yards to my right. I could see Molly quite clearly now. She and Elmer made encouraging, you're-almost-there gestures, as if they wished we could hurry up and be safe, but knew we couldn't rush it.

We were almost to the police line when a gunshot cracked the late afternoon.

Bertram stumbled back against me and we tumbled to the ground in a flailing heap as Georgia and Molly screamed. Bertram's six-foot-four frame was squashing me into the overgrown grass, and I couldn't breathe and I couldn't holler. I tried to push him off me just so I could get some air, but I couldn't budge him. His backside was slick with moisture, and I wondered if we'd fallen in a puddle, even though everything had looked dry when we'd been walking.

A cacophony of sound erupted around us. People shouting, women crying, car doors opening and then slamming shut, the static from a police radio. I heard someone say, "He's been shot."

My hands were painted with blood. Bertram's blood.

Oh, my God. It couldn't end this way. Bertram's soul was trapped in that painting, and if we didn't do the transfer soon, he'd be stuck there forever. And if his body died, same thing. I couldn't live without Bertram. It had taken me fourteen years and two marriages to find him again. And recent events had taught me that having true love in my life was more important than social status or caring what other people thought. I wanted Bertram.

I thought I heard Molly say, "He's crushing her. Can't you see she's not breathing?"

And then I blacked out.

FINALE:

LOVE ME TENDER

CHAPTER SEVENTEEN

Friday, October 31
All Soul's Night

1

Every stone in the wall around Graceland has a story to tell. For almost forty years, fans from all over the world have journeyed to this mecca to pay tribute to a dead king. They've signed their names in paint, permanent marker, even nail polish—all of them expressions of love, echoing the names of his songs.

I imagined the millions of people who had touched this very wall over the decades: women and men, young and old, rich and poor. The clothing styles might have changed, but they all shared one thing in common—a love for Elvis.

I grasped the wall with both hands. From the street I probably seemed like an ordinary fan, coming to soak up the magic of the King's residence. And in a way, that wasn't far from the truth.

The setting sun hit the graffiti-covered barrier full on from the west. No shadows here. But there soon would be. Like the shadow in my heart where Bertram used to be.

The metal gate to my right, commissioned to resemble sheet music, swung open with a clang, and a tour bus full of satisfied Elvis lovers exited the property.

It was almost time.

Our tickets were for six-thirty. By the time we wrapped up the tour at the Meditation Garden, where Elvis and his family were interred, it would be full dark. And it was All Soul's Night, popularly known as Halloween. According to Faye, it was the time of year when the veil between the world of the living and the world of the dead was the thinnest. A time when crossing over would be the easiest.

2

I traversed the four-lane street to the Visitor Center with care. The last thing I needed was to get hit by a car, or God forbid, a tour bus. Wouldn't that be the ultimate irony?

I found my party of six in the gift shop inside the Visitor Center. They'd been passing the time till I returned by browsing the glass shelves lined with Graceland snow globes, Elvis fridge magnets, and all manner of souvenirs, including a board game—Elvis-opoly.

I went up to each one in turn. My voluptuous sister. Her red-headed beau from Florida. My glamorous mother-in-law. Faye Eldritch wearing a beige sweater set and pearls. A white witch from New York City, Peyton Carole—author of *The Rainbow Stone Book* and High Priestess of the Circle of Persephone—dressed in a smart Donna Karan outfit, Nine West heels, and a Dooney & Bourke clutch.

And a tall scarecrow of a man with a gimp leg. He'd been lucky. The bullet had passed through his thigh and missed his femur. No major arteries or veins had been struck, although there had been a lot of blood. And he had to walk with a cane. But the doctors thought he wouldn't need it in a few months.

"It's time," I said.

3

Everyone on the crowded tour bus slipped on the headsets provided. Everyone, except me and Molly. We shared a seat, while Faye and Georgia sat one up from us and Peyton Carole sat across the aisle. Elmer and the man I used to call my husband sat right behind us.

I leaned over and half-whispered to my sister, "So, how did you find us?"

I'd been wanting to know for days, but had been preoccupied with other matters. Like hovering over my husband's body in the hospital. And keeping the Velvet Bertram safe. And brainstorming with Faye and Elmer on how to make the switch before Bertram was stuck in black velvet forever. Which was how Peyton Carole had come to be involved.

"You bear down hard when you write, Cleo. We found an impression of the directions to Lee Munford's on the motel note pad in your room."

I nodded sagely as if I'd known the answer all along. Nice to know a crappy pen can save your life.

The tour bus rumbled from the Visitor Center across Elvis Presley Boulevard and through the entrance gate. We rounded the horseshoe driveway and came to a stop in front of Graceland, a two-story, faux-stone house with a front porch in the Greek-revival style—sorta like a plantation house, but much smaller. In fact, most first-time visitors to Graceland are amazed at how much smaller the house is when they see it in person.

Everyone got off the bus and gawked.

A tour guide directed us inside to the foyer. "Photographs are allowed, but please, no flash photography or video."

I patted the oversized purse hanging over my shoulder. I'd carefully removed the Velvet Bertram from the canvas stretcher, rolled it up, and stowed it in my bag, but not before taking a razor blade and scraping some of the dried paint into an envelope. That envelope was tucked into my bra at the moment. I wasn't taking any chances.

4

My first impression was that I'd stepped into Gaudy-land. Whoever had decorated The Love Me Tender Motel had been right on the mark. Graceland was just old and sad without any charm. Groovy that had lost its groove. I normally would have made cutting remarks about the tacky decor, but held my tongue since the man responsible was right beside me.

Our little group meandered through the parts of the house open to tourists, giving Jesse Garon plenty of time to visit his home one last time and say goodbye. We looked into the living room with its snowy white carpet, and his mama's bedroom with the deep purple curtains and bedspread, and the dining room featuring a table that could easily seat ten, set as though dinner were about to be served at any moment. Everything was so pristine, but then each room on the tour was roped off with Please-Do-Not-Touch signs.

Graceland's second floor was off limits to everyone but the Presley family. So we passed through the surprisingly small kitchen where Elvis's cook had made many a fried peanut butter and banana sandwich, and down to the basement to see the TV room with its bar and three televisions—considered hi-tech in Elvis's day.

After that it was on to the billiards room. The walls were covered in a busy, paisley fabric that didn't make me want to spend any time there.

Then it was back upstairs where we walked past the jungle room, complete with faux-greenery, a stone water fountain along one wall, and furniture upholstered in faux zebra and leopard.

Jesse Garon was quiet and thoughtful the entire time. He lingered in the museum room where many of his possessions were on display. Then we toured the grounds out back, stopping in for a peek at his father's old office, and on to the gold-album museum, the tiny outdoor pool, and the racquetball court that now housed his jumpsuit collection and more gold records.

I'd given Jesse Garon a photograph of Bertram to carry with him. From time to time he'd pause to look at it. I wanted to remind him that the man he currently saw in the mirror had been a real person with a family who loved him.

And we wanted him back.

5

We came to the final stop on the tour, the Meditation Garden, where Elvis, his parents, and his grandmother were buried. His mother's casket had been returned to its rightful place beside her son's body. The officials were still baffled as to how the Blue Shoe Loonies had been able to get a coffin out of the ground without disturbing the earth or alerting any security guards, but when you're dealing with black magic, anything's possible, I suppose.

I've never thought of burial sites as "pretty," but this one was. A circular wrought-iron railing surrounded the four marble slabs that radiated like spokes on a wheel from a circular pool full of dancing water fountains. A beautifully engraved metal inlay covered each slab with the particulars about each of the deceased. Flowers of every color left by adoring fans decorated Elvis's grave, along with cards, letters, and teddy bears. The lawn had obviously been re-sod as the grass appeared undisturbed.

Jesse Garon hung back. During his hospital stay, I think I'd convinced Jesse Garon that he was doing the right thing. It was important that he be willing to surrender the body he'd stolen. To help him see the true man in the mirror, we'd gotten his hair cut and shaved the sideburns off, and I'd given him clothes that Bertram would have selected: khaki pants, polo shirt, windbreaker, and tennis shoes. His glasses were still back in Alabama. But he did have the makings of a beard again.

This was hard on him. But stealing was just plain wrong. And body snatching was virtually unforgivable. He was actually a decent man when you got to know him, and under different circumstances I might have been able to love him, but Bertram was the man I loved. And Bertram deserved better than eternal entrapment within a piece of black velvet. I reached out my hand now to this man who wore my husband's clothes, body, and face.

"You know what has to be done," I said.

He nodded solemnly and tucked Bertram's photograph into his back pants pocket. Then leaning on his cane, he took my hand and stepped up to the rail before Elvis Aaron Presley's grave.

6

Peyton Carole joined us. Tall and elegant, she possessed the physique of a retired ballerina. "This place is magic," she said to Jesse Garon. "Your fans have made it magic. Can you feel their love?"

Jesse Garon closed his eyes, his expression beatific as though he were listening to sweet music that only he could hear.

"Yes," he whispered.

Since Faye was a relatively new and solo practitioner of the occult without a network of like-minded souls to call upon, she'd contacted Peyton Carole via the email address in the back of *The Rainbow Stone Book* and convinced her (with the help of a few greenbacks) to fly down to Memphis and conduct the body switching ceremony. When I'd picked her up at the airport, I'd blurted out, "You don't look like a witch." She'd smiled at my faux pas and said, "And what do witches look like?" Touché. Elmer had told me getting dead people out of live ones was not one of his powers. So he was just here for the emotional support ... and Molly.

Peyton said, "You know your rightful place is with your own body ... in that grave before us."

Jesse Garon blanched, but nodded. "Yes. I know."

"Are you willing to surrender this mortal shell so that its true owner may return?"

When Jesse Garon didn't reply, I wanted to kick him. He better not back out on this.

After what seemed like several agonizing minutes, but was more like a few seconds, he said, "I'm willing."

Peyton smiled warmly. "You may say your goodbyes."

Jesse Garon tipped my face up with the hand not holding the cane and gently pressed his lips to mine. "I'm glad I got to know you, Cleo Tidwell. I'm sorry about all of this."

"Apology accepted," I said quickly. I was antsy to get on with things.

He nodded at Peyton. "Okay."

She took my place to his left and joined hands with Jesse Garon. I stepped around to his right shoulder, ready to do my part.

"Blood is the key. Follow the blood and I will guide your energy."

That was my cue. Blood *was* the key. Elvis had followed the blood tie from the painting into Bertram. To get Elvis back into the grave, we needed his blood. But using Bertram's blood would take Bertram down into the grave, too. At first, I'd panicked, wondering how the hell we were going to get blood from a man who'd been dead for several decades. Then I remembered Lee's story about how he'd mixed a pint of Elvis's blood into his paints. And a flare had gone off in my brain.

I reached into the V-neck of my shirt and slipped the envelope containing the dried paint flakes out of my bra. Then I slit it open with a fingernail and leaned over the wrought-iron rail to sprinkle the contents on Elvis's grave marker, saying a prayer that all this would work.

As for getting Bertram back into his body, Elmer's theory's was that once Elvis was out of the way, Bertram would snap back into himself like a stretched rubber band that's been released. That was the hope, anyway.

I'd tuned out the crowd noises, but now as I waited, cameras clicked and whirred, and people murmured sentiments of awe and love at getting to behold the King's final resting site. If only they knew the King was standing right beside me in another man's body!

Jesse Garon sagged against the rail as if all the strength had gone out of his legs.

Someone behind us said, "Is he okay?"

Georgia said brightly, "He's just a little dizzy. He'll be fine."

The same person said, "He doesn't look fine."

"He'll be okay," I said a bit too sharply. But would he?

The cane clattered to the concrete. Jesse Garon gripped the railing so hard, the veins in his hands stood out in relief. His body started doing a shuck and jive like when you first fall asleep and your muscles jump and jitter.

Another concerned citizen said, "Is he having an epileptic fit?"

Elmer said, "He's going down," as a security guard headed our way.

Jesse Garon sank to the ground like a sack of potatoes, his eyes rolling back in his skull.

Instead of giving us some space, people crowded in around us. It was positively claustrophobic.

"Is he okay?"

"What's wrong with him?"

"I think he *is* epileptic."

The guard pushed his way through the lookie loos. "Do you folks need an ambulance?"

"He just got out of the hospital," I said, holding my husband's hand. "I think he overdid it a little."

"All right, folks," the guard said to the onlookers. "Move along and give them some room."

The wind kicked up its heels, spritzing us with droplets from the fountain, and swirling dead leaves and flowers into the air and across the graves. A wreath on a metal tripod toppled over onto the grass as my hair whipped about my face. The people crowding around us gathered under the covered walkway curving around the outer edge of the Meditation Garden. Peyton's chignon came loose and she looked like Medusa with her blonde hair buffeting about her head.

I thought I heard a voice in the wind saying, "Thank you. Thankyouverymuch."

And then it was gone.

And the wind died down.

Molly said, "He's coming around."

My husband's eyelids fluttered, then opened.

Who was in there? Bertram or Elvis?

He struggled to sit up and we helped him. He smiled at me, an utterly unselfconscious smile that made my stomach leapfrog.

"Cleo?" he said, sounding confused. He looked at each of us in turn, then at Elvis's grave. "What are we doing at Graceland?" His voice rumbled, a rich bass.

Just to be sure, I tugged the painting from my purse and unrolled it. The black velvet was totally blank.

Elvis had left the building.

And Bertram had come home.

ENCORE

It's Over ...

As far as the media knew, the haunted Velvet Elvis was never recovered. To this day there are still people searching for it. They really need to get a life. Bertram and I burned that blank piece of velvet in our barbeque grill. From time to time I still have bad dreams about it.

Jailhouse Rock ...

The members of the inner circle of The Church of the Blue Suede Shoes, including ring-leader Lee Munford, were convicted of several counts of kidnapping and murder in both Tennessee and Alabama, including that of Ruth Gruber of Memphis. Like Aaron and his brother Jared, she'd been another one of their guinea pigs in their quest to put the dead into the living. Always a bad idea in my opinion.

Can't Help Falling in Love ...

Elmer returned to Florida without the oddity he'd come to Allister to collect, but he left with my sister's heart, an item immensely more valuable. He wants Molly to come visit him in Sarasota and meet his four girls during Spring Break. She said yes.

And speaking of falling in love, Bertram and I renewed our wedding vows at the Chapel in the Woods at Graceland before returning home. If our marriage can survive a haunted painting, a crazy cult, and a possession by a dead rock-n-roll star, it can survive anything.

Hound Dog ...

Bertram's brush with death has got him talking about having a baby. Me, I'm not so keen on the idea. At least, not yet. So we adopted a dog, an American Staffordshire Terrier, known in other circles as a pit bull terrier, that we named Luna. We're taking her down to Florida with us for Spring Break, along with Molly's girls and Georgia. What a merry bunch we'll be soaking up the sun down at Sugar Sand Beach on the Florida Gulf Coast.

Faye just called and told me to "beware the moon and watch out for bad fish" while we're in Florida.

I told her she'd been watching too many old horror movies.

Wrongo bongo yet again.

ABOUT THE AUTHOR

Susan Abel Sullivan lives in a Victorian house in northeastern Alabama with two dogs, way too many cats, and a couple of snakes. When not writing she likes to get her groove on by teaching Zumba Fitness classes. She is a graduate of the Odyssey Writing Workshop for speculative fiction. Her short fiction and poetry have appeared in numerous online and print publications, including *Asimov's Science Fiction Magazine, Andromeda Spaceways Inflight Magazine, ASIM Best of Horror: Vol II, Beyond Centauri, New Myths, AlienSkin,* and *Writers' Journal.* She is the author of *Cursed: Wickedly Fun Stories* and *Fried Zombie Dee-light! Ghoulish, Ghostly Tales,* and the Cleo Tidwell Paranormal Mystery Series. Visit her website at susanabelsullivan.weebly.com or twitter @susan_abel.

Also available from World Weaver Press
by Susan Abel Sullivan:

CURSED: WICKEDLY FUN STORIES

"Quirky, clever, and just a little savage!" — Lane Robins, critically acclaimed author of *Maledicte* and *Kings and Assassins*

A collection of four wickedly fun short stories featuring witches, werewolves, limericks that can change fate, and a sinister vine bent on murder and the destruction of Alabama! Inside quirky settings with creepy plots, characters discover new and unsettling powers as their worst fears manifest. You'll laugh, you'll shudder—you'll think twice about taking a deal from a bucktoothed woman.

Turn the page and read the first story for free!
Or pick up the digital edition from any major ebook retailer

GETTING THE CURSE

Enjoy this quick bite from Susan Abel Sullivan's collection of short fiction *CURSED: Wickedly Fun Stories*, available now as a digital edition.

It's Ladies Night in the little town of Foggy Hollow. You won't be attending, of course, not yet, not until you get the curse. Your mom, and all of your girlfriends and their moms, will be out painting the town red tonight while you sit home alone, doing your algebra homework at the kitchen table. Being a late bloomer just isn't fair, you think.

What had been a light pitter-patter of rain quickly turns into the drumming of a torrential downpour. You get a small sense of satisfaction in knowing it'll be cold and wet in the woods tonight. But you still wish like crazy that you were out there with the other women.

The grunting ding of the doorbell gives you a start and you spill hot cocoa on your sweatshirt. Who in their right mind would be at your door on this of all nights?

The answer turns out to be Jason Lamb, the hunky new senior from school. Your breath hitches up a notch at the sight of him on your front stoop. Your insides feel all warm and goopy. He moved in down the street a couple of weeks ago, and already he's in the popular crowd. "New blood," your girlfriends like to say. But what's he doing out on Ladies Night?

A flash of lightning momentarily turns the night inside out, followed a thunderous boom that shakes your very bones.

"Come in, come in!" You gesture frantically. "You shouldn't be out tonight."

He leaves his umbrella on the porch and steps inside. You close the door. A dozen witty repartees flit through your head but what comes out of your mouth is, "So what do you want?" Inwardly, you wince.

Jason runs a hand through his spiky, blonde hair and flashes what you've already come to think of as his trademark grin. "My mom wanted to know if she could borrow a cup of sugar."

A cup of sugar? For a moment you don't know what to say. The silence stretches out like so much salt-water taffy.

"Your mom's *home*? *Tonight*?" you finally say.

"Well, yeah," Jason says, as if everyone should know this. "Isn't yours?"

"No." You're shocked to your core at the very idea of your mother, or any woman, staying home on Ladies Night. But the Lambs *are* newcomers; they don't yet know the ways of the town. "Um ... what does your mom do about ..." you want to say *getting the curse*, but you'd rather be caught dead in your ratty old underwear than have to talk about the curse with a guy, especially a hottie like Jason.

He gives you a mystified look. "What does she do about what?"

"Nothing." Apparently the other women haven't told Mrs. Lamb about Ladies Night. You find this both interesting and disturbing. "Come on, this way."

Jason follows you into the kitchen. "Hey, nice house, Kirsten. It is Kirsten, isn't it?"

"Yeah."

You search the pantry, wishing you'd worn make-up and something a little better than sweat pants. The scrape of a chair on linoleum floor tells you Jason's taken a seat at the kitchen table. Even though he's behind you, you have a heightened awareness of his presence, as if your aura has expanded to touch his, raising the fine hairs on your arms and the back of your neck. He smells faintly of sweat, and the cologne-like Mennen speed stick that your father used to wear when he was alive.

Your stomach rumbles. Some kidney pie or fried liver would hit the spot right about now.

Jason says, "Have you lived in Foggy Hollow long?"

"Just my entire life."

You see the sugar behind several cans of Vienna sausage and deviled ham, and as your reach for it, your guts cramp, twisting into white hot ribbons of pain. *Oh, dear God*, you think. Not here, not now.

"I'll be right back," you say as you run to the bathroom, one hand clutching your abdomen.

Once safely within its confines, you lock the door and sit on the toilet seat, hugging your knees. Oh, why did he have to come over on this night of all nights? He can't be here when you get the curse for the first time. You wonder if you shouldn't just camp out in the bathroom and take your chances.

Jason raps on the door. "Hey, are you okay in there?"

Oh, crap. Why couldn't he have just stayed put?

"Yeah, I'm fine. I'll be out in a sec." And just like that the cramps subside. Maybe it's a false alarm. You certainly hope so. You open the door, mortified that you had to run off and lock yourself in the bathroom.

Jason's smile is dazzling. "Was it something I said?"

You pat your belly. "Nah, something I ate."

The two of you return to the kitchen. You can't think of a single thing to say. The silence presses against your back like a pair of invisible hands. As you fetch the sugar and scoop out a cup's worth, you glance out the window over the sink. The storm has blown over. Dark clouds part briefly, exposing a pregnant moon.

Jason says, "Hey, have you seen that new horror flick, *Nightmare's Daughter?*"

"Not yet. But I want to." You're relieved that the two of you are talking again.

"Well, maybe sometime, if you're not busy ..."

But you don't hear what he says because another round of cramps gouges your insides. You sag against the kitchen counter, wanting nothing more than to lie on the floor in a fetal position and scream until your throat is raw. Jason's got to leave—*now*—before there's blood.

"Jason—" Your voice is husky.

"Hey, should I take you to the hospital?"

You wave him away. "No. Please go. I'll be okay." But the shriek that slips out says differently.

"That's it. I'm dialing 911."

Jason really should have listened to you. Your moon time is finally upon you, and you're no longer a girl anymore.

Your skin ripples, bulging here and there. Wretched agony, you might as well be laid on the rack as bones, muscles, tendons are impossibly stretched and rearranged. Your face is a study in pain unto itself. Your nose and jaw feel as if they are being torn from your face with a meat hook, your ears sundered from your skull.

Your sweats split with an acute rip. The rest of your clothes follow suit as course hair sprouts all over your body like rampant weeds. The rainbow-colored dishtowel beside the sink is now only so many bands of gray. The cockroaches in the wall sound like a legion of soldiers marching.

You whip around, and now Jason is the one screaming.

Terror rolls off of him in wave after delicious wave. You can't help but salivate. He takes a step backward, one hand still holding the back of a chair, and you leap, knocking him to the floor. He tries to ward you off with arms crossed over his face. His legs thrash and kick. You rake claws down his chest, shredding his t-shirt and the flesh underneath as you bite into a forearm. His bones crunch like peppermint sticks; his blood is sweet syrup.

But enough with the foreplay. This is your first time, after all, and you can't hold back any longer. You sink your canines into his throat, whipping your head from side to side. As his life force spews forth, you let out a frenzied howl.

You've finally gotten the curse.

Get this story and more in _Cursed: Wickedly Fun Stories_ by Susan Abel Sullivan, available now!

ALSO AVAILABLE
FROM WORLD WEAVER PRESS

Shards of History

a novel by
Rebecca Roland

"5 out of 5 stars! One of the most beautifully written novels I have ever read. Suspenseful, entrapping, and simply ... well, let's just say that *Shards of History* reminds us of why we love books in the first place." — Good Choice Reading

"A captivating tale of a deadly clash between matrilineal and patriarchal cultures in a pseudo Native American setting replete with dragons! Roland delivers the goods with engaging characters, innovative world building, and plot twists galore!" — Susan Abel Sullivan, author of *The Haunted Housewives of Allister, Alabama*.

Like all Taakwa, Malia fears the fierce winged creatures known as Jeguduns who live in the cliffs surrounding her valley. When the river dries up and Malia is forced to scavenge farther from the village than normal, she discovers a Jegudun, injured and in need of help.

Malia's existence—her status as clan mother in training, her marriage, her very life in the village—is threatened by her choice to befriend the Jegudun. But she's the only Taakwa who knows the truth: that the threat to her people is much bigger and much more malicious than the Jeguduns who've lived alongside them for decades. Lurking on the edge of the valley is an Outsider army seeking to plunder and destroy the Taakwa , and it's only a matter of time before the Outsiders find a way through the magic that protects the valley—a magic that can only be created by Taakwa and Jeguduns working together.

Specter Spectacular: 13 Ghostly Tales

Edited by Eileen Wiedbrauk

Spirits, poltergeists, hauntings, creatures of the dark—*Specter Spectacular: 13 Ghostly Tales* delivers all these and more in thirteen spooky twists on the classic ghost story. From the heartwarming and humorous to the eerie and chilling, this anthology holds a story for everyone who has ever been thrilled by the unknown or wondered what might lie beyond the grave. Step inside and witness ghosts of the past, tales of revenge, the inhuman, the innocent, the damned, and more. But be warned—once you cross the grave into this world of fantasy and fright, you may find there's no way out.

Featuring work by Amanda C. Davis, A. E. Decker, Larry Hodges, Sue Houghton, Andrea Janes, Terence Kuch, Robbie MacNiven, Kou K. Nelson, Jamie Rand, Shannon Robinson, Calie Voorhis, Jay Wilburn, and Kristina Wojtaszek.

"Like a ghost tour through a hundred towns, this was one ride I wanted to last forever." — Alex Hughes, author of *Clean*

Available now!

For more on these and other World Weaver Press titles, visit www.WorldWeaverPress.com.

Made in the USA
Charleston, SC
26 July 2013